FOR LOVE OF THE

PHANTOM

by

Davyne DeSye

BOOKS
BY
DAVYNE DESYE

HISTORICAL ROMANCE

The Phantom Rising Series:
For Love of the Phantom
Skeletons in the Closet
Phantom Rising (forthcoming)

SCIENCE FICTION

The Aggressor Queen Series:
Carapace
Warmonger (forthcoming)
Aggressor Queen (forthcoming)

Short Story Anthology:
Soap Bubble Dreams and Other Distortions

ACKNOWLEDGEMENTS

First, thanks to Gaston Leroux for his original *Phantom of the Opera*, a story so compelling that I couldn't stop my mind from taking the next step.

Thanks, also, to all the "phans" of *Phantom of the Opera* for being such a devoted group and for their wonderful acceptance of this continuation of the story.

Special thanks to Ann and Bit for the immense encouragement and feedback at the very beginning.

I can never thank John enough for everything he does for me, but in this case, for being my first reader and most devoted fan. His questions and suggestions helped make this a better book. And thanks, too, to my wonderful children for their unflagging enthusiasm as I spun them this tale.

To John
Thank you for always believing in me.

Contents

CHAPTER 1
PAIN

The Opera Ghost wept with the desolation one might expect of a specter, but the crashing and splintering of the effects surrounding him was caused by the man.

Erik, the devastated man. Even as tears coursed unnoticed down his sunken, pale cheeks, sound roared from his powerful throat, giving good credit to the terrible wailing of a wounded soul:

"Christine! Christine!"

Echoes of his cries through the underground caverns of the Paris Opera House returned as the sound of ghosts sobbing with him. Christine was gone. His wife-to-be had left in the arms of another. But he had had to let her go. His love for her demanded it.

"Christine!" As he roared, he gripped the edge of the table, shaking the delicate crystals of the small tabletop candelabra. The tinkling of the crystal, usually such a merry sound, now came to his ears as a sad, pathetic noise.

Erik moved to the bed and sat amidst the tatters of the thick, tasseled velvet drapes. For some time, he stay there, broken glass pressing into the palm of his bone-thin, white hand, letting

1

the pain ooze out with the blood of his several gashes. His breathing was the loud wheeze of a breathless, voiceless accordion.

With sunken eyelids pressed closed over tortured eyes, he remembered Christine – his Christine – pressing her face toward his forehead. He felt her soft, warm lips against his parchment skin. One thin, white hand moved to his deformed face above his closed eyes.

In his mind, he heard her voice: "Poor, unhappy Erik."

She cared. Surely, she cared. She had loved him for himself. He was sure of it. She would have come, in time, to accept his vile visage as she had already accepted him into her heart. It was that dandified blackguard, Raoul, who had poisoned her heart against him. Raoul, who cared nothing for the precious flower, the unique and perfect angel, that was Christine. Raoul, who cared for nothing but to collect her as a bauble.

Erik cut off the howl that escaped him and cocked his head to listen, certain he had heard something, certain, suddenly, his Christine was returning. Had she called to him? Had he heard her sweet voice saying his name? He stood, quiet, poised in the still attitude of statuary, not daring to breathe, waiting to hear his name from her lips. No sound came to his ears, though he stood for minutes, frozen, silent. Silent – for the first time since Raoul had taken Christine's hand and pulled her from the room.

Again, Christine's voice came to him – this time only in memory – sighing over the space between them, "Thank you, Erik," as she was pulled from his sight, eyes wet, eyes focused without fear on Erik's unmasked face. "Thank you, Erik." So sweet. So sad. Surely, she cared.

Although he strained to hear her return, the sound of the voice he had heard through his bellow — her voice calling his name — he heard nothing. No movement. No whispered name.

"I am going mad!" he said. "Now it is I, the Opera Ghost, who am hearing voices!" The irony burst from him in rich laughter, which rang and danced through the underground caverns. He was only able to stop the laughter when he heard its tones rising toward hysteria.

Lowering himself again to the bedstead upon which Christine had passed her nights in his home, he sat, observing the devastation. His sanctuary, his home, his peace… destroyed by love.

Thus did Erik pass his first night. For all the strength in his limbs, he was powerless against the waves of emotion that crashed through him.

"Christine…"

Spent, weak, beyond exhaustion, he crooned gently swelling songs of his love. Finally, he slept amidst the debris upon the bed that still smelled so wonderfully of his Christine. He dreamt the lustrous tones of the wedding mass, dreamt forlornly of his bride… and her monster.

CHAPTER 2
THE LOVERS FLEE

As Erik wept, Christine, still clasping Raoul's hand, looked back at the dreaded, beloved façade of the Opera House. Her breath left her in harsh gasps, as did Raoul's. Raoul pulled her toward the street fronting the great building.

We have escaped!

Dropping her hand, Raoul signaled to a passing cabby. Christine fought the impulse to clutch at Raoul and instead raised the back of her bare wrist to her face, surprised, still, at the tears that littered her cheeks.

Surely I do not cry for Erik! But even as she thought this, another thought, *Poor Erik*, brought a fresh blur to her vision. She closed her eyes and dabbed at the corner of each eye with the knuckle of one gloved hand. When she opened her eyes, she looked upon Raoul – her beloved Raoul! – holding the door to the cab and reaching a solicitous hand toward her.

"Raoul. Raoul, you have saved me," she said. Fresh tears flooded her eyes and cascaded down her cheeks. This time, Christine knew, the tears were those of extreme tension and relief.

4

Not joy. Not yet. Her freedom was too newly won, too nearly beyond belief, for Christine to weep for joy.

"Come, my love," Raoul said in softly urgent tones, "Let's away, before we discover he has reinstated your evil sentence."

Christine gratefully accepted Raoul's hand and pulled upon it as Raoul lifted himself in beside her. Then, they were in each other's arms.

"Raoul, Raoul," she murmured against him, her head pressed to his chest.

"My darling," he whispered, but instead of continuing to nuzzle her, his head swiveled to gaze out the windows of the moving cab. With Raoul's watchfulness, and his arms around her, Christine felt safe.

I wonder how long we will both be peering over our shoulders for the specter of Erik. I wonder how long I will still hear him moving, as he once did, in the walls around me.

Christine shuddered, and Raoul tightened his arms about her and spoke into the curls of her lustrous, golden hair. "Hush, my love. You are safe at last."

Christine wished she could believe this simple statement, so confidently and quietly delivered. The energy that powered their escape – always with the nightmarish feeling that they were being followed by mere inches, that a hand would close upon them at any moment – still kept her breathing rushed, her cheeks flushing with heat.

She inhaled a long and tremulous breath, held it, and slowly released it. She forced herself to relax, to sink more deeply into Raoul's arms.

This — this! — is warmth and safety and love.

Hot tears sprang to her eyes and littered Raoul's torn shirtfront. When the cab stopped, Christine reluctantly released Raoul and gathered her skirts to debark.

"No, Christine, you go on. I must make arrangements." Raoul did not look at Christine, but glanced back and forth, first up, then down the street, as if he expected to meet Erik bounding toward them.

Fright descended upon Christine with a crashing weight, and she nearly leapt from the cab into Raoul's arms. "Raoul! You cannot leave me!"

Her frantic tone, and her unseemly scramble across the seat of the cab toward him awakened Raoul from his own hurried thoughts. He signaled to the driver to wait, and re-entered the cab. Christine clutched him to her, again hiding her face against his chest.

"Christine, my darling, my love," he crooned, as he stroked her hair. "I will never leave you." Raoul disentangled himself from her arms and pushed her back until he could look into her eyes. "I am going to make you my wife. We will be exquisitely happy together." He waited until Christine nodded, but — all gentleness — pushed her back as she tried to reattach herself to him. "I must procure our coach. I would not stay another day in this city!"

"But where…?" Christine began.

"You will go to Mamma Valérius." Raoul's warm eyes held hers, and she could feel the power of his commandment. "You will be safe there. I will call for you as soon as I have made the necessary arrangements." Raoul turned and glanced out the cab's open door. Speaking almost to himself, he said, "At this time, I don't know what they have done with our traveling barouche or the luggage I prepared. …"

Raoul shook himself, and looked to Christine. "So, you will go?" he asked, peering at her from beneath his brows, his chin pulled toward his chest. Christine felt herself a child being spoken to simply by this beloved man.

"Yes, Raoul, I will go to Mamma." The weak tones of her simple reply confirmed the wretched feeling of being a child, as did the indelicate sniff that followed. She straightened her shoulders to regain the attitude of a woman about to be married – and to a vicomte – and repeated, more strongly, "Yes, Raoul, I will go."

"Good girl!" Raoul said with an encouraging smile and exited the cab.

Christine leaned toward him, her body unwilling to relinquish his closeness, although her mind had consented to go. From the street, Raoul leaned toward her and kissed her lips, warming her insides. Then, with his charmingly confident smile and a wink, he dashed to the driver, gave directions, and strode away.

Christine watched him through the back window of the cab until he was out of sight around a corner, still trembling, but feeling in control of her fate for the first time in a long while.

***

Mamma Valérius was scandalized at the news.

"But, my child, where will you go? What of the Angel of Music?"

"Mamma, I have told you, there is no Angel of Music." Christine sat beside Madame Valérius' bed, holding the old woman's frail hand. "I have slipped his clutches, and I am finally free to indulge my affection for Raoul." Her eyes fell to the gold ring upon her finger – Erik's ring – the ring she had promised Erik to wear until his death and then to bury with him. The promise seemed a small price in exchange for their lives and freedom.

"Are you to marry? I am fond of Raoul, but. ..."

"Yes, we are to be married. Immediately." Christine knew the haste of the marriage would raise inappropriate questions – perhaps even in Mamma Valérius' mind. "I have not been compromised," she said.

"No, no, of course not dear. I am perfectly aware of your virtue." Mamma adjusted her position under her coverings, while absently patting Christine's hand. Then, as if the question had only just reoccurred to her, she wailed, "But where will you go?"

"We originally thought to go to Brussels, but I have convinced Raoul this is not far enough." Christine's expression brightened before she continued, the smile genuine enough for what was to follow. "Raoul is taking me home. Sweden!"

"Oh, my dear, how lovely," Mamma responded, a beatific smile creasing her features. The two gazed at each other, smiles mirroring each other, hands clasped over the blossom-pink eyelet coverlet between them. Then the old woman seemed to awaken from a daze, and she began to pull back the coverlet.

"What is it, Mamma?" Christine asked with some concern. The frail woman was not often found outside of her bedchambers.

"Why, I must pack, my dear! It has been years since I visited my home country, and I will not live here, packed away in this wretched house, without the one person left to me in the world." She labored to move her legs to the side of the bed.

"Mamma! You are far too ill! I will not stand for it!" Despite her words, Christine moved to support the woman in her efforts.

"You will. Now, if you wish to prolong my life, assist me." Mamma Valérius gained her feet, and humming, moved to the door and called her young servant.

Christine continued to sit by the bed, torn between helping the old woman who had already thrown open the armoire and fearing to assist in an endeavor that would, without doubt, be dangerous to the woman's precarious health.

"And you shall be married at the little church in Perros-Guirec. Your father would be so pleased." The old woman turned to Christine, and holding out a handful of cotton and lace underclothing, said, "Help me with these, my child. There, put them on the bed. That's a dear."

"Perros-Guirec," Christine echoed. With the uncanny events of the last day, she had not given any thought to where they would be married. Her current circumstance was completely unforeseen to her, and her mind had scarcely begun to grasp her new future – even the future looming one day from today.

"Certainly!" boomed Mamma Valérius, seeming to gather strength as she moved.

"Perros-Guirec," Christine repeated. With a smile at the perfection of this simple idea, she crossed the room to assist the woman in unloading the armoire. "Yes, Mamma, it is a perfect notion. I will marry within sight of father's grave, and he will smile upon us from Heaven."

"Yes, and to a vicomte, no less!" Mamma said, huffing – and finally relinquishing the packing to a confused but compliant young servant girl. She settled on the lounge beside the bed. "We must see to the arrangements at once!"

CHAPTER 3
WRAPPING UP

Erik had always been a man of action. This was as much due to temperament as it was to the fact that he could analyze six, eight, ten steps ahead in a flash — as insight rather than through plodding, sequential, rational steps. For this reason, Erik did not long wallow in the misery of his absent Christine. He would not worry at the absence, as a tongue worries at a gap in a gum from a dislodged tooth — he would fill the empty space. Fill it with the vision and voice of his Christine. As any lover might do, he would leave the now-empty hollow of his home in the Opera House to be near her.

Erik knew he could trace the route of Christine and the simpleton, Raoul, and find where they had settled. But first, he must throw the ubiquitous Persian from his trail. The daroga — police chief — although now retired, was ever the detective, relentless in his surveillance of Erik, determined as ever to assure himself Erik was no danger to others — or more precisely, to continue in his role as savior of the public against what the Persian viewed as Erik's violent nature. Sadly, Erik knew the goings on at the Opera House of late had done nothing to alleviate the Persian's perception of Erik's murderous nature.

Of course, Erik knew, the easier course would be to kill the Persian, thus living up to the Persian's expectations of his nature. But the easier course was less than palatable to Erik, both because the Persian had saved his life and eased his escape from the sultanate of Mazenderan – at considerable cost to himself – and because it was too easy. The idea and the ease with which he could carry out the murder simply bored him. The murder also defied the resolution Erik had made after his exploits in Asia to stop committing or assisting in the atrocities of others – the blood lust of the Turkish Sultan (to say nothing of the Sultana of Mazenderan) had finally soured Erik to such exploits. His quiet home in the Opera House was his attempt at the serene life of music and leisure he felt he had earned.

Erik caressed the small wooden jewelry box, which was a gift to Christine, warming his fingers against the smooth, rich surface, and sighed. "Until Christine," he said, speaking to nobody but himself.

Until Christine, he thought, with melancholy, *my home had been enough.*

He had been surrounded by artists, by music, by dance, by beautiful – if shallow and ignorant – aristocrats and had delighted in charging "rent" to the universally silly purported owners of the above-ground layers of his home. He had reveled in the coarse but honest gaiety of the theater workers, the earnest, hard labor of the scene-shifters and constructors, the sublime perfection of the society gatherings with the uniformed servants gliding food and drink to the glittering fingers of the wealthy. He had crept so smoothly amidst these vastly different tenants of his home that he often forgot he crept – he felt a part of their world, as they were a part of his.

And then came Christine.

"Christine," he said aloud again, cherishing the sound of her name, the feel of her name breathed over his tongue and thin lips. Her name on his lips felt as velvety as the rose petals he now slowly crushed from a stem with his fingers.

"Enough," Erik said, as though waking from a dream. He swept the crushed petals from his pant legs to the floor. "First, the Persian."

Almost at the same instant as the statement, his plan to deceive the Persian was formed and complete within Erik's mind. An elegant plan. His lips stretched into a death's head smile.

The days passed, as Erik made the necessary travel plans. He did not know yet where Christine and her (damnable!) lover had settled, but he knew enough to know he would be leaving France. He emptied one of his numerous and large bank accounts (after all, Sultans pay well, and in gold – if one can escape still alive), and on a whim, he crept back to the manager's office to return the forty thousand francs he had extracted from the new owners. Certainly, the entertainment the two ridiculous men had provided him the night of Christine's disappearance was worth the return of the meager sum – they had proved his only entertainment on a night that would end in such disaster, with Christine gone.

Erik spent what he knew to be his last evenings ensconced in Box 5, enjoying the performances played out for him. His only wistfulness was due to the fact that Christine was not performing. Carlotta performed in *Faust* with her typical overblown and haughty prancing, and he could not keep himself from laughing as she gingerly approached the lines during which the famous croaking "Co-ack" he had caused had previously escaped her rounded mouth.

Immediately following his laugh, there was a brief moment when it seemed the entire house paused for breath – musicians, audience, and actors alike – and Carlotta glanced tremulously toward Box 5. The moment passed. Carlotta took up the next lyrics, perhaps even more gingerly, and Erik had to clap his hands over his mouth to keep from laughing again – perhaps this time, even using his ventriloquist's powers to place the laugh just beside Carlotta's jeweled ear. But no. Erik controlled himself, rather than create another ruckus. He was leaving his house. He would leave it in peace.

On the evening of his last attendance at the theater, Erik spoke to his devoted (if dim) friend, Madame Giry. At his first words, she moved with her normal stiff formality, the skirts of her dark dress rocking about her feet, to the small shelf at the front of the box. She faced toward the seats of the theater below her, her hands clasped before her in her usual attitude of deference and respect. The rustle of her skirts quieted, and her whole person took on an attitude of listening for a whisper. He spoke, throwing his voice to an intimate spot near her ear.

"Madame Giry," he said.

"Yes, Monsieur," she responded, with the same obedient tones of her usual service to him.

"I am leaving this Earth," he said.

Erik was touched as a small gasp escaped the stolid woman, and her hands fluttered toward the shelf before her. Her hands returned to gripping each other, and she said, "Where do you go, Monsieur?"

"Where all ghosts go who seek happiness away from this world."

"Ah, to Heaven, Monsieur, surely. This is best." Her words rang with sincerity. The feathers of her hat bobbed drunkenly as she nodded in emphasis.

"I am leaving you with a gift," Erik answered, but before he could get further in his explanation, Madame Giry interrupted with fervor:

"But no gift is necessary, Monsieur! You have prophesied that my little Meg will be empress, and this is all the gift a mother needs!"

"Aaah," he answered with one long, rolling syllable, for the moment sorry for the small lie he had relied upon for years with Madame Giry. Gently, he broke faith with his lie, hoping his explanation would suffice. "Meg will indeed succeed, Madame, although perhaps, without my efforts on her behalf here on Earth, empress may be a bit out of reach."

With a small puff of breath, the woman crumpled slightly from her proud posture, the feathers above her head drooping with her, but after a moment, she straightened again.

"This is just," she said, and before Erik could wonder what she meant, she turned the slightest bit toward the column where he was hidden, and said, "I have betrayed you in discussing you with my employers and with the Commissaire de Police. You are kind not to punish me – or my little Meg – further."

"No punishment, Madame," Erik answered. "You acted rightly in all matters. I simply shall no longer be here to assist."

The woman answered with a small sniff, which sniff betrayed the tears that Erik could not see, but knew were there.

"Madame, I go now. With all thanks for your faithful service, I leave your gift. With this gift, you will have the power to assist your daughter in all things." Erik silently moved the small envelope to the richly upholstered cushion of the chair behind Madame Giry, the chair she considered "his" chair.

"Thank you, Monsieur," she said, without turning. And after a hesitant pause, "May God bless you, Monsieur."

Erik watched, moved by the woman's kindness (although if she saw his face, perhaps even she would be moved to cruelty and distrust) as she continued to stand at the front of the box.

"Monsieur?" she asked. Receiving no answer, she turned and looked to the envelope on the chair, red-lettered in his large hand with her name.

She pressed the envelope to her breast and again sniffed. After bringing out her pressed handkerchief and wiping primly at her nose and the corners of her eyes, she opened the envelope, undoubtedly expecting to see his usual gift of five or ten francs. Her expression as she read and re-read the passbook for the bank account he had established for her, and there at the top, the very large figure contained in the account, was most satisfactory. He stayed and watched as she sank to her knees before his chair, and lowered her head, face in hands, to the cushion, pressing the passbook to her cheek and sobbing in a low voice.

He crept away down his secret passage as she finally controlled her sobbing and repeated over and over:

"For little Meg, yes, Monsieur … thank you, Monsieur … God bless you, Monsieur."

It was the only moment when Erik felt regret at his decision to leave his home. The regret burned away in the bright knowledge he would soon be near his beautiful Christine.

CHAPTER 4
A WEDDING

Christine was seized by a paroxysm of joy when Raoul arrived at the home of Madame Valérius only days after her own arrival. The packing of Mamma Valérius was completed, since they could not take most of the old woman's belongings on their flight, and arrangements had been made for the sale of the house and effects. The proceeds would be forwarded to their new home in Sweden.

"Raoul, isn't it wonderful?" Christine asked after they embraced.

Raoul gazed at Christine, eyes shining and dancing over her face as though they would devour her, and answered, "Wonderful, yes, to see you again, my bride." They kissed briefly before following a servant into the small sitting room, where tea things stood ready.

"Then you have not turned your mind away from marrying me, in your absence?" Christine asked, smiling, tilting her head at him and looking at him from the corner of her eye.

Raoul bent and pressed his lips to the back of her hand. "Never. You are the only woman for me. You tease me. You know how long I have loved you."

Christine giggled, and felt her face go to flame at the lovely utterance. "I would like to be married here," she said.

"Here? At the home of your matron?" Raoul's eyes took in the small, dark room with its heavy drapes and ponderous dark furnishings.

"No!" Christine giggled again. "Here in France. At the birthplace of our love. At Perros-Guirec." She paused, searching Raoul's demeanor for his reaction, hoping he would agree.

"Brilliant!" he responded without hesitation. Then, in the tone of ultimatum: "So long as it can be done today."

"Today?" Christine asked, confounded as to how this could be accomplished, at Perros-Guirec, or anywhere. "But I did not even know you were to arrive today. Raoul!" Her querulous tone was followed by a pout.

Raoul's rich laughter filled the room. He stood, extended his hand to her, and when she had risen, folded her into his arms. Bending and speaking into her ear, he asked, "So, how long must I wait for my hard-won bride?" His breath, warm on her ear and neck, sent a delicious shiver through her insides, and she felt the skin prickle on her arms.

"Well … with the musicians, and the guest list, and the …"

"Musicians!" Raoul exclaimed, releasing her. It was Christine's turn to laugh.

"Will the day after tomorrow do?" Christine asked in a small, warm voice, taking him into her arms again. She wished for him to speak again in whispered tones into her ear. The thrill was all the greater when he fulfilled her wish.

First kissing her ear, he murmured in a warm hiss, "Yesss."

Raoul seemed worried but pleased when he learned Madame Valérius would be traveling with them. He graciously explained to the old woman that her presence would complete their happiness and that her willingness to join them was just as he wished. The energy and healthfulness that had come over Mamma Valérius since Christine's unannounced arrival comforted Christine greatly.

Because the wedding was to be a small affair – no musicians (Christine laughed to herself, remembering Raoul's reaction) – there was no difficulty in completing the arrangements. The priest, being well acquainted with all the parties, was quite self-satisfied in his agreement to perform the ceremony, almost as though he had been merely awaiting a foreseen event.

***

Before the small ceremony, Raoul and Christine walked upon the sands of the inlet of Trestraou, where the two had met so many summers ago. The wind off the water caressed Christine's cheek, and the sea smelled of freedom as it sighed to them from the shore.

Raoul stopped and lifted his eyes to the horizon. "Do you wish to throw something into the water for me to rescue again?

Shall we marry as we met, with you as beautiful as the morning dew, and I as wet?"

Christine paused as if she were considering his question. Then she looked askance at him and said, "I think not, Raoul. You are far too handsome today."

Raoul bowed playfully to Christine, and again they walked, slowly, in silence, happy in each other's company.

Upon their return, Christine found Mamma Valérius waiting in the pews, head bowed in prayer. She raised her head as they approached.

"Oh! These old knees of mine. Do you think God will forgive my impiety?" The old woman slowly rose to her feet, and smiling, embraced Christine, then Raoul.

"Are you ready, my children?" she asked.

"I have been ready many days hence," responded Raoul. After a brief kiss to the wrinkled cheek she presented, he said, "I will find the priest."

Mamma Valérius motioned to the servants who stood at the back of the small church, and they came forward with slow solemnity. "Are you happy, my dear?" she asked. Rather than look to Christine as she spoke, her eyes roved over the stone walls, the numerous candles, the scant statuary, the one colored glass window.

"Oh, Mamma. So happy!" Christine embraced the woman again.

"Good. It is all I have ever wanted for you." The old woman leaned in closer to Christine, apparently trying to keep her words from the servants now standing quite close. "Although I wonder about your Angel of Music. Will you still sing with such beauty? Such joy?"

"Mamma, please," Christine answered, not quite curtly, but certainly with a tone of quiet admonition. "Speak not of the Angel of Music. Not here. Not today, of all days. I have explained he was no angel, but merely a man."

"An extraordinary man, to have been mistaken for an angel, I should think," Mamma replied. "And still you wear his ring, I see."

Christine felt a flush of sadness pall her features. She held her hand away from her body, fingers tilted up and splayed, and glanced down at the bit of gold adorning her hand.

"I cannot explain," Christine answered, feeling some small part of her joy infused and eclipsed with a darker emotion. Guilt? Sadness? Fear?

Mamma leaned toward Christine and, clutching the unadorned hand, squeezed it. "But, look at me! Here, on this day of happiness and union, darkening your brow with unwanted subjects. Forgive me, my darling. I will not speak of such nonsense again, so long as I live." The old woman raised herself to her toes and kissed Christine on the forehead. "Be gone!" she said, with a flutter of her hand, as though warding off the spirit that creased Christine's brow.

22

Suddenly, Raoul was beside Christine, and he took her hand, some small concern touching his features. "Are you well?" he asked.

"Better than well," Christine answered with happy cheerfulness. The vision and touch of Raoul washed over Christine with the warmth of summer sun. "Aflame in your love."

"Radiant, certainly," Raoul answered with a glowing smile, and he led her to stand before the priest.

The ceremony was brief and sweet, and the vows Christine made the sincerest of her life. Her eyes filled to overflowing with tears as she heard the sincerity of Raoul repeating the vows to her upturned face. Although her eyes were only for Raoul, Christine heard the sniffing of Mamma Valérius seated behind them and knew this day had caused more than just her own sublime happiness. She imagined her father there, seated beside Mamma Valérius, and imagined the strains of his sweet violin filling the small church. She was so entranced with this imagining, she was nearly startled when Raoul pulled her to him for the kiss, the marriage kiss between the man and his wife.

As their lips met, inexplicably – and with a touch of guilt – Christine also imagined Erik there, standing tall and dark at the back of the church. In her mind's eye, his unmasked face twisted in grief, tears glistening on his sunken cheeks as he watched the lovers united, Christine's lips sealing her commitment to another man. For a moment, Christine heard a reluctant echo of Erik's voice raised in sorrowful song.

This is what comes of Mamma's idle curiosity, she thought, as Raoul released her. *I am cursed to ruminate upon that poor, unfortunate creature while accepting the marriage kiss from my husband.*

Christine could not bring herself to irritation of the old woman, however. She turned with Raoul to face the almost empty pews and smiled at the sniffling matron. She raised her eyes to search the shadows at the back of the church for the figure of her imagination.

Erik was not there.

The servants smiled and offered obsequious congratulations to the couple, and Mamma Valérius wept and embraced them, pulling them together in her two, stout arms and embracing them as a whole, as though they were brought together by her arms instead of through the marriage sacrament.

Raoul laughed and offered Mamma Valérius his arm, leading her down the main aisle of the church toward the entrance. Christine lingered for a moment, a childish despair washing through her at being so quickly abandoned by her husband, and then she shook herself and followed, chiding herself for her ungraciousness.

As she moved from the candlelight of the church into the sapphire and amethyst sky of early evening, she was struck by the fact that her thoughts of Erik were not colored by fear or horror, but by melancholy with the hue and sensitivity of a bruise.

Poor, unhappy Erik. I have escaped you and found sublime happiness. Some part of me feels I have wrongly abandoned you.

Raoul stood, mere feet away, arms held out toward her, smile shining more luminously than the retreating sun through the trees. She rushed to his arms, and he lifted her from her feet, spinning her in a full circle. They laughed together, a beautiful duet.

Yes, sublime happiness, she thought, banishing the uneasiness that had attempted to gain entrance to her wedding.

"We are married, my love!" she shouted, reveling in the sea air and the freedom and freshness that surrounded her.

With an overwhelming joy she thought she might never recapture, she joined her husband in the nearby carriage, and they laughed together through the ride back to the house, the seemingly implausible fact of their escape finally made real.

CHAPTER 5
ERIK AND THE PERSIAN

Erik dressed and donned his death's head mask, feeling around the edges of his face to be sure of the proper coverage and fit. He had no mirror with which to check the lay of the mask over his features – he had seen enough of the horrified expressions as others looked upon him to want to see that horror himself. He placed a hat upon his head and pulled it down over his white forehead. Finally, he swirled the heavy, black cloak he favored around his shoulders and, after securing the clasp at his neck, pulled the oversized hood of the cloak over hat and head, drawing the hood far enough forward to hide his masked face from all who might try to plumb the shadows.

He took a cab through the early evening shadows, down the darkening streets to the Persian's little flat on the Rue de Rivoli. After paying the cabby to wait, he stood in the wan light of the gas lamp and glanced up at the lighted window, behind which, he knew, the Persian sat. Given the brightness of the lamps behind the window, Erik pictured the Persian reading or perhaps writing. He took a moment to compose himself for the act he would perform this night – to an audience of one – and once ready, rang at the door.

He had barely obtained his slumped and exhausted attitude at the door when Darius, the daroga's trusted servant, opened the door.

"Sir?" the servant asked, in his subdued and respectful tones.

"I beg your pardon," Erik said, breathing as though fatigued and debilitated, "I wish to speak to the Persian."

"May I say who is calling?"

"No, you may not," Erik answered, striking a pose of somewhat greater strength before slumping again against the doorway.

"Sir, I must announce you," answered Darius.

"You may announce that I am here to see the Persian," answered Erik.

"If you will not give your name, perhaps if I saw your face, I would recognize my master's acquaintance and could properly announce you." Darius bowed with all appropriate formality, clearly trying to take any offense out of the request.

"I will not give my name, I will not show my face, and I will not leave this door until I have seen the Persian." Erik moaned and slumped further. In a weakened tone, almost a whisper, he said, "I insist, my good man, announce me. Your master will see me."

After a hesitation, Darius bowed, pulled the door open further, and gestured that Erik should step inside. "May I take your

27

cloak, Sir?" Darius asked, standing resolute upon the gleaming wood floor of the entryway, arm extended for the task. When Erik, head dipped forward, did not so much as look at him or answer him, the servant turned and made his way up the carpeted stairs. Waiting, Erik inhaled the sweet scent of the Persian's clove-scented cigarettes.

Presently, he was shown into the presence of the Persian. Erik pushed back the hood of the heavy cloak and removed his hat, pausing between the two actions to lean against the wall, feigning weakness, illness, or both. Before he could say a word, the Persian leapt to his feet, outrage coloring his dark features, and spat the words at him:

"Monster! Abomination! Murderer of Comte Philippe! What have you done with the Vicomte, his brother, and what have you done with Mademoiselle Daaé? Do they yet live?"

Surprised at the vehemence of the verbal attack (this was most unlike the retired police chief of Mazenderan), Erik slid down the wall as though he might collapse to the floor, then pulled himself toward the nearest chair and fell prostrate there, completely without decorum or posture.

The daroga was relentless, jabbing words at Erik like an angry parent who has discovered his child is a criminal, asking again and again after Raoul and Christine.

Erik knew his script, however, and despite the angry jabbing, told of the last hours of Raoul and Christine in his lair. He huffed and grunted through his words, affecting a great weakness, as he explained he was "dying of love." He told of Christine's ultimate resolution to stay with him and to marry him, all in sacrifice to her beloved Raoul. He told of Christine weeping and calling him "poor Erik," of her small, warm hand taking his cadaverous fingers in her own, of her tears warm against the cool, hideous skin of his face as he lay at her feet. He told of Christine allowing him to kiss her forehead with his own lips and of Christine returning the kiss on his own forehead as she left him.

Erik wept and moaned and hissed harsh, hiccoughed breaths through the retelling of that awful night, and the passion and sorrow of his heartbreak at reliving the night was the one part of the performance he did not need to pretend. Drawing the words and the touches and the visions of that night into his mind, he felt anew the anguish that wracked him again, here, in the retelling.

Even in the midst of his own distress, Erik remained cognizant enough to watch the daroga, to gauge his audience, to determine whether he was being convincing. And when finally he saw the glistening, tear-filled eyes of the daroga, he knew he had won. The performance was that of a virtuoso – unparalleled and perfect.

Erik finished by explaining to the Persian the arrangement he had struck with Christine – that when he was dead, she would return to yield his ring and bury him in his home. He extracted from the Persian the promise that when Erik, close to death, sent the Persian Christine's meager personal effects still in his possession, the Persian would inform the young couple of Erik's death and publish a notice in the paper.

Satisfied by the pallor of the Persian's dark features that he was not only convinced of his sincerity but also moved to pity, Erik took his leave. Aware his audience still studied him minutely – the habits of a life-long policeman were difficult to escape – Erik weakly made his way to the cab that still waited and dragged himself into its dark enclosure.

"Go to the Opera," he said, voice low and ponderous.

The cabby looked concerned at the sudden, profound change in his fare and, with a mix of caution and speed, returned to the Opera House. His confusion when Erik bounded from the cab and smartly paid the man drew a laugh from Erik.

The Persian dispensed with for the time being, Erik began his search for his beloved Christine. Tempted as he was to search personally for the wayward couple, to start immediately for the train station from which he knew they started their journey, he constrained himself, and instead, used funds and spies to search them out. Time did not permit him luxury for his own cautious personal inquiries – for cautious they must be to maintain his hidden identity. Soon enough – mere weeks – and with fewer payments to detectives and fewer bribes than he had imagined necessary, he located them. Christine, bless the dear girl, had returned to her childhood home in Sweden. The father of whom she spoke so frequently and with such esteem would be touched if only he watched Christine from Heaven, as she supposed.

Erik was angered but not surprised to learn also Christine had left France as the wife of the absurd vicomte. Had the rogue forced her? Or had she been so ready and willing upon abandoning her music tutor to take up with this insipid patron? Irrelevant. Erik would soon be with his Christine again.

And now for the preparations of the final act with the Persian. Then, at last, Erik would be free to seek his new life with his bride (for she was his and no other's) – or at least within sight and sound of her.

Inside Christine's beautiful wooden jewelry box, he placed a lone shoe buckle that Christine had missed in the haste of her leaving; a small, fine pair of Christine's gloves; and two dainty, perfumed pocket handkerchiefs that still smelled so wonderfully of the beautiful girl. Erik's misshapen and nearly nonexistent nostrils throbbed with the scent of her for hours after the jewelry box was sealed.

Erik bundled Christine's letters to Raoul (which she had inexplicably left with Erik) to the top of the jewelry box. These he sent to the Persian with a brief and almost illegibly printed note explaining that he would be dead within the day and containing a reminder to inform Christine, along with the newly obtained address.

Do me the honor, my noble daroga, Erik had written at the bottom of the note, *of announcing my death in the Epoque. If you can bring yourself to show this respect to such a scoundrel as I, it seems fitting – after the inimitable life I have led – that I die with such a notice.*

FOR LOVE OF THE PHANTOM

Impatient for Christine, but filled with the necessity of seeing the matter through to its finish, Erik waited for the Persian. Indeed, the concluding trap was nearly sprung.

CHAPTER 6
SWEDEN

Christine was happier than at any other time of her life since the hazy, lustrous days of her youth when she traveled and performed with her father in the carefree protection of the man and of music. Those days were difficult to remember with any clarity, being before her "adoption" by Professor and Madame Valérius, and remained tinted with the misty and halcyon glow of life seen through a beloved child's eyes.

Her return to Korsnäsborg, the little market town in which she was born, was rendered magical by half-remembered vistas and smells. She could not locate the farm on which she and her father resided for the first years of her life (she could not remember her mother except as a misty, indistinct picture of a smiling woman tucking her into bed) until she asked and received directions from an old townsman who recalled the musical farmer with fondness.

Even having located the old holding, Christine could find nothing familiar outside of the large, branching tree at the edge of the field, which tree she had repeatedly and unsuccessfully attempted to climb. The now-faint scar on her arm above her left elbow testified to her most successful attempt – an attempt that left her white-faced and breathless on the ground, peering at the spinning sky through leaves.

The freshness of the sea air surpassed even that of Perros-Guirec, and the cerulean ocean called to her in a song of dreams. The pastoral beauty that surrounded her fulfilled her. She hoped for her father that his perch in Heaven, from which she knew he watched her, was a paradise modeled on Korsnäsborg.

Much to her chagrin, Raoul did not seem to share her appreciation of the quaint little town. "You will come to love it as I do," she told him one evening, helping to remove his coat.

"Undoubtedly," he answered glumly, "when I am dead and buried under some paltry part of it."

Surprised at the bitter statement, Christine was unsure how to respond. Raoul had given small hints of his unhappiness, but had never spoken so boldly against what she thought a charming town. She turned away with his coat and, taking it to his bedchamber to gain a moment to think, hung it in the wardrobe. Returning to where Raoul slouched in one of the chairs of the sitting room, she stood, watching him brood. After a time, he glanced up and noticed her there.

"Oh, never mind, my darling," he said, with a swishing gesture of one hand. Straightening his posture, he said in a brighter tone, "Come to me," and rakishly patted his thighs, indicating she should seat herself upon them. Arms out to receive her, he continued, "How can I protest anything when I have such a pretty young wife?" And after she had seated herself and received his kiss, "Your beauty is a credit to your husband's excellent taste."

"You are kind," Christine said, this time speaking in the language of her home, trying in this small way to supplement and reinforce Raoul's slight knowledge of the language.

His suddenly furrowed brow matched her own. She remained confused with his vehement condemnation of her home. Their home.

Christine excused herself to check on Mamma Valérius, who seemed, after a remarkable show of strength during their travels, to be weakening again.

After a quiet dinner during which Raoul continued to brood, Christine brought him a glass of sherry, determined to fathom his melancholy. She sat in the nearly darkened room, waiting for Raoul to acknowledge her. The clock on the mantle ticked an unhappy beat, and the quarter hour chimed desultorily into the silence. Raoul sipped at the sherry, but continued his distracted distance.

"What troubles you, husband?" she said. Her own voice in the quiet room seemed loud, despite her resolve to speak softly into the depths of his gloom.

"Hmm?" He seemed a man coming out of sleep. "I beg your pardon, my dear?"

"Something is troubling you out of all proportion to the lack of cosmopolitan characteristics of Korsnäsborg." She was ashamed that her tone contained a hint of hurt and accusation.

"You have not spoken a dozen words to me this evening. Have you become tired of your wife so quickly?"

Her question seemed to bring Raoul out of his distraction. "Never! Never, my darling," he said. He sat forward with such abrupt speed, he nearly upset the sherry at his elbow. He placed his hands upon hers as they moved and fidgeted upon her knees. His eyes were focused upon hers, and she happily accepted the glimmer of love that seemed to shine at her from the semi-darkness.

"What troubles you, then?" she asked. "Can you not tell me? Perhaps in my own small way, I could assist you."

She pulled her hands from under his and placed them on top of his, where they now rested upon her knees. She shivered, warming at his touch, even felt through the layers of her dress. Raoul's features soured, and he grunted as he pulled his hands away from her light grasp and sat back in his chair, again staring off into the gloom. Christine was patient. She waited for Raoul's answer, knowing her patience would outlast his stubbornness.

With bitter tones, Raoul broke his silence. "I chose better than you chose for yourself."

"I cannot imagine what you mean," she answered, a nervous fluttering beginning in her stomach.

With a heavy sigh, Raoul continued, "My funds are nearly depleted. I, a vicomte, *and I cannot support my wife!*"

Christine waited while he took another sip of the sherry. She understood Raoul's anxiety – for he had lived a life of ease – but she could not share his apprehension, having never experienced wealth. She rose and poured herself a small glass of the rich, golden-brown liquid, and then she returned, signaling that she was prepared to wait for him to continue.

After another long moment, he spoke. "I have written to a trusted friend asking after the status of my brother's estate, asking if it seems possible to obtain funds, but have received no response as of yet. And although Mamma Valérius has placed her estate in my hands for your and her support, even those funds are diminishing." Again, Raoul sank into his brooding.

Tentative and careful to speak with gentleness, Christine asked, "Can you find nothing here in Korsnäsborg that would provide a means of support? Surely, our lifestyle does not require much."

"What is to be done in this wretched town, besides digging in the dirt or wrestling fish from the sea?" Again, Raoul spoke in anger, but Christine now understood his frustration with their choice of town and forgave him.

"You are a sailor, Raoul," she said.

"A sailor, yes! Not a fisherman!" he answered.

"Could you not – " Christine started.

Raoul interrupted, "No, I cannot! I am the Vicomte de Chagny. I will not debase us both with such an untoward endeavor."

Raoul took a sharp breath and then softened. His chin fell to his chest, and his eyes closed as he exhaled a loud sigh. Although he did not speak of it again, Christine knew he thought on his lost position as a member of the official expedition to the Arctic Circle. He reached blindly toward her with his hand, and she gave hers into his gentle grip.

With another sigh, he said, "I am sorry, my darling. I am certainly not angry with you. I should not speak to you thus. I am angry with myself, with my failure as your husband."

Christine felt her throat tighten as tears threatened. Her voice quavered as she answered, "You are my savior, Raoul. Not a failure. I am happy as your wife, rich or poor."

Her eyes were fixed on him with a firm intensity, although she had to blink several times to clear her vision. Raoul had not spoken of it since their marriage, but she was always aware of the inappropriate nature of a vicomte taking a peasant girl for a wife. In some indistinct way, she felt she was to blame for his current dilemma.

He lifted his head and met her eyes. "Thank you, my dear. Thank you." His eyes fell to their hands, clasped between them, bridging the air between them. His thumb moved back and forth over the gold ring she wore, and his eyes narrowed.

"Rich or poor, I will get you a new ring, however. I'll not have you wearing *his* gift as a symbol of our marriage." His voice was a harsh rasp.

"Raoul!" For reasons Christine could not comprehend, she was offended by his suggestion and the jealous tone with which he addressed the matter. She pulled her hand from his. "He released us. This ring was his wedding gift to us. I do not need another or newer symbol of our marriage and our love, especially as you have just explained that we do not have the funds for such trivialities." After a pause in which she attempted to lower her pique, she said, "Erik is behind us."

"Do not say that man's name in this house!" The volume of Raoul's response shocked and startled her.

"Raoul, Raoul, he cannot hear us any longer." Her voice pleaded for his return to the reality of their new life.

"I know that," Raoul said, voice soft again. He leaned back in his chair and sank out of the lamplight into darkness.

After a moment, during which confusion boiled in Christine's stomach and brain, Raoul sat forward again, eyes piercing. "You are my wife. You will not wear another man's ring. I will buy you another, and you will dispose of that ring. I will not even accept the monies that might be received from its sale."

Christine did not respond because she could think of no response that would suffice. She also knew she would not throw the ring away. It had become for her a symbol of … she did not know. It conjured memories of her father, of her brief time of happy belief that the Angel of Music was her guide and guardian, sent to her from Heaven. It rested as a weight of culpability she knew she would not dispel even after burying the ring with the dead Erik, as she had promised.

But she would not throw it away.

CHAPTER 7
A FAREWELL

Travel preparations completed, Erik was free to dog the Persian as he chose. The Persian's home was more difficult to navigate than his labyrinthine and trapdoor-riddled Opera House, yet Erik had the opportunity, the time, and certainly the skill to spy as he needed.

Of an afternoon, when the Persian left his home in the company of the devoted servant Darius, Erik combed the Persian's personal effects, stifling the instinct to play tricks such as leaving belongings in slightly rearranged positions.

He was pleased to discover that the Persian's account of Erik's life, living arrangements, and actions within the Opera House – written with the purpose of being published, it seemed – was now consigned to the back of the drawer in the large but utilitarian and undecorated desk. Erik was also pleased to note that the Persian's account correctly reported that Joseph Buquet had hanged himself (albeit after falling into and being trapped in the Opera Ghost's torture chamber) and that the chandelier had fallen of its own ill-maintained accord.

Erik was more amused than saddened by the Persian's misapprehensions regarding the death of Raoul's brother, Philippe, Comte de Chagny. "You give me too much credit, Sir," Erik mused and chuckled.

The truth – which the Persian would now never learn – was that the foolish, foppish count had never rowed his own boat, nor even been in a boat so small, and could not swim. In the Comte's agitation over the disappearance of Christine and his brother the Vicomte, he had swamped the small boat and drowned in the underground lake.

Erik spoke aloud while lounging luxuriously in the Persian's private sanctum: "But you are correct that the Siren sang him to sleep rather than making an attempt at rescue. Sirens tend to be heartlessly indifferent to the lives of men." He chuckled as he tapped his foot against the hassock and rifled through the pages of the long, detailed account before returning it to the drawer.

On another occasion of spying, Erik read the short but pleasant letter the Persian wrote to Christine and her husband. It contained hopeful congratulations on their presumed marriage and informed the couple of the Opera Ghost's death:

> *…Who would have thought the intractable and*
> *unforgiving Erik would die of love in the end,*
> *my dear Madame Vicomte? But do not let this*
> *fact rest a mantle of guilt upon you. You were*
> *wrongly lured to the beast, and undoubtedly this*
> *outcome is the best end, if a melancholy one. It*

seems the master was a man, as well as a beast,
but only learned this of himself at the brim of
his demise.

The Persian wrote of his final pledge to Erik to remind Christine of her promise to come bury the poor man, although he did so only out of a sense of duty to the dead, not as a command or suggestion that Christine should indeed travel for so solemn and distasteful a task. Erik knew for a certainty Raoul would never allow Christine to return for her promised task.

The letter sat upon the Persian's desk for many days, and Erik at first wondered if the Persian intended, in the end, to keep his promise and send it. However, on the day after the short notice of the Opera Ghost's death appeared in the *Epoque*, the letter was posted. (The notice said simply, "Erik is dead," which Erik thought stingy of the daroga.) Clearly, the Persian was waiting only to include a clipping of the notice for Christine's benefit.

And still Erik waited. He knew the Persian was not finished. He knew the inquisitive blood of the police hound would not rest until the matter was truly and finally settled in his mind.

Erik watched and dogged the Persian. At nights, Erik viewed his random, banal movements through his rooms, his evenings at his writing desk, or reading until sleep claimed him where he sat. During days, Erik trailed him through streets and shops, waiting always, always, for the final closing of the book of Erik's life. When it did not come, Erik – more impatient now than at any other time in the process of purging the Persian from his life – decided to take action. He would force the final scene.

For a week, perhaps ten days, Erik reinvaded the home of the Persian. This time, he did not refrain from the small tricks that would awaken the daroga's uneasiness. A cigarette case was moved from one side of the mantel to the other. Slippers were placed farther under the bed than was the Persian's or his servant's wont. A lamp was left burning that had been unlit when the two men left the small flat, but in a back room that could not be seen from the street. Erik never moved or changed anything that could not have been moved or changed by either the Persian himself or the servant. Perhaps the Persian had simply forgotten where he placed his cigarettes or kicked his slippers. Perhaps both men had forgotten to extinguish the lamp.

Erik could see the daroga was unsettled in the alert posture and wary attitude of the Persian as he now moved about his errands around town or the surreptitious glances out his windows night and day. The Persian would not wait too much longer before confirming for himself Erik was indeed dead.

Erik mischievously provided the final touch one evening by lowering himself to the balcony outside the Persian's bedchamber and peering in, as he had once done to torment Raoul, and with much the same effect. The Persian, readying himself for bed, glanced toward the window and, with a shout, dashed across the room to where Erik knew his eyes were reflectively gleaming in the low gaslight of the bedside lamp.

Erik barely managed to remove himself from the balcony and cling below it in time to avoid the man. He struggled to contain a laugh as he heard the Persian pant heavily above him and say, "Erik haunts me even now."

The following morning, Erik was pleased to follow the Persian from his breakfast to the Opera House. After speaking briefly and politely to the man cleaning the foyer floor, the Persian slipped into the back of the great building and into the bowels of the Opera House. Already ensconced in his home, Erik awaited the Persian's arrival. Erik was confident that, while the Persian knew many of the secret routes and passages and spy-holes, he did not know them all.

The Persian crept into the home of the Opera Ghost. His stealth was such that it was quite clear the poor man half expected to find Erik in residence. The shambles Erik had left of his home soon convinced the daroga he need not creep about the abandoned rooms. The Persian carefully – almost reverently, Erik thought – searched the underground house, checking the armoire and cupboards for anything Erik might have packed before leaving. It was only when the Persian found the finished score of Erik's *Don Juan Triumphant* among the wreckage that the Persian seemed convinced.

"Ah, Erik," the Persian said aloud, with a heavy, sad sigh. "You would not have left this."

With the score wrapped, tied, and carried under one arm and a lantern in the other hand, the Persian renewed his search, this time outside the rooms of the house. After another hour, the Persian found the final persuasive evidence: a freshly dug grave, set far back from the shore of the underground lake, hidden in the shadows of the deep domain.

Erik watched, rather touched, as the Persian stood at the end of the grave for many minutes, neither moving nor uttering a sound, as if breathing the aroma of the freshly turned and mounded earth, as if imagining the epitaph on a headstone that did not exist. After a time, the quiet words of the Persian reached Erik's ears.

"Christine. You were good to the end, I see."

The Persian walked the few steps to the side of the grave, knelt, and placed the score of *Don Juan Triumphant* upon the center of the mound. After a moment more, he said, almost sadly to Erik's hearing, "Erik was a burning coal in all our lives. My body still senses the after-image." With a nod and a breathed "Farewell, Erik," the Persian rose to his feet again, and with no delay or lack of energy, with no looking back – almost as if ghosts chased him – he hurried from the darkened realm.

Finally, finally, Erik was free.

CHAPTER 8
COMTE PHILIPPE'S REVENGE

Christine opened the curtains allowing the bright sunshine into Mamma Valérius' room.

"Ah, thank you, my dear," Mamma said, full of obvious good cheer. "These old bones may not let me wander the beautiful vistas of my home country, but still, the sun that washes through the window is as warming as a mother's arms." She leaned forward as Christine pulled up the pillows and then raised herself to a sitting position.

Christine put the luncheon tray across Mamma's lap and pulled a chair to the side of the bed. Mamma hungrily eyed the tray and waggled her fingers above the food as if playing a piano, unsure of where to start.

"You certainly are an excellent cook, my dear. However did you learn?" Mamma plucked gravad lax from the plate and popped it into her mouth with a smile and an appreciative roll of her eyes.

Christine laughed. "Papa was a good many wonderful things, but he was not a talented cook."

"Mm. Mm," Mamma said around another mouthful.

46

Christine felt the praise too high and added, "It is the freshness of the food here – fresh fish, fresh vegetables – which give the good flavor."

"And good Scandinavian sunshine!" After another mouthful, Mamma said, "Aren't you going to eat, child?"

"I ate as I prepared your luncheon." After a pause, Christine asked, trying to mask her worry, "How are you feeling?"

"Stronger today. Yes, I shall be up again before you know it."

Looking at Mamma Valérius, Christine could not believe this happy statement, although Mamma's appetite seemed healthy today.

"Have you been singing, my dear? I never hear you singing," Mamma asked. She did not take her eyes from the tray before her and so did not see the visible pang that Christine felt sure crossed her face.

"There is no opportunity, Mamma," Christine answered. After a pause, she said, "That was another life."

"Nonsense! There may not be an Opera House here in Korsnäsborg, but you can sing. It is your gift! You must sing for me," Mamma replied. "I miss the house full of music as it was when you and your father lived with the dear Professor and me."

Christine had to admit she missed singing, missed it as she would miss a limb – a part of her, which gone, left her less than whole. She had not sung since leaving the Opera House and Erik, for singing had been too intimately connected to horrible memories

of fear and escape. But now, with Mamma's innocent statements –
unrelated to the tragedy of her escape from Erik – Christine
recalled that singing had always been a part of her life. To stop
singing forever would be to disrespect her father's memory … and
God, who had given her the gift.

"Well, perhaps…" Christine said.

"Only if it would make you happy, dear. I certainly will not
insist," Mamma said, smiling and reaching to pat Christine on one
cheek.

"I think it would. Thank you, Mamma." Eyes closed,
Christine trapped Mamma's frail hand against her cheek with both
of her own, then released it and smiled gratefully at the old woman.

"Will you sing now, dear? Accompaniment to my meal?"
Mamma cocked her head, pleading with her smiling eyes.

Christine at first thought to sing a passage from *Faust*,
which she had always enjoyed, but memories of the fateful night of
her disappearance from the stage flooded her, and she decided
against it.

*I must sing something that will remind me of singing with Father. I
must reweave my memories of singing until singing is simply my joy again.*

Christine stood and, humming a brief scale, sang a
melodious little song her father had taught her and which he always
told her emphasized her range. Mamma bobbed her head and kept
time with one hand as she ate.

Christine stopped when she heard the slam of the front
door. Raoul was home earlier than usual. She did not resent his

days socializing with the town leaders, as the only elite to be found in Korsnäsborg, but she was always happy when circumstances brought him home early. She wondered if he had eaten. She had prepared too much food and could give him a meal in just moments.

"I will sing for you another time," Christine said, smiling apologetically. "If you are finished, I will take your tray."

"Yes, go, go," Mamma said, making shooing motions with her hands. "I have reading to catch up on."

As Christine, tray in hand, turned to leave the room, she heard Mamma, talking to herself say, "The enthusiasm of young lovers. Ah, Professor, would that you and I could be together again and young. Young!"

Christine turned to Mamma, and Mamma winked with great exaggeration. Christine laughed, and feeling herself flush at the insinuation, hurried from the room.

"Raoul! You're home!" Christine held the tray to one side and greeted him with a kiss to the cheek. "Have you had luncheon? We could eat together." She knew she would not eat much, but preferred to eat with Raoul as a shared experience, rather than to watch him eat alone. "We could sit outside – the weather is lovely."

Raoul did not take her in his arms with enthusiasm, as was his wont, and his expression was stern and distant.

"Raoul?" Christine put the tray down on the side table. "Is something wrong, my love?"

Raoul peered at Christine with a closed and enigmatic expression and said, "I'm not hungry." When Christine did not move, he stepped to her, kissed her on the forehead, and wandered away, lost in thought.

Christine took the tray to the kitchen and then went in search of her husband. Something was bothering Raoul, and she would do her best to soothe him. She found him in the sitting room.

"Can I pour you a dr … Oh." This last utterance was made as he waggled a small glass of wine in her direction, nearly sloshing the ruby liquid over the edges.

She went to where he was sitting and knelt before him, face turned up for a kiss. Raoul obliged, although not with the slow, lingering kiss Christine hoped for.

"What is it, my husband?" she asked again, as she stood to take the chair near his.

Raoul put the wineglass down on the small table between them with a loud bang. "I am ruined," he answered.

"How …" she began.

Raoul pulled a letter from his inside coat pocket. He brandished it in a slow, watery wave and said, "This arrived today."

She reached for it, but he pulled it away.

"What is it?" she asked.

Raoul sighed deeply and stood to pace before her.

"It is a letter from my trusted friend. A letter explaining the provisions of Philippe's will."

50

When he seemed reluctant to go on, Christine prompted, "Yes?"

"I suppose you know Philippe did not approve of our marrying." Still he paced.

Christine felt a pang, but maintained a calm voice as she answered. "Naturally, I did not know, but I hardly find that surprising. You are, after all, a vicomte, and I am merely ..."

"An opera wench." Raoul uttered the words quietly and with such calmness – without the passion that would have solidified the insult – but this did not keep Christine from gasping and uttering a small cry.

Raoul turned to her. "Darling, darling. You know that is not how I think of you." He raised her, took her into his arms, and caressed her back, rocking her, with his face pressed into her hair. "I say only what my brother thought."

Christine despaired of believing him, worried perhaps he had merely spoken his mind, spoken his regret at having married her. Somehow, she controlled herself and managed to banish her threatening tears unshed. She took a deep breath and controlled her voice, as she said, "Surely this is not all your letter tells you."

"No!" Raoul took a step away from her and smacked the letter against his pant leg. "No, of course not!"

Raoul resumed pacing as he opened the letter and again surveyed its contents. "Philippe's will states specifically that I cannot inherit the title of Comte if I am married to you. He named you, specifically!"

Christine inhaled a deep breath, and said, "Go on."

"The title will be held in abeyance until there is a male heir born – he allows that it may be mine – and that child will inherit."

Christine understood the hurt Raoul must be feeling, and thought to console him that he still retained the title of vicomte. Philippe could not take that away from Raoul.

Before she could speak, Raoul continued. "And the worst and damnable part of the whole affair! The assets of the estate are frozen, except for allowances for my two sisters, if necessary, because the Comte is dead, and I am presumed so." Raoul panted and paced, making a complete circuit of the room.

"But that can be easily solved, can it not? Can you not merely present yourself and make proof the wrongness of this allegation?" Christine could not see how anything could be simpler.

"Of course not," Raoul growled. His anger and frustration only seemed to be growing with his pacing, which also gained fervency and speed. "My friend tells me I am implicated in my brother's death! If I present myself, it may only be to be arrested!"

"But …" Christine started.

"No!" Raoul roared, stopping his relentless movement to glare at Christine.

Christine raised her hands to her mouth, and the tears, which she had controlled thus far, spilled onto her cheeks. Raoul sighed and returned to his chair. He placed his elbows on his knees and his head into his hands.

"How could I have allowed jealousy and your song to seduce me? My pride merely wanted to remove my beautiful childhood friend from the clutches of a man she loved more than me. I wanted to win you from him." He did not speak with the volume meant to direct his words to Christine, but seemed to speak to himself.

Christine, hands still over her mouth, tears flowing freely, felt as if a great weight settled on her chest. She wanted to say something, wanted to scream his name and beg him to erase the words, but her throat constricted, barely allowing her to breathe. She ran from the room and fought her way through slashing beams of sunlight to her bedchamber, where she threw herself on her bed and wept with abandon.

An endless time later, Raoul knocked and, calling her name, let himself into her room. Christine turned away and hid her swollen face in the bed linens.

She listened as he apologized in the most fervent tones, as he caressed her and held her. "I love you, Christine. I love you. Forgive me. It was anger speaking, not my heart. My heart is forever in your hands. Forgive me."

She allowed him to undress her, having no energy to be scandalized by the early hour of the day. He made love to her with every bit of tenderness available to his strong and knowing hands. He repeated sweet endearments through his kisses to her neck and shoulders, and she could not doubt his sincerity or even his love.

Dinner that evening was full of small touches and endearing glances between the two. Mamma Valérius joined them at the table, and smiled knowingly at the couple, especially when Christine blushed as Raoul caught her eye and caressed her hand.

In bed later that night, Christine smiled to herself, remembering the afternoon and Raoul's sweet affection. But, after settling into the bed linens, her mind treacherously recalled the statement that had led to the apology and affection, and her smile faded. She pushed the memory of that pain to the bottom of her mind, but knew, as a slow tear escaped her eye and rolled in a lazy path toward her pillow, that she would never truly forget.

CHAPTER 9
ERIK TO SWEDEN

Erik's voyage to Sweden was tedious due to the small size of his cabin. It was not the first such voyage he had made, but it had been years since he had been on the sea. He had grown used to the expansive spaces of his home in the Opera House and his relative freedom in the arms of his adopted city of Paris. Had it not been for the books he read during the voyage, giving him at least a mental freedom from tedium, he might have thrown himself overboard.

His adopted persona as a member of the Moorish royal family granted him the largest of the personal cabins and allowed him freedom from prying questions and eyes, but the need for secrecy kept him shut almost continually in the small, dark room. The black cream he applied to his skin to complete the illusion caused his skin to itch abominably. His only pleasant moments aboard ship were those nights when he stole to the deck and allowed the ocean spray to dash against his uncovered face. The crew was sufficiently in awe and fear of his rumored persona to keep well away from him during these midnight expeditions.

After making port in Kalmar on the southeast coast of Sweden, Erik's impatience was tempered only by the knowledge that his Christine grew closer by the day and that he at least now stood upon the earth in the same country as his love. He made his way aboveground north to Stockholm enclosed in a luxurious private carriage. In Stockholm, he exchanged his lavish appointments and disguise for that of a poor laborer and traveled overland north, stopping at a small fishing village he knew to be near his final destination. He went to the docks and loitered, hoping to catch a modest fishing vessel north to Korsnäsborg, Christine's new home. It was here Erik experienced the first real freedom in his life from the curse of his mangled features.

He stood at the pier, sole bag of possessions shouldered over a tattered, hooded rain cloak, recalling from his travels the cadence, the music, the rhythm, and song of the Swedish language. Having spread the word of his desire for passage, he could do nothing but wait, so he amused himself by watching the various sailors and fishermen as they passed. He noted several with missing fingers or hands, one man with a missing foot, and several with hideous scars upon their faces, arms, or bared legs. He surmised that ocean fishing was a dangerous occupation and that sharks or other large and brutal sea creatures often fed on the unlucky.

He had only just reached this conclusion when a rumbling bass voice behind him said, "Oy, are you the fellow wanting to get to Korsnäsborg?"

As Erik turned to face the speaker, his hood was pulled from his head, and Erik stood, bareheaded and barefaced, before a large, golden-haired, and hairy man, wearing sailor's pants and an open shirt. Erik stood motionless, torn between the now-ancient instinct to cover his face with an arm and the more newly won habit of arrogance that had attended him in his Opera House. Arrogance overcame the instinct to cower, and Erik waited, without speaking, for the inevitable reaction. He had not yet determined if he would strike the man when it came.

"Whoa, friend. There's a face. Sharkie get you?" The enormous man smiled, showing small, childlike teeth, spaces visible between each pearl. He raised his left hand, and said, "Got me, too."

The large hand was missing the smallest finger and the next, and a portion of the meat of the palm. The shock of this amiable reaction, this unhorrified reception of what Erik had come to accept as his revolting visage, left Erik with no words for response. His mouth opened and then closed.

"Guess I was luckier than you," the man said, laughed in round tones, and remarked, "Or maybe not. You were lucky enough to be standing here today. That's damned lucky, I'd say!" He laughed again.

When Erik still said nothing, the man held out an enormous slab of a hand as if to shake, and said, "Mattis is the name."

"Erik," Erik answered and hesitantly shook Mattis' engulfing hand. His surprise at the encounter did not leave him with the wit to give another name.

"Korsnäsborg, eh?" Mattis said. "I'm headed that way." He cocked his head on an enormous neck and said, "Say, if you're willing to work, I won't charge you for the trip. Anybody who can survive a sharkie has to be a fearless fisherman."

Still reeling from the impact of this man's good-natured acceptance, Erik responded, "I haven't worked the trade in some time."

"'Salright. It's like walking; you never forget." He clapped a hand to Erik's back as though they were old friends and led him down the pier toward a small fishing boat rife with activity. Upon boarding, Mattis, hand still upon Erik's shoulder in comradely regard, announced, "Hey! This is Erik. Sharkie got him."

Erik was greeted with general halloos, and he raised a hand in response. Mattis helped him stow his bag, and where he could, Erik assisted in the preparation for casting off.

He slept that night in a common cabin, surrounded by the inoffensive smell of fish and hardworking men as well as various sorts of snoring and grunting. The novelty of such perfect acceptance kept him awake long after the others were dreaming. Not even in his youth, when he traveled Europe in various fairs as "the Living Corpse" had he found such unquestioning acceptance. After all, his purpose in such fairs was to inspire horror in the audience, and his natural aloofness and cadaverous appearance had often prompted mocking aversion even in his fellow showmen.

How strange, after all these years to find a place – a people – who looked upon his tragic features as a sign of strength. Perhaps even as a sign of good luck. The fishermen had certainly reacted to his presence aboard as a favorable omen.

His experience of the afternoon, while he carefully observed the fisherman's trade and offered what meager assistance he could muster, and finally, shared a meal with the men, touched him deeply. During the meal, Mattis hunkered near as though he believed Erik his own discovered treasure, and the men included Erik in their stories and their bawdy jokes and their laughter. Erik had long since given up hope of such open camaraderie.

As he rocked in the hammock, he thought of how easily he could enrich Mattis – in profound gratitude – but then realized no amount of monetary assistance could repay the man's instant and unaffected offer of friendship. In fact, payment would be a gross obscenity in return for such an offering.

No, Erik thought. *This man has earned what I have given no man before: my loyalty and friendship.* Erik wept grateful tears.

In the morning, after a hearty breakfast of dried fish and beer, the labor of these hardworking men resumed. Erik left the task of sailing and tacking to the men who performed these functions as a flawless dance. He believed they could navigate the boat through the local waters even if blinded, using merely smell, the sun, and the wind upon their faces for guidance. Much as he wished to observe the hot, pleasant performance, Erik threw his efforts into assisting with the fishing. He cast empty nets, pulled up cages anchored on their last passage through these waters. He added his strength to pulling up heavy, dripping nets bowing with their sparkling, shivering, silver and jewel-toned catch.

"Quite a bounty," Mattis huffed after one such load was dropped to the deck, hearty smile spread across his roughly handsome features. "'Tis good luck to have you aboard, Erik, I'll swear it."

And later, when Erik had retied a loosed bit of cording, Mattis appeared at his elbow and said, "Now there's no knot I've seen before." The large face screwed into a puzzled squint as he examined the knot and then tested it. After flashing another large grin at Erik, Mattis boomed, "Oy, men! Gather 'round. Erik's got something to teach us." After Erik demonstrated the complicated but infallible knot – learned during his time in India – Mattis clapped him on the back and said, "Asset to the boat, you are."

After another genial evening meal, Erik stretched in his hammock, suffused with pleasure – at a good day's work, at the uncomplicated company, and at the thought of Christine mere hours away – and soon slept.

The morning proceeded quickly, with docking and unloading at the meager docks of Korsnäsborg. The excitement welling in Erik at the nearness of his goal added energy to his efforts. He accepted advice from the fervent Mattis regarding lodgings and declined the offer of a permanent position with the crew.

"I have business to attend to in Korsnäsborg," was his only explanation, though it troubled him not to be more forthright with his friend.

"Business to attend to! Ho ho!" Mattis laughed. "Sounds high and mighty. Much too high and mighty for a market town such as this. Must be a woman!" After another warm laugh, Mattis sobered and, with a hand to Erik's shoulder, said, "You'll have a place if you need one. I stop here often on my sojourns of this coast – although my wife's tucked safely away in Gävle! – and luck is a passenger I'll take aboard happily." And after a pat on the shoulder, "Good fortune to you, Erik."

Moved with gratitude for this simple, open man, and despite a reluctance to touch another, Erik placed his hand on the mountainous shoulder of the other. "Lucky," said Erik, thinking of the danger of using his name in so small a village – Christine would surely perk at the name. "Just call me 'Lucky.' I owe you my thanks."

"Lucky, indeed." The great man boomed with laughter again. "Thank me by joining me again some time." And with another laugh, Mattis moved back toward the boat and the activities that would dock them for the evening. Erik watched the man until Mattis reached the small gangplank, turned, raised a hand, and bellowed, "Another time, Lucky!"

Erik raised a hand in return, pulled the hood of his cloak over his head, and turned to survey his new home. His eyes searched the walkways and open buildings near the docks for Christine. Failing to find her, he walked – eyes searching from beneath the cowl of his hood – toward the lodgings where he would temporarily make his home.

CHAPTER 10
TENSIONS

Christine was happy. She was not ecstatic, not deliriously and sublimely blissful, as she first imagined she would be, but happy. She chided herself for childish dreams of Heaven on Earth in the protective arms of Raoul. She knew married life was full of moments of banality – or thought she knew. She could not remember the marriage relationship of her own parents, but certainly she was aware that the marriage of Professor and Mamma Valérius rarely rose above the merely pleasant. And even *their* rapport was higher in scale than others she had witnessed from time to time.

Raoul was very sweet and solicitous, even through his unhappiness at their dwindling financial resources. He eschewed Christine's suggestions for how either he or she could garner additional funds, but Christine had long lived the life of a wandering peasant performer and managed to limit their expenses in countless hidden ways. She was happy to be of some small assistance, even if Raoul – quite correctly – did not consider her capable of understanding the ways of finance.

Tonight, they were to attend a dinner party being given by the mayor, and Christine had robbed two old gowns of their finery in altering and ornamenting the finest of her dresses. She was very pleased with the results, as the gown reminded her of the beautiful costumes she had worn in her performances in the Opera House. (She limited this brief recollection to the gowns, not the full import of the Opera House in her past. She refused to let her mind turn to Erik.) She chose the most elegant and refined of the jewelry Raoul had lavished on her after their wedding.

Mamma Valérius clapped like a child when Christine showed her the finished result of an afternoon of preparation. "Oh, my dear! You are lovely, lovely!" Mamma paused for another of the racking coughs that had been troubling her more and more frequently of late. "Ravishing! Your dear husband will not keep you long at this evening's entertainments, mark my words. He will want you to himself!"

Christine felt her face redden at the statement, although she had become accustomed since her marriage to Mamma's frequent ribald insinuations. Before the marriage, Mamma had found virtue the most appropriate topic for the young Christine, but certainly the rules of conduct had changed since Mamma's foster daughter had become a married woman. Rather than reproach Mamma for such moments, even in her mind, she relished the warmth provided by these private and familiar improprieties.

Raoul was equally appreciative when he arrived shortly thereafter. "Who is this beautiful creature?" he exclaimed after kissing her thoroughly. "You would steal my soul from me!"

Christine released herself from his arms and turned a slow circle before his admiring glance. "Do you like it?"

"Like it, Madame? You are extraordinarily beautiful! I will have the pride of escorting the most exquisite woman at dinner this evening." Raoul kissed her again, and turning from her, said over his shoulder, "I must wash and change. I must attempt to do you justice, my dear!"

Uncharacteristically, Christine poured herself a small glass of sherry and settled in the sitting room to wait for Raoul. The warm liqueur deepened the glow within her that had been sparked by Raoul's effusive praise.

When Raoul returned to her, handsome in the sharp lines of his eveningwear, he swept her again into his arms and kissed her warmly. Apparently tasting the sherry, he made a show of licking his lips.

"Ah, the honey of Heaven from the lips of an angel."

At the word "angel," Christine gave a small start, but Raoul playfully feigned hunger for her lips and kissed her again, releasing her from her momentary recollection of Erik.

"Raoul, I shall have to reapply my lip rouge!" Christine said, pushing at him and moving toward her bedchamber. "Finish my sherry?"

"Hurry, my love."

The party was a small but elegant affair, boasting the best of the cuisine Korsnäsborg had to offer: pickled herring in wine and mustard sauces, meatballs with lingonberry jam, steamed and fresh vegetables, including a rich cheesy potato casserole, succulent young lamb, and smoked and fresh fish of all kinds. Christine enjoyed the slow elegant dance of the meal, accompanied by the muted music of silver on china and crystal touching crystal over toasts.

Raoul seemed happy and relaxed despite his usual frustration over his lack of command of the language – during one evening at home he had commented vehemently on the "arrogance of the Swedes" and fumed over a snigger he thought directed toward his lack of good accent. But tonight he seemed quite content.

After dinner, the party retired to a large music room, where several of the ladies took turns at the piano, serenading the guests with songs of springtime and young love. It was not the grand music of the Opera House, but Christine was enchanted with the pleasant, if inexpert, performances. The glow that had suffused her upon Raoul's homecoming earlier in the evening had grown – no doubt with the assistance of the wine at dinner – until Christine felt effusive and warmly satisfied. She sat – Raoul standing behind her, hand on her shoulder – allowing the conversations around her to wash over her without meaning. Her spoken name broke her undirected reverie.

"Christine, I have heard a rumor you have a lovely singing voice. Do you play?" It was the mayor's kind, homely wife speaking.

Raoul's hand tightened upon her shoulder. "No, I'm afraid I do not play well enough to do justice to the previous performances," she answered. Raoul's touch loosened. She looked a question up to Raoul, confused at the meaning of the signal.

"Perhaps you can sing for us, then?" The mayor's stout wife took several steps in Christine's direction, hand raised in invitation.

Christine felt herself flush with the excitement of singing.

Before she could decide to rise or respond, Raoul broke in. "My wife has just recovered from a slight ailment to the throat. For her own sake, I am afraid I cannot allow her to accommodate you this evening." He patted Christine's shoulder solicitously.

Christine turned her questioning eyes again to Raoul, but he simply smiled, bent, and kissed her on the cheek. This act was greeted with a general murmur of approval from those present.

"Oh, no, of course," answered the mayor's wife, plump hand coming to rest on her breast. Turning and gesturing at a very attractive, slender young woman, "Perhaps Gunilla might be enticed to honor us with another song?"

Gunilla, looking to her councilman husband, blushed prettily, rose, and with a small curtsey, resumed the piano. In her confusion at Raoul's blatant and incomprehensible lie, Christine did not hear the performance. Throughout, she did not look to Raoul again. He would explain himself later, and the explanation would be perfectly reasonable. Consoling herself thus, Christine settled back into the glow of the evening's pleasantries.

The evening concluded, thanks and good evenings were graciously given, and Christine took Raoul's arm for the short walk back to their house.

"You were beautiful this evening," he said, bringing her hand to his lips and smiling at her out of the corner of his eye.

"Thank you, Raoul," she answered. "It was a lovely evening." She waited for his explanation of his behavior.

"I could eat like that every night," he continued. "Of course, then I would be as round as our dear mayor." He patted his flat stomach and chuckled to himself.

Christine looked at Raoul, and he returned her gaze, still smiling. "Are you cold, my dear?" he asked, pulling her cloak closed at the front.

"No, thank you, I am quite warm," Christine answered. After several more steps taken in silence, Christine could wait no longer. "I have had a throat ailment? I have no recollection of this ailment, Raoul," she said.

Raoul's arm stiffened under her own. His handsome face lost his smile, and he did not look at her. Several more steps.

"Raoul?"

"I will not have you disgrace us by acting like a showgirl or common entertainer!"

The sharpness of his words startled Christine into resuming her silence, which silence after several moments must have satisfied Raoul that the topic was closed. His arm relaxed under her hand.

"Those other ladies did not disgrace themselves or their husbands with their performances," Christine said. Raoul's arm and jaw tightened again, but Christine determined to continue. "They were not the performances of showgirls, but were a pleasant entertainment. We have enjoyed such before."

"I don't wish you to sing in public. Do the wishes of your husband mean nothing?" Raoul answered. He stopped walking, and this time turned his eyes to Christine for her response.

A small coal of anger and defiance smoldered within her – that he should deny her the exercise of her talent! – but was doused by the pain and pleading in his eyes. She need not perform in public. She must attempt to understand the ways of a vicomte.

"Of course," she said, dropping her eyes. "I understand."

The remainder of their walk was made in silence, Christine inexplicably feeling that some small part of her had been crushed between boot and gravel.

The subject, however, was not closed.

Two days later, Christine sang at the request of an increasingly weakened Mamma Valérius. Quite alarmingly, the dear old woman's cough had worsened overnight, and each breath was a wheezing gasp that pained Christine almost as much as it seemed to pain Mamma.

Christine heard Raoul enter the house, but could not bring herself to stop this performance short of completion. The dying woman might never hear another song. She finished the song from *Faust*, which she had managed to distance in her mind from her last performance at the Opera House. She crept to Mamma Valérius' side and pulled the covers to her chin. The old woman seemed asleep.

When Christine turned to leave the room, she discovered Raoul standing in the doorway, legs wide, one hand on each side of the doorframe, undisguised anger festering in his eyes. Christine put her finger to her lips and, gesturing to Mamma with the other hand, walked to the door. Raoul backed and stepped aside to allow her passage. Christine closed the door to the sick room.

"You are angry," Christine said, almost in a whisper. She saw no purpose in any coy misunderstanding on her part. She led Raoul down the corridor away from the sick room.

"You can't keep from singing, can you?" Raoul's answering whisper was harsh in his throat.

"Why should I? You asked me not to perform in public, and certainly singing for Mamma Valérius is not singing in public." Much to her surprise, Christine felt quite in control of herself.

She led the way to the sitting room, Raoul pacing behind her, and pulled the doors closed behind them.

"You miss him! You still love him!" The words burst from Raoul before Christine could turn around to face him.

At first, Christine could not comprehend the meaning behind his words.

"You love Erik! You have always loved Erik! You sing for him still!" Raoul took several panting breaths and continued, "Well, the man is dead. I've had word from the Persian. Your love is dead!"

All the calm control Christine had maintained to this point burst into fragments, and tears sprang to her eyes. Her mind flashed to her promise to return the ring upon Erik's death, but she knew this was not the time – if ever there was a time – to broach this subject.

"Raoul, how can you speak to me thus?" Her hands fluttered between them, unable to come to rest. "He gave me to you, and I came willingly into your arms!"

"Came as he ordered you, perhaps. Was your love for him so great?" The bitterness of his words nearly choked Christine.

"Raoul, Raoul, I loved *you*. I came happily to you. You were my savior. Do you not recall that terrible time?" She stepped toward him, arms supplicating.

"'Loved,' you say." Raoul stepped back and away. His rejection stabbed at her.

"I love you, I love you still!" The tears now poured down her contorted face, and a sob caught in her throat. "Raoul, how can you doubt me?"

"You sing. You sing and remember him." His voice was low and shaded with pain and jealousy.

Christine, heart breaking in her chest, arms still reaching for Raoul, could find nothing to say to such an undeserved accusation. Raoul – seeming determined to avoid her touch – walked in a wide circle around where she stood, frozen in her agony, and left the room. Moments later, she heard the main door of the house open and close. This was the sound that unfroze her.

She collapsed to the floor, face buried in her arms on the seat of a chair.

"I sing for Mamma, Raoul. I sing for Mamma. That's all." She sobbed as she spoke to the empty room. In her despair, she felt some small measure of guilt because she knew her mind did sometimes turn to Erik as she sang. *But not with love. Not with love.*

An hour later, when she had regained her control and some semblance of her usual features with applications of cold cloths, she went to Mamma's room. Much as she wanted to confide in the woman, she knew she would not burden her thus. She could at least hold the woman's hand, she thought as she entered the room, and take comfort there.

Mamma Valérius was dead.

CHAPTER 11
SETTLING IN

Erik leased a small, disreputable shack set apart from any other shacks and nearer the docks than the village proper. He knew better than to affect a higher-class disguise, for this would attract the well-to-do of the small village (such as they were) and would undoubtedly lead to attracting Raoul. Several days' reconnoiter had led to the knowledge that sailors and fishermen often leased these small shacks and that no one would question "Lucky," lately of Mattis' boat (for Mattis was well-known and liked among the seaside peoples), coming landside for a brief stay. Further, the modest sum required for the lease would raise no eyebrows and cause no impertinent questions. In these first few days in Korsnäsborg, Erik did not catch sight of Christine.

Erik was aware he could not ask after his beloved without eliciting the curiosity of the rough people who worked dockside. But most were willing gossips, and he kept his ear tuned for mention of Christine. After several more days, Erik could no longer resist the magnetic pull to find Christine and wandered from the dockside toward the village proper, careful to remain unobtrusive without appearing to skulk. From beneath his hood, his eyes searched faces, figures, gestures for those of a woman so familiar to him that a mere moment's observation would reveal her.

In the cool of one early morning, Erik left his small shack and, walking with the silence of a cat along the wooden boards that raised the path to his home from the muck, saw a vision that sucked his breath from him.

Christine! His beloved Christine!

He continued along the walk, unwilling to draw attention to himself by stopping in the solitary path, and moved into the shadows cast by the makeshift wall of an open-air stall. From this vantage, he feasted upon every detail of his angel.

She was as beautiful as his perfect recollection of her – golden hair gleaming, upturned almond-shaped, blue eyes smiling, full mouth curled in a charmingly open smile. Her dress was simple, yet of better quality than those coarser dresses worn by the women of the docks, as was her shawl. She was gloveless, and her slender fingers danced as she gestured to the various wares of the fishmonger. A basket hung over one gracefully bent arm, and the fine lace that trimmed the covering cloth glowed in the morning sun, accenting the gleaming impression of freshness and youth she exuded.

Erik watched as she chose two fish and spoke pleasantly with the fishmonger. He could not hear her words, but how else could she be speaking than pleasantly, with her smile and the almost child-like tilt of her head as she listened to the response? He watched as she accepted the paper-wrapped packages, and after placing them in the basket, she moved away, stately and graceful, toward the village. Erik moved to the fishmonger's stall and surveyed the wares.

"Which is freshest?" he asked.

"All's fresh," was the short answer.

"Ah. Well, which did the lady decide upon? Perhaps I will take her advice on the matter," Erik said, gesturing with his head to the back of the retreating Christine.

"My best, my best," answered the fishmonger, now smiling, eyes darting between Christine and his wares, as his hands raised a small, white fish toward Erik. Erik agreed to the price, and the fishmonger began wrapping the sale, eyes still darting in the direction of Christine.

"Lovely girl," the fishmonger offered. "Lady, indeed. Hear she's married to a vicomte now, but she doesn't put on airs. Talks to me as though I was her father, God rest his soul. Lovely man, lovely man. Remember his playing and her singing as a child. Doesn't sing now, though, such a shame, such a shame."

Erik did not need to prompt the fishmonger further, for the man seemed eager to babble on about the "dear girl." His wife, when she emerged from behind the hanging curtain at the back of the stall, was more than willing to provide a prompt or another comment when the man seemed to be tapering off.

Erik learned where Christine resided, received directions as well as comments on the nearest neighbors, and even obtained a description of the flowering plants adorning the yard of the modest house – the fishmonger's wife had delivered there once. Erik also learned Christine's foster mother was in residence, and sickly, which was information new to Erik, unreported by his detectives in their report on Christine's whereabouts. Erik maintained his amiable if not too apparently fervent attention and did not waver from his seemingly inattentive grunted responses – "ah" and "I see" – even when the couple insisted on informing him of what a popular figure Raoul was about town. It took great effort, but Erik kept in check the rage that threatened at the flattering description of the damnable Raoul.

"Charming and handsome," said the wife, enthusiastically.

"Enough to turn an old woman's head," said her husband and was answered with a short guffaw from the woman and an elbow to the ribs.

Erik took his packaged fish and returned to his shack. Once inside the darkened one-room abode, Erik flung the fish at the bare wooden wall, bursting the careful wrapping. His rage over Raoul's unfortunate presence and popularity demanded he crash about, pounding walls, splintering the already rickety table, chair, and bed, but the commotion would be heard through the thin walls of the shack.

Instead, Erik paced the small space, determined to regain the radiant flood of emotion that overcame him on sight of Christine. Raoul was irrelevant, a hideous eyesore – heartsore! – upon which Erik would not dwell. He would create a blind spot in his mind and imagination into which the wretched vicomte would disappear. After regaining his self-control, Erik sat at the single table, and eyes closed, reconstructed every detail of Christine as she had appeared before him this morning. Now that he had found her, like a man returning to his opium, Erik determined to see her again and again. To hear her, if proximity permitted.

Over the next month, Erik renewed his faith in his ability to move invisibly through the world – a world defined by Christine. Erik accompanied Christine on her shopping trips in and about the village, watched her work in the flower garden she lovingly maintained, and eavesdropped on her pleasant conversations with Madame Valérius. The weather and Christine's belief in the curative value of fresh air conspired to keep the old woman's window open most days. He swooned on the occasions when Christine sang for the old woman and only kept from replying in song by the knowledge of the disastrous consequences.

In the evenings, alone in his shack, Erik composed long and loving letters to Christine, always beginning the missives with endearments to "my dear wife" and writing as though he was a husband away, returning soon. He never posted the letters for delivery. In all this, he never allowed Raoul to impinge on his awareness. In his mind, Christine's apparent happiness was because she was Erik's wife.

Twice during the month, he allowed Mattis to persuade him to make a day trip on the sea. Although he was torn at the thought of not seeing his Christine for the day, he still cherished the open friendship and affection freely afforded him by the fisherman and returned the friendship by allowing himself to be persuaded offshore. The two days of sailing were made more pleasant by the fact that "Lucky" – as he was now known onboard and off – could relinquish the ever-present hooded cloak he wore in the village. In fact, his habit of remaining hooded in the village was quickly rendered unsuspicious by Mattis' heartily whispered confidence to dock mates that "Lucky" was ashamed of his appearance since his terrible but victorious battle with a "sharkie." (Yet another act of friendship by Mattis for which Erik was grateful.)

One evening, not many days before Madame Valérius succumbed to her illness and died, Erik engaged in the most audacious of his exploits. Observing Christine leaving the house dressed for dinner (a dark, well-dressed shadow at her side whom Erik refused to recognize or acknowledge), Erik entered the house. He moved through the house, touching items here and there as he imagined Christine had touched them. He spent long minutes in Christine's bedchamber, touching her belongings, and intoxicating himself with Christine's scent in the bed linens.

As he crept down the hall to quit the home, he passed the door to what he knew to be Madame Valérius' room. He heard a cough. On a whim, he pulled his hood higher over his head and entered the darkened room. He waited for his eyes to adjust to the gloom of the sick room and crossed to the chair that sat beside the bed. Picturing Christine sitting in the chair holding the frail woman's hand, he seated himself and took the woman's limp hand in his own.

"Christine?" came the woman's voice, as she squeezed the hand that now held her own. "By the saints, child, your hand is cold as ice." The woman coughed with the effort of putting indignity into her words, and the breath that followed was harsh and wheezing. "Christine?" she asked again, voice close to a whisper, once she had recovered.

Erik did not answer.

"Ah, no. Not Christine. It is the Angel of Death." She waited and then asked into the silence, "Is it time?"

"Not yet, Madame," Erik answered. Then: "You are aware that the time is near?"

"Yes, and may God help me, I am often afraid." This statement was followed by another wracking cough. Erik waited until it had subsided.

"Fear not, Madame. Your husband awaits you in Heaven." It was the only kindness Erik could do for the woman who had so cherished his beloved.

"Ah. Ah, thank you." Erik heard the sniffle that let him know tears were imminent.

"Sleep now," he said.

"Christine does not know," she said.

"Surely she suspects, Madame," he answered.

"You must not tell her!" she said, with more force than Erik thought possible, and a tightening of the pressure to his hand.

"Christine will not see me for a long time," Erik answered, smiling sadly at the ironic truth of the statement.

"Good, good. I will sleep now. Thank you ..." The words trailed off to a whisper.

Erik stayed until the woman fell asleep. Then he pulled his now warm hand from the limp grasp of the woman and crept from the room.

"For you, Christine," he sighed as he closed the door and retreated into the darkness of the night.

Not many days later, dazed and distracted by the sound of Christine singing to the old matron in the middle of the day, Erik was nearly discovered by Raoul's early homecoming. Providently, Raoul did not glance to the flowering bushes in which Erik concealed himself.

It was thus that he heard a terrible argument between Christine and her monster husband – an argument that began by informing Erik that Raoul had prohibited Christine from singing in public. This enraged Erik to a degree that he could no longer pretend the non-existence of the scoundrel, and he swore an anger-filled oath to punish the man. Such was the depth of his anger, he was knocked to his knees at the side of the house when he heard Raoul's fevered accusation.

"You love Erik! You have always loved Erik!" Raoul's anger-distorted voice continued, but for many moments, Erik heard nothing, save the clanging repetition of these incomprehensible words in his own head.

Erik remained, frozen, hanging on the words of the unhappy couple, until Raoul left the house again. Even with Christine's fervent denials – for what else could she say? – and the relentless tears that followed, Erik left the house filled with a heretofore unimaginable hope filling his breast. If Raoul accused, perhaps he had reason. Perhaps Christine had betrayed something.

Perhaps I still have Christine's heart.

The following day, Erik left a perfect rose upon the counter in Christine's kitchen, where she would be sure to find it upon her return from the day's shopping. He was made all the more hopeful when Christine did not thank her husband for the little gift.

Perhaps …

CHAPTER 12
DREAM OF A CHILD

The solemnity of the days following Mamma Valérius'
death and burial blurred Christine's mind and separated her from
the reality of her own life. She still engaged in her normal activities
– shopping, cooking, cleaning, mending – but for days, these were
actions undertaken as if in sleep. Raoul was careful of her, spending
more time at the house during the day and urging her to take to
bed, if need be, but Christine moved through her chores as an
automaton.

"Christine, darling, certainly this can wait," Raoul said,
coming into the room where Christine was cleaning the silver.

Christine heard him, but could think of no response other
than to continue polishing the silver.

"Are you well?" he asked, taking the hand that held her rag
and bending close to peer into her eyes.

After a hesitation, during which his question broke apart,
whirled, and reassembled in her mind, she said, "Yes, Raoul, I am
well."

"Perhaps you should lie down for a moment," he said, squeezing the hand holding the rag.

"I must tend to the shopping," she said, putting down the large spoon and the rag.

"Are you still angry with me?" he asked. When she looked to his face questioningly – having, in all sincerity, no thought as to what his question might refer – she saw that his features were contorted with a pleading for forgiveness. The features of a little boy imitating a puppy.

"Am I …?" she said.

"I didn't mean the things I said," he said, words rushed, pleading eyes drawing near, both hands grasping both of hers. "I was jealous. I have always been jealous of that monster and his strange effects upon you. I am merely weak and ridiculous to continue such foolish thoughts now the man is dead. Forgive me?" Again the pleading eyes. "Please, forgive me?"

Now Christine remembered. She wished she did not. She did not wish to dwell on that horrible conversation again. She made every attempt to sweep it aside.

Trying to smile, wondering if the awkward twist of her mouth would seem to Raoul like a smile, she said, "Of course I forgive you." She embraced him. His arms were tentative as they enfolded her. She had not said enough. "I am merely sad – no … heartbroken! – over the loss of Mamma. I would give much for even another day with her. Now I have lost my father and the only mother I remember." She pulled away from Raoul so he could see her face as she smiled again. "At least I still have you." She leaned toward him to kiss him.

After an uncertain hesitation, Raoul's eyes searching hers, seeking her sincerity, Raoul lowered his face and kissed her. Partway through the kiss, his arms tightened around her, and his kiss gained eagerness. Christine was breathless when he released her. He clutched her to his chest and murmured into her hair.

"I love you, Christine. I love you so."

"I love you, Raoul," she answered. She hoped the tone of her answer did not betray the numbness she felt inside. She knew it was no weakness of Raoul's, but at this moment, his love did not comfort her.

Over the next weeks, Christine felt a slow return to the semblance of herself. She missed Mamma Valérius, but created an image in her mind of Father and Mamma Valérius smiling down on her, watching her as she went about her chores. She felt their love and their eyes upon her as she worked in the flower garden and strode in the sun to market. She collected the flowers Raoul secretly left – he was such a loving man! – into magnificent bouquets around the house. But still she seemed tired and without energy.

It was not until some weeks later that Christine realized the reason for her sudden, constant exhaustion. She wished all the more that Mamma Valérius were here. …

No. I mustn't think like that. Mamma is with me, as Father is always with me.

She forced her exhaustion aside and worked diligently at her chores and ended by preparing an exquisite meal with which to celebrate at dinner with Raoul. She was in the kitchen when he arrived home.

"My, my!" he said from the dining room, his appreciation apparent. "What is the occasion, my beautiful wife?" He was standing beside the dining table and gesturing at the good linens, the gleaming silver and crystal, the numerous candles she had placed there. He came to her without hesitation and kissed her. She pulled back from his embrace and smiled at him, wondering if he could read the occasion in her eyes.

"You certainly are ravishing this evening. I am pleased to see my wife appearing so happy again."

As the meal ended and Raoul sat back, satisfied, in his chair, he said, "So? What is the secret? You've been smiling at a secret all the way through dinner. You've only half-heard what I've said. Tell." His smile was infectious, and Christine felt her own smile growing.

"Raoul," she said.

"Yes?" he answered, leaning forward to clasp her hand.

"You are to be a father!" The words came almost explosively from her, the pressure to utter them having built almost beyond endurance over the day.

"I ...?" Raoul said. A great laugh burst from him, and he bounded from his chair, knocking it to the floor behind him, and swept Christine into his arms. He lifted her and spun in a circle, still laughing.

"How perfectly wonderful!" he said, as he replaced Christine on her feet. He embraced her again and showered kisses upon her head and cheeks. Then he released her and said, "Oh, my. Oh, I'm sorry! Should I be careful?"

Christine laughed, full of delight. "No, Raoul, you need not be careful of your kisses. Your kisses led to this lovely development, after all." Christine felt her features flushing as she uttered these words, and she thought again of Mamma.

Yes, Mamma is still with me. I hear her ribald words from my own mouth.

This thought was followed darkly by the thought that she did not hear her Father's music from her mouth, but she pushed the thought away as unworthy of this happy moment.

Raoul laughed again and again kissed her cheek, although this time without the squeezing embrace. "This baby shall be a boy!" Raoul said, pacing excitedly away from her and back again, heels clicking as he moved from the carpet to the floor. "And he shall be handsome, and make his father proud!" He held his hand up, one finger pointed to the ceiling, like a lecturer making a profound point.

Christine giggled again, hands clasped before her chin. "Or a girl. A wisp of a girl, who shall play by the sea and collect sunshine in her hair."

"Yes, yes, Christine. But a boy! A boy! He would inherit the title! Don't you see?" Raoul put his hands to her arms just below her shoulders and threw his head back and directed another laugh to the ceiling. Then he paced the floor again, away from Christine and back to her, rubbing his hands together.

His words, and his hand gesture – like a miser counting his gold – sent a small chill through Christine, and she stood, a little afraid and speechless, feeling her smile droop from her face like a flower without water.

With a tremor in her voice she could not prevent, she said, "This is the reason for your excitement? The title?" She was terrified to hear his answer.

"What?" Raoul answered, as though he had not heard her question, and then he spun and strode back toward her, arms thrown out to embrace the world. "Oh, no! Of course not! My goodness, Christine – boy, girl, I will be happy! This is the best news in the world!" He wrapped his arms around her, lifted her, and spun her again, kissing away her breath as they turned and turned. They embraced, Christine inhaling heavily against his chest, happy again.

Raoul took her chin between thumb and forefinger and lifted her face to his once more. After gazing into her eyes, he winked and said, "But a *boy* would certainly solve our problems, eh?" And he laughed as he released her.

Christine's happy bubble deflated at his words.

"To bed, to bed, woman!" he cried as he strode from the room. And over his shoulder, "You need your rest!"

Christine heard his chuckle as he moved away from her and forced herself to forgive his seemingly cunning ruminations.

He is happy we are bearing a child. He is simply considering finances as well. There is nothing wrong with such a consideration.

But she went to bed that evening wishing she could raise her spirits to her previous ecstatic condition.

***

Christine spent the next several days becoming more and more excited at the prospect of raising a child on the same shores as those of her childhood. Her mind danced over memories of her father: velvet evenings outdoors near a roaring fire, gazing into the darkness with the hope of catching sight of the fairies – or korrigans, as she and her father called them; playful mornings in fields of flowers; quiet afternoons listening to his wonderful stories. And singing. Of course, singing.

But the memories of singing brought a dull ache that Christine did not feel appropriate to her wonderful condition. She pushed these uneasy thoughts of music away and built beautiful fantasies on her memories until she felt she was building future memories of herself with her child to come.

She was delighted when Raoul burst through the door one early afternoon carrying a huge colorful bouquet of flowers that filled both arms and covered his face. He made a show of not being able to find Christine through the floral lace enfolding him and then said, laughing, "I'm sure there's a vase here somewhere!"

Coming to the vase on the sideboard and discovering it already full of flowers, he said, "Ah, I see we hardly needed more."

Christine giggled at his spectacle. "And now, dear husband, it is my turn to ask after the occasion." Smiling, she knelt, brought another vase from the cabinet, and gestured with her head that he should follow her to the kitchen.

"News! I have news!" he said from behind the bouquet that filled his arms.

"As good as my news to you of days past?" She glanced over her shoulder at him and giggled again at his face framed by blossoms.

"No, certainly not. How could it be?" Raoul deposited the bouquet next to the sink, where Christine was filling the vase with water from the nearby pitcher. "How are you feeling, by the way?" He put one hand on her still-flat stomach.

"Still tired. But perfect, just perfect." She accepted his kiss to her cheek. "Are you to keep me in suspense all evening?" she asked, her back to him, now arranging the flowers into the vase. The luxurious fragrance of the fresh bouquet filled the corner of the small kitchen and she inhaled deeply.

"I," Raoul took a breath, held it, and then said, "have found a position!"

"Raoul!" she spun toward him, thrilled at this wonderful, if surprising, news.

"Yes!" He strutted a bit, before continuing. "In London. They've told me that my sailing experience …"

"London!" Christine exclaimed.

"Yes," he answered, smiling.

Christine shook her head as if to clear an unpleasant buzzing. "London?" she said, turning back to the flowers in the sink. The scent of the blooms now seemed overpowering.

"It will be grand! Back in a proper city, money for the spending." Raoul was too excited to notice Christine's unhappy silence, and the explanation poured from him. "It is a large shipping house, and while they won't often call me to sail – I'm a bit beyond that, I should think – they feel my experience and contacts would be invaluable."

He stopped and looked around, as if wondering why they were standing in the kitchen. "A toast! A toast! I shall return!" Turning suddenly in the door, he said, "No. I shan't return. Leave that. Come, let us sit and congratulate each other!"

Tremulously, Christine turned from the sink to follow. By the time she reached the sitting room, Raoul had already poured a small aperitif of fragrant orange liqueur and was holding one cut crystal glass toward her.

"A small drink, to celebrate. Come."

Christine could neither bring herself to smile nor to move any more quickly than her dread pace allowed. "Raoul?" she asked. She could hear the tremor in her voice, but clearly, he could not.

His teeth glittered in his broad smile. His hand still held the glass toward her.

"Raoul," she sniffed, "I don't want to go to London. I want to stay here. This is home."

"Nonsense!" Raoul said good-naturedly. "Didn't you hear what I said? A *city*, for goodness sake – not Paris, but still. And money. No more of this rarified country air. No more of this inadequate house. Servants again, although perhaps not right away. Beautiful new clothes for you … and the baby, of course. It shall be Heaven!" Raoul settled himself into a chair with an arrogant lift of his chin. He was a new man, reborn from the ashes of an exiled vicomte in a backwater market town.

In Raoul's distant eyes, Christine could see the recollections of his previous life rushing upon him, could understand his desire for a return to a life more genteelly lived. But she could not bring herself to accept leaving her home.

"Raoul, *this* is Heaven. I want to raise our child here. I …"

"As a peasant?" he answered. He immediately recognized his mistake and rose to take Christine in his arms again. "I didn't mean that. We don't live as peasants, and I certainly did not intend to raise an old argument. But we could do better. We shall."

"But I …" Christine started. She could feel tears of frustration and unhappiness filling her eyes.

"But nothing. We are going, Christine. Just as soon as we can." Raoul settled himself into the chair again, a satisfied smile gracing a face whose eyes were far-focused, imagining London, imagining his new future. He did not seem to notice when Christine excused herself and went to bed.

CHAPTER 13
A NEW PATH

Erik thought he might lose his mind waiting for Mattis to bring his boat to the docks. His meager belongings had been packed for two days, and his need to get to London by the fastest possible means had filled him with an energy that might well have sufficed to propel him across the ocean on nothing but his own feet.

Erik felt a renewed upwelling of pity for Christine as he recalled her broken-hearted sobs over leaving Korsnäsborg, but – knowing there was nothing he could do to affect Raoul's decision – he accepted and found the good in the situation.

First, Korsnäsborg was a small market town, and his constant surveillance of Christine was bound to end in disaster at some point. Second, he could not erase the sound of his name from her lips as she wept in her bed that evening.

She had wept inconsolably for some time, with interjections in a shaking, throbbing voice, of "Oh, Father." He understood that she was calling on the spirit of her father for strength, for support, for help from his assured position in Heaven. Erik had wanted to climb through the open window and hold her in his arms, but he had not even dared to raise his head to the level of the sash for fear either Christine – or worse, Raoul – might see him.

"Oh, Father," she had whimpered and continued sobbing.

Perhaps it was thoughts of her father and of Heaven and of the Angel of Music her father had promised to send her that caused her, quietly, to say later, "Oh, Erik."

His mind had run a smooth, circular path thinking over and over of her small utterance. Small in words, but tremendous in his ears, in his heart – Christine had uttered his name.

By the time Erik had returned to his shack that night, the plan was fully formed in his mind. He had packed before sleeping and then lay abed, wanting sleep to come upon him if only to speed the passage of the night, yet unable even to close his eyes.

And now two days of waiting.

"Oy, Lucky!" The bass rumble of the words seemed to clap Erik on the back of the head as he bent over a lunch of fish stew and rich, warm bread at one of the dockside establishments. He turned and leapt from his stool, almost throwing back his hood in his search for the source of the voice.

"Oy!" Mattis walked toward him, with bag over one shoulder and hand raised in greeting.

Erik forced himself not to run to the man. He could not control the glad embrace he threw around the mountainous man's shoulders.

"Mattis. Good to see you," he said.

94

"Missed the sea, did you? Can't ever get her out of your blood once she's had you," the large man said with a bawdy wink, and laughed.

"I was hoping. ..." Erik began.

"I was hoping for luncheon," boomed Mattis. "May I join you?"

"Yes, yes, of course," Erik answered, although he wanted to drag the man bodily back to the boat and cast off at once.

Over luncheon, Erik listened as Mattis discussed his travels, and when he knew he had restrained himself for a polite expanse of time, Erik made his request.

"London, eh?" Mattis said. "Don't go so far. Mine's not a big boat, as you know."

"I know. I just thought, perhaps, you could take me as far south as Kalmar, or if that is too far, to Stockholm." Erik tilted his head back to watch Mattis' face from beneath his hood.

"Stockholm, eh?" Mattis paused, bread lifted partway to his mouth, and said, "Certainly, I can get you that far." With a grin and an elbow to Erik's elbow, said, "You help us fish along the way?"

"I would rather make a quick trip, Mattis, but. ..." Erik paused to think how he might entice Mattis. "What if 'Lucky' could guarantee you a better than fair price in Stockholm for whatever you bring there? Not just this trip, but always? I have an acquaintance in Stockholm who pays extremely well for fresh produce. I could put in a word."

In fact, Erik knew nobody in Stockholm, but he also knew he could make an arrangement that would make Mattis a moderately successful man over the years. It would not begin to repay the fisherman for his kindness in the short time Erik had been in Sweden, but Erik did not believe he would be returning. It was the least he could do. And with Mattis' simple lifestyle, the outlay Erik would need to make for each purchase would be negligible to his holdings.

"Hmm," rumbled the large man around a mouthful of stew. "You seem quite rushed. I'll get you there. Not for a 'better than fair' price, but because you asked, friend. If I get a good price in the bargain, I'll consider myself lucky, 'Lucky.'" Mattis laughed uproariously at his own joke as he clapped Erik on the back.

Erik determined that Mattis would get the incentive promised. And perhaps he would even return someday to see Mattis settled in a bigger house, laughing (always laughing) at his good fortune with his pleasantly plump wife.

After making the necessary arrangements in Stockholm and watching a very happy Mattis return to his boat with fat pockets, Erik bought a ticket on the fastest steamer available and took the long journey to England.

***

Once in London, Erik worked to secure his ability to re-enter Christine's life less dangerously. Through intermediaries, he made discreet inquiries to discover both where Raoul had secured his position and where others of Raoul's ilk housed themselves. He knew Raoul and his kind well enough to know the man had the instincts of a sheep. Wheresoever Raoul's peers and compatriots gathered, so would Raoul go. His ego demanded the support of other similarly inutile gentlemen.

He searched the area north of Whitechapel and the London Docks, in the nicer areas north of the district, until he found the perfect house. It was a large stone house, far larger than Raoul (or his peers) could afford, separated from the nearest houses by a large expanse of yard, tall hedges, and a wall, yet far enough from the slums closer to the docks to afford a feeling of graciousness and safety. The feature that made the house perfect was the presence of a small separate cottage for a gardener at the far back of the yard.

Erik purchased the house from its absent owner, paying far more than necessary to insure a quick transfer, and began the necessary adjustments. The rooms were large, the smallest being a square five meters to a side. Erik could take nearly a meter, perhaps a little less, from one side of the room without unduly reducing its size, and afford himself (on the other side of the false wall he would build) an adequate two-thirds-meter passage. Erik studied the house, determined which rooms might require such passages (certainly the two largest bedchambers, for he had no notion of which Christine might choose) and set to work.

Recreating the surfaces of the false walls, even allowing for hidden doors and spy-holes, was no great problem. In fact, the greatest problem he faced was the fact that the high ceilings were elaborately molded and scrolled and, in some cases, beautifully painted. The blending of new moldings and scrollings as well as the creative modification of paint – so the ceilings appeared complete instead of truncated by his new wall – required his most careful work.

As he worked, he kept close communication with the contacts who would provide information regarding whether (or perhaps when) Christine and Raoul had arrived in London. His first work was completed hastily, although not without the perfection required, as he felt the unbearable pressure of completing his task before their arrival. As time stretched – had Christine persuaded Raoul to stay in Korsnäsborg? But no, his contact at the shipping house assured him Raoul was still to come – Erik gained the leisure to work more slowly, perfecting the niceties of the hidden passages he had thought he might need to leave for later.

Finally, the news came that Raoul and Christine had arrived. They were staying in a sumptuous hotel with which Erik was acquainted from his previous travels in Europe. He thought to go there, if only to catch a glimpse of his Christine, but determined that patience was the better course.

Erik wasted no time. On Raoul and Christine's second day, while the couple was still at their breakfast in their rooms, Erik sent a land manager to meet with Raoul. Raoul, quite excited at the prospect of settling so quickly in London, agreed to have the man show him prospective houses, all of which were open for lease. As instructed, the land manager showed Raoul several houses, all much smaller than Erik's house. While two of these seemed to pique Raoul's interest, nothing matched the excitement with which Raoul reacted to Erik's perfectly prepared house.

Erik eavesdropped on the conversation from within his prepared passages as the two discussed the lease arrangements.

"No question. The house is magnificent," Raoul said, turning in place to survey the largest of the bedchambers, with its dark wood trim and flocked damask velvet wall coverings. "And furnished?" he asked.

"Indeed. Unless, of course, you wish to furnish the house yourself?" the land manager asked.

"No, no. The furnishings are adequate," Raoul answered. A small squint entered one eye as Raoul asked the important question: "The rent must be … significant?"

"Strangely, no," answered the land manager. "This is why I felt I simply must show you this property. The estate contains provisions that if the heir and his family do not reside in perpetuity, they may neither sell the land nor charge more than a specified rent. If they attempt to do so, the property reverts to an illegitimate child of the original owner. Naturally, the family has determined to accept the income from the property rather than have it revert." The land manager gave a small cough into his fist, as though the impropriety of the subject faintly disgusted him. "Naturally, this is not widely known."

"Naturally!" exclaimed Raoul. "And the rent?" Raoul did not react beyond a carefully controlled "hmm," when the land manager named a sum significantly less than the rent of the smaller houses Raoul had already been shown.

After another circuit of the house, Raoul shook the land manager's hand and proclaimed he would accept this house.

"Ah, yes. I'm afraid I neglected to mention one condition to the lease."

"And that condition?" Raoul asked. His sour expression showed that he expected the condition to be so unpalatable that he would be forced to retract his acceptance.

"You may have noticed the gardener's cottage at the back of the yard?" the land manager asked.

"Yes," Raoul answered hesitantly, this clearly not being the subject of any of his nebulous conjectures.

"It is currently occupied by an old gardener, a magnificently knowledgeable man. He still maintains the grounds."

"Yes, and splendidly, I will agree," Raoul answered, still waiting for the unbearable condition to surface.

The land manager again coughed into his hand. Raoul clearly took this as a sign of the man's discomfort at the bad news he had yet to deliver, and his agitation grew, visible in his posture and the twitching of his hands.

"The lease requires the gardener be retained," the land manager finished.

"At what cost, may I ask?" Raoul clearly imagined the cost to be prohibitive, bringing the total of rent and gardener's wages to an unaffordable amount.

"Oh, no cost to you, Sir. The gardener's wages are paid from the estate."

"The estate!" Raoul repeated. "So the condition to the lease is that I allow the gardener to remain to do his work? That is all?"

"Indeed," the land manager answered.

"Is the man a scoundrel? A problem?" Raoul asked, still quite convinced a hidden obstacle existed.

"Hardly. He is quiet and quite respectable," the land manager answered, stopping an inspection of his fingernails to look at Raoul with sincerity.

"Ha! Then, as I said, I accept! When can we finalize the paperwork?" Raoul shook the man's hand again and, with a great smile and a hand to the man's back, led him to the waiting carriage, discussing the final formalities.

Erik crept from his secret entrance to the house and crossed the yard to his new home in the gardener's cottage. Now, he must finish perfecting his new mask.

CHAPTER 14
A LOSS AND A FRIEND

For reasons Christine assumed were related to her delicate condition, she was violently ill on the voyage to England. Her illness was neither assisted by the dark mood with which she left her beloved home, nor her subtly masked disappointment in Raoul's refusal to consider her wishes.

Yet who am I to challenge the wishes of my husband and master? The nausea that descended upon her with the rolling of the sea and her own internal chiding brought another thought. *Perhaps I am being punished for my ungracious attitude toward Raoul.*

After several days of illness, sudden pains in her abdomen set in, and Christine trembled with fear that these pains may indicate more than simple illness. With luck, there was a physician aboard ship, but this was the extent of her luck. The physician was on hand to assist Christine in the loss of her child, but could do nothing to prevent the terrible happening.

As she lay, cold and yet filmed with moisture, she allowed the physician to put the small cabin to rights in silence. The kind man came to check her, touching her forehead, feeling for her

102

pulse, and then quite efficiently examining her nether regions before leaving her to her private agony. As he reached the door, she asked the question that had tormented her all the time the quiet man worked.

"Was it a boy?" She knew how important a boy was to Raoul, although privately, she had wished for a girl. Her mind was a jumble of the fantasies she had contrived for the child: a boy, golden hair thick like her own, in short pants and tie, walking proudly with his father. A sweet-faced girl, hair fairer like Raoul's, carefree and beautiful and clever. She wished a method of extinguishing these fantasies forever. Now they were so many dead leaves in the winds of fate. But still, she had to know.

The physician turned his stout figure toward her before answering. "These things are best …"

"I must know," Christine interrupted, voice calm yet commanding.

With a sigh, the physician moved back to the bed to peer down at Christine over his small, round glasses. He rubbed his eyes beneath his glasses as she waited. Softly, he said, "The child would have been a girl."

A girl!

Christine felt she might crumble in upon herself, fantasies caving in upon her, but she maintained her control to the extent of only allowing a solitary tear to escape one eye. "Thank you, Doctor," she said, and turned her face toward the wooden wall at the side of her bed to let the tears come.

At least Raoul will not be devastated, she thought, and followed the thought with another: *That is unfair of me.* Somehow, in her pain, the second thought was unconvincing.

Raoul entered after the physician left her. His face, when she turned to him, was a mask of pain and regret.

"Oh, Christine, Christine," he murmured, as he dabbed at her tears with his handkerchief. "Has the voyage caused this? Have *I* caused this?" The pain lacing his voice was genuine.

"The doctor says not," she answered. *Surely seasickness did not help*, she thought, but did not say.

Raoul dropped his head to where his hand held hers at the edge of the small bed, his fingers pressing her hand to his forehead.

"It was a girl," Christine said, her voice dead and flat in her ears. "Did he tell you?"

"No," he answered, lifting his head and searching her eyes. "I am so sorry. So sorry." Raoul lifted her head and shoulders into his arms and cradled her there before letting her carefully back down to the bed. Christine searched his face to see if his indications of pain had lessened upon learning he had not lost his son. She imagined some small sign of relief, and the pain in her heart sharpened.

"Sleep," he said. And then, "Or would you prefer something to eat? I could bring you something."

"No, I will sleep," she answered.

Raoul squeezed her hand and leaned forward to kiss her cheek. As he stood, he asked, "Will there be others?" The gentleness in his voice implied that his concern was for Christine, but she imagined she knew the real meaning behind his question. *Will you be able to bear me a son? My son, the Comte de Chagny?*

She turned her face toward the wooden wall before she answered. "The doctor tells me there was no damage." Her tears began anew.

She did not turn her head back until she heard Raoul close the door. She did not sleep.

***

Christine was still weak, although much recovered, when Raoul helped her into the lavish rooms of one of London's best hotels. She did not ask how they could afford such luxury and did not care. She cared only that the ground did not rock beneath her any longer and hoped the food would be fitting to the setting. Raoul did not leave their rooms that first day and pampered her unfailingly, with frequent small meals and a delivery to their rooms of fruit and flowers. He ran her a bath and brushed her hair when she had dressed and rejoined him. He held her hand, and asked often how she was feeling.

Yet the thrill was there in him, just under the surface, Christine knew. He stood frequently at the windows looking with evident excitement down the three stories to the busy street below, taking in the traffic, the street lamps, the crowds, the towering buildings.

On the second day, just as Christine finished her breakfast, a man came to the door, and after a brief conversation with Raoul, took Raoul away. She was glad to be alone at last. She took her own turn at the windows and sighed at the repulsive panorama spread before her. Cobblestone streets and raised walks covered in filth, squat ugly buildings, garish signs, black street lamps, carriages, and everywhere people. No trees, few flowers. She was happy that a morning fog obscured the harsher outlines of the view.

"My new home," she said aloud. "Yet, I must come to love it. I must. I will."

She returned to her bed and slept a while longer. After luncheon, she dressed and spent the remainder of the afternoon wandering restlessly from one chair to another, one room to another, looking out the windows, and forcibly recalling all she found good in a city. The excitement, the pace of life, the restaurants, the many shops, and their wares.

Perhaps even an Opera House or theater! she thought, but then angrily turned her mind away from the accompanying recollection of the joy she found in singing and the pain of her denial. In a moment of rebellion, she began her favorite passage from *Romeo and Juliet* and recalled the triumph of her debut in Paris. Thinking of Raoul and his injunction against singing, she came to a sad, quiet halt only phrases into the beautiful aria.

Surely Raoul cannot forbid me to sing solely for myself! But she knew, as she thought this, that Raoul would undoubtedly rage if he heard her. Raoul took her singing to reflect her fondness for Erik.

Fool! she thought. But even as she denied that she sang to recall Erik, she did recall the ecstasy of joining him in song or of listening to him sing, and she wished briefly for the simplicity and joy of the days when the Angel of Music ruled her world. She stood, thinking to sing again, but upon inhaling for the first note, realized she could not face Raoul's wrath, should he return at this moment. Instead, she went to the desk and thought to write a letter, but could think of no one in the world to whom she wished to write. All the people who meant most to her were no longer in the world.

Raoul returned in the late afternoon bursting with excitement. Already he had found them a beautiful home, and he spoke of all its amenities.

"It has exquisite gardens," he repeated, "and it is astoundingly private!" Christine admitted that gardens and privacy would certainly be an improvement over the almost completely treeless, flowerless, greenless view from the window of their hotel. She hoped without much hope that the sky above the house would not be the same brown shade she saw from the window of the hotel.

***

Christine did, indeed, love the house Raoul found. Again, she could not imagine how he could afford such a magnificent place, but she determined not to involve herself in matters outside her comprehension. She took the smaller of the two largest bedchambers and arranged their belongings in their separate rooms. Her view from her bedroom window looked toward the back of the house, where the yard was larger, the flowers and trees

more plentiful, and containing no view of the house next behind
them.

Raoul was often out all day and many evenings – at first,
settling into his position at the shipping house, and later, exploring
the city with which he seemed so enamored. Christine hated
London. The smell and filth of London did not compare at all
favorably to the fresh sea air and country beauty of her home in
Korsnäsborg, but also did not compare favorably even to Paris.
The city was a teeming mass of people too many for its expanding
borders. Christine did not often allow Raoul to entice her into
London's "many entertainments," (as he called them), although she
did dutifully dine with him when propriety and obligation
demanded. She never once thought of offering to sing at these
occasions.

She did often sing at home, however. Raoul had obtained
servants – a butler who ran the house and served as Raoul's valet;
two young but disciplined girls – Peggy, who acted as Christine's
personal maid when needed and otherwise assisted the other girl,
Missy, with the household chores; and a cook. Christine did not at
first think much of the cook, until she learned the woman could
duplicate some of Christine's favorite French dishes and certain
foods from her homeland, instead of merely producing the tedious
and often tasteless foods representative of English cuisine. Because
of the servants, whom she did not believe she could trust not to
speak to Raoul, Christine only ever sang in the garden.

At first she eschewed of doing even this much, due to the rather constant but non-intrusive presence of the old gardener. However, the pleasant old man quickly earned her trust. This trust began on a pleasant afternoon, when she wandered amongst flowering hedges, thinking herself alone. The sun warmed her head and back. She was startled when she rounded a hedge and found the gardener there, kneeling on a thin padded cushion, pulling at weeds with a quiet, expert hand.

"I beg your pardon," she said. Her voice was harsh as she was irrationally angered by being startled.

"I beg *your* pardon, Madame," the gardener answered in a low, pleasant voice, as he bowed from his knees. He spoke with a heavy Londoner's brogue. "I imagine you were attempting to escape, and now I have discomfited you."

The uncanny way in which the gardener's words matched her feelings made her feel silly for her abrupt words to him. She decided to answer him with honesty.

"Yes, actually. You have stated it perfectly." She glanced back toward the house, and then returned her eyes to the bent old man. She stood silent, noticing the peculiar waxiness of the wrinkled skin on the old man's face and the shining baldness of his head. In contrast, his hands almost looked like the hands of a young man. She took a step toward him and held out her hand. "I am Christine," she said.

"Madame," he answered. He held out a hand to show her the dirt on his fingers as an excuse for not taking her hand and shrugged apologetically.

"Ah, yes," she said, and wiped her hand on her skirt without thinking, although he had not dirtied it by touching her. There was an awkward silence as they looked at each other.

"I'll let you get back to your work," she said and turned to walk back to the house.

"Madame!" he said, rising to his feet as quickly as his advanced age would allow. "Do not let me chase you from your solace. I will retire until you have recharged yourself in my garden."

At first Christine was taken aback by the pronoun proclaiming the garden *his* garden, but then she recalled he had been working this garden for some time – years, decades, perhaps. "Yes, your garden," she said. "And as such, you should not let me chase you from it either." She smiled shyly at the old man. He smiled in return.

"We shall be secret escapees then, Madame," he answered, voice lowered as though they were conspirators.

"Christine," she prompted. "If you can bring yourself to call me Christine, we shall be secret friends, as well."

"Christine," he said, his voice low and resonant, and bowed rather formally to her, hands and arms clenched to his sides as though this were the most ceremonial of occasions.

She decided she liked the old man. She giggled lightly, lowered herself in a deep curtsy, and said, "Well, friend, what shall I call you?"

"Peck, Madame," he said, then smiled and corrected himself, "Christine."

"Peck, then," she said, gave another small curtsy, and smiled over her shoulder at him as she turned to continue on her walk.

When, on another day, she nearly stumbled upon the gardener as she strolled, singing, through the garden, she felt immediate apprehension for her song. "I ... I was just ...," she stammered.

Seeming to understand her at once, he responded, "It shall be our secret, Christine." He turned back to his pruning with a smile.

From that day forth, she often took to the garden when the urge came upon her to sing. The gardener's appreciative smiles returned some fragment of pride to her. Their brief but ever more frequent conversations created in her a feeling that she truly had a friend in London at last.

CHAPTER 15
ERIK AT HOME

Erik as Peck was a happy man. Christine, released from her household chores by the hired help and uninterested in the city, came often to the garden as to a cherished refuge. Sometimes she even trod its paths during the rain, which rain was fortunately infrequent and never significant, except in the occasional burst. Erik turned his skills toward making the garden the magnificent colorful aerie Christine so obviously cherished. This labor of love was also an excuse to be near Christine, sometimes to speak to her, sometimes to hear her sing. Even when she sang quietly, and without the full force she had called upon in his Opera House, she still sang like the angel he cherished. His only pain in this regard was his inability to join her song, for he refused to permit himself to raise his own voice in song, even when in the privacy of his gardener's cottage. He knew his voice to be so powerful and so recognizable – to Christine at least – that the small cottage would provide no lockbox to his music.

Erik never worked in the rain, as even the most industrious of gardeners would not venture forth in such weather, but the rain did not keep him indoors any more than it kept Christine there. He followed her, silent and unseen, and, thrilled by her nearness, kept warm in the desolate drizzle by the sight and sound of her. She often sang with more volume and passion in the rain, knowing the windows of the main house to be closed to the weather.

The only unpleasant part of his role as Peck was the discomfort of the mask he wore – a mask that encompassed the whole of his head and wrinkled the skin of his already repulsive face with the moisture of its closeness. Thankfully, the volume of the artfully constructed nose left him air enough for breathing so he did not need to breathe solely through his mouth.

Erik as ghost was happier still. Peck, after all, was imprisoned by his mask and by the confines of the garden; Erik was not imprisoned at all. He made free use of the main house, and maskless, truly free, he lurked through the passages between the rooms at will. (His mind could not help but wander gratefully to Mattis and to the freedom the sailor had introduced to his life. He wondered whether he would ever again feel such freedom in the presence of another.) At times, he followed Christine through the house, watching her progress from one room to the next, observing her as she paused to engage in some small activity. More than even in the Opera House, she was his constant companion, and the familiarity of even her smallest gestures enhanced his love for her. There was never a moment when she was not graceful, kind, beautiful.

At other times – for example, when he knew Christine to be sitting in a window, reading – Erik left her to roam an empty room she had recently relinquished. At these moments, he was alert and careful of the household staff's whereabouts, yet calm and refreshed by the light, clean scent of Christine in the air of the room.

Many a night, Erik let himself into Christine's bedchamber, and there, seated in a chair in the shadows of the far corner of the room, he watched Christine sleep. He felt confident that should she awaken, she would not see him there in the shadows. If he had allowed Raoul to impinge on his thoughts, he might have been pleased at the infrequency with which Christine shared his bed, but during his hours in Christine's bedchamber, his thoughts were only for her.

One night, late, as Erik rose to return to his own small home for the few hours of sleep he needed, Christine began thrashing amidst her bedclothes, apparently caught in the throes of a nightmare. She moaned as she pulled and pushed at the coverings, and Erik imagined that her dream included night-translated feelings and images of being bound and tied in the twisted cloth. Unwilling to leave her as she struggled, Erik waited and watched for her nightmare to subside. Again and again, Christine calmed, and moments later, began her dream-powered struggle anew.

Finally, feeling he must do something to assist Christine in her imagined plight, he crossed the room to her bedside. Reaching with care and moving with agonizing slowness, he loosed the bed linens where they twisted around her limbs and body. With reverence, he pulled the linens smooth and replaced them atop her body, leaving her pale arms uncovered. He stood, watching for signs that her nightmare had left her. Instead, she thrashed again, rolling and coming to rest on her side, a mere hand-width from the edge of the mattress, and barely more than a hand-width from where Erik stood, bent solicitously over her. Her face contorted, and she cried out, almost forming words amidst the low moaning.

Without thinking – other than of how he might comfort his sleeping bride – Erik reached his cool fingers to her forehead and stroked away the renewed furrows. Breaking his own self-imposed fast, he crooned the phrase of a melody in a low voice, quiet and soothing in its tones. Christine stopped her struggles, and her eyelids fluttered … but did not open. Erik hurriedly stood back a pace, scandalized at his own flagrant actions, angry that he should have taken such a risk. He stood without moving from his place a mere meter from her bedside and waited to see if she would awaken further. What he would do if she did, he did not know, but he was unwilling to make the slightest noise by moving when she was teetering on the edge of wakefulness, not when the minute noise might complete her rise to consciousness.

Christine's face smoothed into the soft aspect of sleep, and now her face was childlike in its serenity, the nightmare apparently defeated. Still Erik did not move, torn as he was between the emotional desire to touch her again and the rational desire to flee while still undiscovered. When he did move, it was to her bedside, where he lowered himself to his knees, the closer to bring his face to her own. There, he lingered for several minutes, not touching her – not so ruled by his emotions as to reach that level of foolishness again – but breathing with her, mingling their two breaths as she inhaled and exhaled.

Drunk with the scent and the flavor of her breath on his tongue and in his nostrils, he crept from the room. He stood for minutes watching her from the passage, allowing his mind and body to fully possess the ecstasy of the moment, for he knew he would never allow himself to act so senselessly again. He could not afford to endanger his life with Christine in such a way.

In control of his senses again as he crept across the cool lawn to his home, he marveled at the thought that his touch and his voice, instead of eliciting nightmares in the dear girl, could instead comfort her and bring her peace. He fell instantly to sleep, lingering lovingly, even in sleep, on the extraordinary events of the night.

***

Christine was early to the garden in the morning, a phantasmagoric figure moving through the dense morning fog. She hummed as she moved among the flowers – touching one here, smelling one there – and at times interspersed song with her humming. She seemed happy and bright, even in the dismal light of the diffused morning sun.

"Hello, Peck," she greeted him cheerily. "Lovely morning, as usual," she said and laughed at the ludicrous statement.

"Christine," he answered with a bow. He felt possessive toward her after the intimacy of the previous night, and ashamed at having exacted such intimacy without her knowledge, without its being freely shared. He swore anew never to repeat the incident, first, due to the risk involved, and now because he found his violation intolerable. "You brighten the morning," he said, turning back to his work, "surely you will clear the fog even without the help of the sun."

Christine giggled and, turning, picked a small rose and held it to her nose. "You flatter most beautifully," she said. He wondered if she found it strange that with the strong Londoner's brogue, the old man still spoke as a gentleman might. "But, I *feel* bright this morning. I had a most pleasant dream last night and woke with its pleasure still upon me."

Erik looked to her face to see if he could detect any sign she was toying with him, that she had in fact been awake and had known he was there and what he had done. He could detect nothing. Then he realized she could not be toying with him. Had she seen Erik, she would not be teasing about the fact with the gardener Peck.

"I slept peacefully, as well, and dreamed pleasantly," he answered, still watching her face, "both unusual for a man of my advanced age. P'haps there were fairies afoot last evening."

"Mmm," she answered dreamily, rose still pressed to her face and, turning, moved slowly away from him into the fog. "Korrigans," she said, almost as though she spoke to herself.

117

"When I was a child, my father and I called them korrigans." She turned to face him through the whitening mist. "Do you have korrigans in England?"

"Undoubtedly," he answered, "though p'haps not in London."

Christine tucked the rose into the band at her waist and took several tentative steps toward him. "If there are fairies in London, they would certainly find home in your garden," she said. She took another step and peered into his face as though looking for a sign of some expression. "Thank you," she said.

"For what do you thank me, Christine?" he asked, and some part of him thrilled with the notion that she was thanking him for his actions of the night.

"For not laughing at me about korrigans," she said. "You aren't laughing, are you?" She tilted her head to one side as she waited for his answer.

"And why should I laugh about korrigans?" he asked. At this close distance, he was mesmerized by the sparkle of mist dew on the long, thick lashes framing her beautiful eyes.

After studying his face – his mask, he reminded himself – she said, "You are a good friend." Another pause, this time contemplative, as she studied the ground at her feet. "You never seem to find me silly." And this time, she turned and faded slowly into the fog.

CHAPTER 16
A DISCOVERY AT DINNER

The crystal chandeliers sparkled magically in the brightness of the gaslights as they floated above the gathered company. The glittering crowd, strewn like brilliant gems throughout the elegant hall, moved slowly through a hidden dance of interwoven conversations and known and unknown allegiances. Despite the fact that dinner had not yet begun, Christine wished for the end to the evening and the return to her home.

As she stood with several other young wives, smiling and nodding – although she had no idea of the subject of the senseless conversation – she caught herself fingering the large cool necklace at her throat. She despised the draping ornament for its garishness. She felt it too large for her features but Raoul had insisted she wear it, meeting her objections with the statement: "Your beauty is so fine you diminish any jewelry you wear, and yet, I wish to demonstrate my success here in London. Wear it." This last statement was unmistakably a command, although Raoul had delivered the phrase with a gentle hand to her shoulder and a kiss to her cheek. Christine found these small physical endearments enchanted her less of late, seeming merely a practiced language in which Raoul was fluent but perhaps less than sincere.

Smiling and nodding again as the ladies laughed with refinement into their handkerchiefs, Christine brought her hand away from its restless motions at her throat and down to rest against her cool taffeta skirts. She had to force herself not to smooth the fabric in yet another uneasy gesture. She had endured the questions regarding her activities in London and then had endured the hand-patting and the you-poor-dears showered upon her when these perfumed, bedecked ladies assumed Raoul was not allowing her full access to the entertainments of the city. She did not care what they thought of her. She could neither explain the loathing she felt for the dark city, nor the comfort she took in remaining cloistered in her quiet home.

Christine excused herself to the powder room, pleased that none of the ladies offered to accompany her. Having made her momentary escape – she knew it could not be for long, as she must play the part of the sociable guest and refined wife of Raoul de Chagny – she glided slowly at the edge of the room from harpsichord to harp to piano with the attitude of examining the displayed instruments. She paused at the piano, a melancholy washing over her, thinking of the pleasure she would experience to be singing once more to its accompaniment.

Guilt suffusing her, she swept her eyes over the room for Raoul. She found him engaged in an animated conversation with a group of young ladies, charming them with some amusing story that left them all laughing from behind dainty handkerchiefs and lace fans. Wishing to prolong her escape, she moved behind a slender pillar gilded at its base with two enormous potted plants.

She stood with her back to the cool pillar and then moved to step around it again for fear someone should find her concealed there and wonder at her behavior. The voices of two women stopped her, for she had no way to explain her presence, hiding as she was. No excuse for her location behind the pillar presented itself to her mind – there was no window from which she might have been admiring the view.

"I think he is indescribably handsome," said the high, sweet voice.

"As does every other woman in London who is not on her deathbed," answered a lower, huskier voice.

"And I have heard nothing but praises for his loyalty to his wife and his steadfastness. It makes me admire him all the more. So many men dally – men will be men – but he seems not to be the sort."

"Although," and here a low, intimate chuckle punctuated the husky-voiced statement, "perhaps the man you are admiring so much for his steadfastness is merely extraordinarily discreet. Perhaps I may find the truth of the matter with a little … prodding." Again, the low chuckle.

"Elizabeth!" came the shocked and amused response, the sweet voice breathing the words between a squeak and a whisper. "You wouldn't!"

"Have you ever noted there would be no dalliance for a man without a woman willing to succumb to his charms?" answered the husky-voiced woman.

With again the low chuckle and the timorous response of a high-voiced giggle, the two moved away, leaving Christine panting tensely behind the pillar. With a deep, calming breath, she moved around the plant at its base and back into the crowded open space of the grand hall.

This filthy city is peopled with filthy inhabitants. How can Raoul stand it? Yet, clearly he does. They might even have been discussing Raoul. He is certainly handsome and loyal to me. Her heart warmed to Raoul, despite his insistence on her attendance at this gala. *Perhaps to get through the rest of this evening and the odious dinner to come, I will lean on him for support. Raoul will be my tower.*

Her eyes again swept the room for Raoul. This time, he was quite alone, arms clasped behind his back, body bent forward, admiring a painting located several steps down a far corridor.

Ah, even Raoul takes refuge from the crowd at moments. I must learn from him.

Christine drifted in his direction, imagining the instant when her hand would close on his strong arm and they could enjoy a moment of peace together amidst the glittering company. She forced herself to move with the decorum she knew Raoul expected from her and allowed herself to be detained in her goal by small pleasantries. When next she searched for Raoul, she could not see him. In her need, she was tempted to rise to her toes in her search for him, but knew she could not disgrace herself with such a childish and inappropriate stance.

She wandered into the midst of a group of ladies and, with as little attention to what they discussed, smiled, nodded, and unobtrusively continued to look about the room for Raoul. He was nowhere in sight.

My tower! Where are you? I need you!

Christine stifled a momentary feeling of dread and chastised herself for her uneasiness. She forced a façade of false gaiety as she moved from one group to the next, counterfeiting bright engagements in several conversations. All the time, she searched for Raoul. Finally, she found herself standing with a gentleman of the shipping yard whom she knew to keep regular company with Raoul.

"Darren," she asked with a demure curtsy, "have you seen Raoul about? I wish to introduce him to a new acquaintance." She gestured vaguely to one side with a hand, as though indicating a member of some nearby group. She could not confess to merely wanting his strength and easy geniality to help her endure the remainder of the evening.

The man smiled with a charming flash of teeth and said, "I'm afraid I have no idea where he has gotten himself to. Perhaps he is exploring the house? I would be most pleased to accompany you in any search." He bowed over her hand. Christine was appalled to see how his eyes unabashedly lingered on her breasts as he rose. With eyes moving to her necklace and a hand reaching as though to touch it, he said, "How lovely." He extended his arm to her as though ready to escort her on the proposed exploration. "May I?"

"Oh, no," she answered brightly, "there is time later, and I would hate to take you from your conversation." Turning to her side, she said, "Oh, I see Cecelia; I simply must say hello. Please excuse me."

She moved toward the group of women with whom she had started the evening, as Darren murmured, "Of course."

As soon as she could, Christine moved to the passageway where she had last seen Raoul. She would far prefer to explore the house with Raoul than endure any more of this detestable event. After a last searching glance through the crowd for Raoul, she moved down the half-lit passage. She had not moved far into the passage when she heard a feminine giggle ahead of her and to the left. She froze, horrified at the thought of interrupting an elicit encounter, which interruption might well prove embarrassing to all.

If Raoul came this way, it cannot be anything too untoward.

Slowly and quietly – and with the full intention of backing quickly away should she be wrong in her assumption – she moved toward the origin of the giggle, which came again, from an alcove just ahead.

As she reached the alcove, she held her breath and moved her head around the edge, one eye blinded by the wall before her face, and the other taking in the scene in the alcove.

The shock of what met her eye choked the breath from her.

Raoul. And a girl younger than Christine, with a décolletage so low as to escape any pretense at modesty. Her head was thrown back as Raoul kissed her neck, his hand wandering over a large breast barely covered by the dress she wore. As his kisses moved from her neck toward her plumped bosom, the girl squeaked and giggled again. The startling sound brought Christine back to herself.

In an instant, she pulled her head back to its concealing place against the wall outside the alcove. She did not remember to breathe until the next giggle tumbled from the alcove down the passageway.

Staying close to the wall, humiliation rising to her throat and heating her cheeks, Christine moved back down the passage toward the brightly lit hall. Her anger and hurt as she moved toward the noise of gay conversation transformed into sadness as she realized she was more concerned with the disgrace of being a pitied woman than with the heartbreak she did not feel. Betrayal, yes. Humiliation, yes. But no heartbreak.

Christine moved through conversations as distracted as she had been, although her current distraction was for quite a different reason. She did not notice when Raoul re-entered the room, but he was immediately at her arm when dinner was announced. His manner toward her seemed not changed in the least. She hoped the heat that rose to her cheeks again at his touch would go unnoticed.

Dinner was lavish, and Christine feigned an appetite. Raoul, seated beside her, was sweet and attentive as usual, even kissing her knuckles at a moment between courses. He did not look to the young lady who had giggled in his embrace earlier, although Christine noted several coy glances toward Raoul from the girl's place farther down the table. The face of the matronly companion seated with the young girl seemed set in a permanent scowl.

Christine smiled, and spoke with charm – perhaps even more so than at any other point in the evening. She took a fierce pleasure in the challenge presented by knowing Raoul's nature and still performing her role as the brilliant diva she once was. She could detect no amorous glances from others at the table, which led her to believe she was not the only accomplished actress at the table. Certainly Raoul had a heretofore unknown talent for discretion.

Christine's sadness returned as they sat together in the carriage for the ride home. She clasped her hands in her lap and examined the ring with which Raoul had replaced Erik's gift.

"Are you quite well, my dear?" Raoul asked after a long silence.

"Yes, I am fine. You know I do not enjoy these occasions," Christine raised her eyes to his and smiled as she continued, "but I do hope you had reason to be proud of your wife."

"Proud, certainly!" Raoul crossed the carriage to sit beside her. He clasped her hand as he said, "You are the most beautiful prize in Christendom. How could I be anything other than proud?" He smiled and kissed Christine on the cheek. She pictured his lips on the neck of another and heard the echo of the abominable giggle on the air.

"I just worry, my dearest, that you tire of your wife. Certainly, a more social creature would suit you better." Christine said this brightly and with no melancholy downcast of her eyes.

I should be ashamed of myself for teasing him thus, she thought. *It is unworthy of me, and Father is undoubtedly mortified with me.*

Raoul took her face in his hands and pulled her toward his own. Before he kissed her, he whispered, "You are the only woman for me."

Ah, how many times have I heard these words from Raoul? And for what period of time were they true?

Raoul embraced her again in the hallway between their rooms. "Would you share my bed with me, wife?" he asked in low tones, running a hand up and down the bare skin of her arm. Christine shivered, but not for the reasons she had when first they were married.

"I am afraid I fairly stuffed myself at dinner," she responded, eyes downcast. "Will you forgive me?"

Raoul drew her close and granted absolution with another deep kiss before moving down the hall away from her. Christine retired, confused at the melee of emotions that wracked her. Hurt and betrayal, anger directed at herself for her own foolish naiveté, relief, sadness … and fear. Insecurity and fear.

She cried herself to sleep.

CHAPTER 17
ERIK BLUNDERS

Erik rejoiced in the coming of summer. Raoul was gone on one of his short trips away from the city, which – this time, in this season, and for no reason that he could discern – provided a heightened level to Christine's spirit. Christine, on her languorous walks through the garden, now shunned any cloak or gloves and walked instead with an umbrella to protect her from the ravages of the sun or the brief summer showers.

This day, she brought a book to the garden and sat at the stone bench under the shade of a large oak tree as she read. When after a decent interval Erik came into view, she spoke immediately, as was her custom in their friendship.

"Shall I read to you?" she asked, without polite preliminaries, but with the warmth and naturalness of a continued conversation. She did not spare him more than a glance from her book as she asked the question, as though she expected and accepted his presence as comfortable given.

Erik dared not gaze at her as he longed to, dared not take in the dance of the leaf-dappled sun on her lovely features. He moved to a patch of flowers not far removed from the trunk of the tree and answered, "I would rather you sang."

Christine laughed gaily, as at a private joke, and said, "Tomorrow, dear Peck. Tomorrow I shall sing."

Erik did not understand her enigmatic gaiety, but answered immediately, "Then of course, you must read."

Christine read from a book of poetry, sometimes sitting, oftentimes pacing near him, and Erik lost himself in the tedium of his work and the pleasant light hum of her voice. When one of the house girls brought out a cool pitcher of iced water, Christine asked for another glass and insisted Erik stop his labors and sit with her as they drank.

"Here," she said, patting the bench beside where she sat. Erik marveled at the fact of her willingness to be so close to him, after all his time of wanting nothing more than her proximity. But of course, he reminded himself, she could not see his face.

In a moment of quiet reflection, Erik's eyes fixed themselves upon the ring Christine wore on her hand – not his own ring – and anger flared in him at the disloyal substitution. He had not noticed this new ring before today, most likely due to Christine's normally gloved state out of doors. Without thought, his hand rose briefly and hovered toward the ring, before he drew the hand back to his lap.

"Pretty, isn't it?" Christine said, lifting her hand from her lap and spreading her long, thin fingers.

"Quite lovely, yes," he answered, making every effort to loosen his clenched teeth around the words and to keep his tone normal.

"I don't think so," Christine answered and moving her fingers as if to catch the stray dapples of sunlight in the red gems, she said with a small laugh, "I suppose that makes me mad. It is meant to be magnificent."

"You don't like your wedding ring?" Erik asked, anger fading to surprise.

"Not particularly," she answered. "I find it vulgar."

Erik could find nothing to say in response. Nothing, at least, that would not give him away. He forced his eyes to move away from Christine and focused instead on the flagstones beneath their feet and the trim grass beyond them.

In a distracted tone, she continued, "I had another. A simpler ring. I suppose I think it suited me better." After another long pause, during which she continued to move her fingers while she gazed at the ring, she said, "But my husband did not like it." She dropped her hand to her lap as though the muscles of her arm had deserted her.

Erik smothered the instinct to growl and pushed away the now rather infrequent vow to strangle Raoul in his sleep. He stood and replaced the water glass on the tray next to the pitcher.

"Thank you, Christine," he said, with a slight bow to her. He knew he was not thanking her for the water so much as her unwitting admission and the subsequent release of his anger. But she did not know that.

"Nonsense. This is hot work," she answered with a small wave of her hand. She lifted the book from the bench beside her. "Have more if you need it."

Erik excused himself to cover the trembling that came with the implications of her simple confession.

The following day, Christine was nearly giddy when she came to the garden. It was early in the day, but past the time of the morning fog and not yet to the stifling warmth of the afternoon. She came to Peck and stood before him, shaking with suppressed excitement.

He stood and faced her without speaking, allowing his expectancy to grow as he watched her build toward whatever announcement might be coming.

"Peck," she said, first wringing her hands and then forcibly placing them at her sides, "Today, I sing."

Erik smiled and said, "Of course. But forgive my confusion, my ... lady" – he had almost said "my darling" – "you often sing."

"Yes, but today I shall *really* sing. I have dismissed the staff for the day, and today I shall truly be free!"

"I see," he answered, and then, "I will also retire, Christine, so as not to ..."

"Nonsense!" she responded with vehemence. "I can see in your eyes when I sing that you ... appreciate ... my song, and so it is for you that I sing today." Erik thrilled at her words, recalling the Christine of the Opera House days swearing she sang only for him. She walked a slow circle, happy, self-confident in a way Erik had not seen since Paris, and said, "You may work, as you always appear so driven to your craft, or you may sit or do whatever you like. We shall both be at leisure to enjoy ourselves today!"

Erik bowed low and said, "I shall work in my garden while you sing for me, Christine. You provide a garden for my ears as I work."

Christine laughed and watched as he returned to his weeding and pruning, giving him time to settle into his work before beginning. She began her private concert with a beautiful piece from *La Juive*. She built from the beginning gently, but for the first time since the Opera House, she used the full power of her voice to a glorious conclusion. Erik swooned as she sang, and his hands loitered amidst the flowering bushes, accomplishing little.

She moved from *La Juive* to a piece from the prison scene in *Faust* and finally, triumphantly, to the wedding-night song from *Romeo and Juliet*. She walked as she sang, moving with grace, as though on stage, having lost no strength of voice or stage presence through long lack of use. Erik wondered if she had contrived to practice at volume before this triumphant performance – he could not imagine when or how.

In his delirium during her final song and without thought or intention, Erik began to sing a low harmony, a simple, syncopated rhythm to underscore her song. He was brought to his senses by the abrupt cessation of Christine's song.

She looked to and fro, head cocked in an attitude of listening. Erik immediately realized his mistake and damned himself for his impulsiveness, while at the same time excusing himself for succumbing to Christine's song. Above all, he knew he must recover from this blunder.

"Christine?" he asked. "You stopped. I wish you hadn't. You were sublime. I felt carried away." The statement was truth.

Christine looked at him, face stricken with confusion, and again turned her head from side to side as though even now hearing some faraway music.

"Were you singing?" she asked him.

Erik laughed. "I, Christine?" He laughed again. "I swear to you, my lady, my song is not a sound you would care to hear in this garden." When still Christine did not move, he asked, "What is it? Do you hear singing?" He made a show of rising to his feet and listening.

Christine shook her head, golden locks shining in the sun, as if shaking a distracting thought from her head, and said, "No." She walked a short distance, peered behind a tree, fingertips resting on the rough trunk, and then up along a row of hedges. "I thought I heard. … I thought. … No," she said, returning. She sat on the bench and, wiping her brow with the back of one hand said, "My mind is playing tricks upon me. My song has taken me back. …"

When she did not complete her sentence, Erik offered, "Back to a better time, I hope."

"Back, yes," she said. She rose, said, "I'm sorry, Peck, for interrupting your performance. I will rest a while. Perhaps I will sing again later." She moved toward Erik and placed a hand upon his shoulder, still seeming dazed, unseeing of the old man before her.

"I was. …," she said, as she turned to the house, "I was thinking of a friend."

Christine did return to the garden in the late afternoon, but she did not sing. She walked along the cooler paths of the garden and did not speak to Erik even when she passed within feet of him. She did not seem sad, but lost in thought. Erik did not speak to her either, for he was distracted by his own ever-more-hopeful thoughts.

That night, as Erik watched Christine sleep, free from any worries of discovery other than by Christine herself, he both nursed his hope and chided himself for it. Despite his most fervent wishes, he could think of no way to approach Christine in a manner that would allow her to love him. He left her room just before dawn the following morning, careful to avoid any early arrival of the returning servants.

CHAPTER 18
CHRISTINE WRITES A LETTER

After Raoul's return home, Christine found herself anxious for him to leave again. Not because of his infidelities – she discovered the effects of this betrayal faded quickly. Raoul was pleasant, wonderful to her, in fact. In addition to his reported discretion while out on the town, Raoul was also respectful enough to dote on Christine in the comfort of their own home. She repaid his kindness with cheerful attention to his stories of his work and other entertainments, even agreeing from time to time to accompany him to the theater or an afternoon at the museum. She dutifully shared his bed, as and when he requested, although she did not offer or come quietly to his bedchamber as she did when first they were married. In a moment of humorous self-chiding, she reminded herself Raoul needed rest from such exertions some time.

No, Raoul's behavior was not the reason she longed for him to leave the house again. She wanted another opportunity to dismiss the servants and sing in the garden again. She wanted – even if it was only her imagination, for surely it could be nothing else, the poor man was dead! – to hear Erik's voice again.

Reluctantly, when Raoul gave no immediate indication of further travel plans, she let go of what had become for her an almost feverish desire. *It is not fair to wish for Raoul's absence merely so I can indulge the mad desire to keep company with a phantom of my imagination.* She laughed to herself at the thought. *Phantom, indeed,* she thought, recalling the ballet girls and their talk of Erik as the "ghost" of the Opera House.

She continued her forays into the garden for the pleasant company of the dear old Peck, and she sang, although never with the volume of her one day of freedom. Even in the *sotto voce* she used as she sang in the garden, a part of her tensed and searched for the sound of Erik singing with her once more. She never heard him again, although the mere thought of the possibility drew her more and more frequently to the garden until, weather permitting, she often took luncheon out of doors. But still, even with eyes closed and imagination at its fullest, she did not hear him.

Except in her dreams. She began to dream of Erik – she and Erik – singing rapturously, their song lifting her to heights of ecstasy she had never achieved before or since that brief, lovely time in the Opera House. She often woke with the trembling, aching rapture of their dream-song still upon her.

One day in the garden, she spoke to Peck about Erik, with caution, avoiding declaiming the full extent of her current confused feelings about the dead genius.

"Peck," she said, as she picnicked near where he worked. "Do you recall the day I sang in the garden? Truly sang?"

"The day is unforgettable, Christine."

"You are kind." She took another small bite of her sandwich, adjusted her skirts to cover her shoes, and plucked at the blanket under her, lost in thought. As was Peck's usual nature, he waited for her to continue, leaving her in comfortable silence as she attempted to sort out what she might say.

"You will recall," she continued, "that my song was interrupted."

"A mournful moment," he answered, with what seemed to Christine a sincere sadness and without any hint of reproach. She watched him as he dug with care at the base of several flowers, presumably to move them to a better location.

"I imagined a voice singing with me that day," she said.

"I recall," Peck said with a laugh, and Christine knew he was referring to her suggestion the voice was Peck's.

"A beautiful voice. The voice of an angel," she continued. After a pause, she asked, "Do you think me silly to imagine such things?"

He looked to her for the first time. "How can I, when I felt I was hearing the voice of an angel issuing forth from you?" he answered.

Christine laughed at his flattery, although she had become accustomed to his frequent compliments. She still never failed to be delighted with his kind words, even when she felt they were undeserved.

After another few moments in which she continued her leisurely luncheon, she spoke again. "I had a friend, once," she said. "I had a friend who sang like an angel. At first I believed he was an angel – the Angel of Music."

"I see," Peck answered. When she did not continue, he prompted, "and you believed the voice you heard was that of this friend?"

"Yes," she said.

"Is he here, in London?" Peck asked. He worked as he spoke, not looking at her.

"He is … dead," she answered. A great sadness washed over her as she realized anew that she would never hear his voice again.

Peck looked to her and said, "I'm terribly sorry."

"I find I am terribly sorry as well," she said. "I would … I would hear him sing again. I fear I am conjuring him. Do you think I am losing my senses?"

"No, no, dear Christine. There is no madness in a pleasant memory," he said. Then with a brighter tone, clearly trying to dispel her melancholy mood, he said, "For example, if you and your husband were to leave this house, I would have your song with me always. Does this make me mad?" The old man laughed.

"You are not mad, dear Peck. Merely kind beyond anything I might deserve."

"Hardly," he answered.

After another stretch of silence between them, Christine spoke of other things. She sang for the old man before going back to the house, and in her own ears, her song was filled with longing.

That night, not only did she dream of singing with Erik, but she also dreamed he had visited her in her room, standing over her while she slept, like a watchful spirit. In her dream, she had no fear of him, although she could not fully picture the awful deformity of his face that had so frightened her when she beheld it in the Opera House. She woke after the dream, and her mind circled on Erik. Indeed, in thinking back to the horror he inspired in her with his behavior at the end, she realized nothing had come of Erik's threats. Perhaps that was all they were? Threats to induce her to stay with him? Was any of his behavior so terrible?

In the morning, unable to remove Erik from her thoughts, she determined to write to the Persian. She thought perhaps if she disposed of the unfinished business between them, she could banish the ghost that had come to haunt her mind and return to the normalcy of her life. The torture she endured at Erik's memory was both exquisite and unbearable.

After the opening pleasantries she felt necessary – the Persian was nearly dead when last she saw him, and she must ask after his health – she came to the true purpose of her letter: Erik. She asked the Persian if he had taken care of Erik's body, according to his wishes. With an expression of some small regret, she explained that Raoul had not initially informed her of Erik's death, and that once she learned of the event, Raoul had not permitted her to fulfill her promised obligations and return for the burial. She wrote:

> *I am tied by the dual obligation of promise to a man who would have killed my husband but not for my promise, and obligation to the man whom I married. I would have you put my mind at ease, if that is possible, and relieve me of this small dilemma.*

She paused in her writing to consider the predicament of Erik's ring, but decided there was nothing to be done about the fact that Erik had not been buried with it, as promised. She could not contemplate the gruesome idea that perhaps Erik had not been buried at all. She hoped the Persian could at least put her mind at ease with regard to this horrific possibility.

She deliberated over the final statements, wanting on the one hand to divulge her sorrow that Erik was no longer of this world, and on the other, not wanting to say too much. She was still uncomfortable with the confused feelings that filled her when she thought of Erik. Finally, determining there could be no wrong in expressing her sorrow to the Persian – with restraint, of course – she wrote:

I must write, as my own paltry eulogy to poor Erik – she had wanted to write "dear Erik" but knew the phrase to be too sentimental, and certainly "poor Erik" was appropriate – *I find myself saddened, despite all, at the passing of this wonderful (if psychotic) master. As you and I know, at least his music was above all criticism.*

Christine considered whether to ask the Persian to answer her directly, as the lady of the house, rather than to answer to Raoul – she had an instinct to avoid any upset that might be caused, should Raoul discover she had written of Erik – but she decided it would be a foolish and shameful end to her letter.

Despite the quickness with which she hoped for a return answer, Christine meditated over sending it. There was so much she felt she needed and wanted to say about Erik, and what she had written seemed insufficient. But in the end, she posted the letter, and prayed the Persian would be kind enough to reply with some haste.

CHAPTER 19
CHRISTINE'S DREAM

Erik was torn with a curious dilemma of jealousy. Since the time he had inadvertently sung in the garden with Christine, she seemed haunted, distracted, less inclined to stop and speak with him in his guise as the gardener, or to read to him. She sang more often and spent more time in the garden – a wished-for treasure – but less and less did she involve herself with Peck. And when she sang, it was to and for another creature, no longer solely for her own pleasure or the pleasure of the trusted gardener. As such, Erik as Peck found himself in the curious position of being jealous of himself. Erik the Angel of Music had stolen some measure of Christine from him.

Erik reminded himself to patience – what other course did he have? – for Christine would certainly return to herself (and to Peck) with the passing of time. But for the unfortunate Erik, Christine's pulling away from him only increased the ever-present desire for him to reach out to her, physically as well as emotionally.

Erik began to wonder if he could endure the torturous half-life of his current friendship with his beloved. The pain that coursed through him as, distracted, she passed by him seemed unendurable after the work of winning her trust and friendship. For a day, in a sulk, he avoided the garden while she walked it. His sullen mood was not improved when she gave no apparent notice to his unusual absence. He did not allow himself to go to her room to watch her sleep that night.

Yet, he felt a puerile pleasure when she spoke to him, quite sincerely, the following day, after making the effort to seek him out where he worked.

"I missed you yesterday, Peck. I cannot recall a day you were not laboring to make the gardens more beautiful. Did you have an errand?" she asked. She bent to smell an iris then lifted her head to gaze at him, seemingly interested in his answer.

"I was not well," he answered, in all honesty.

"Oh dear. Are you better?" she asked, stepping closer and putting a hand upon his arm.

"Better, Madame, yes," he answered. He did not notice until the words were out that he had used the word "Madame" to address her for the first time since the day they "met." It was a measure of his feeling that their friendship was languishing.

Christine seemed to notice the address as well, for she scowled prettily at him. Then her face cleared to the same distracted, dreamily smooth countenance she had presented since he sang, and her eyes wandered away from him.

"I am not well, either, of late," she said. "I find myself faced with an insoluble difficulty."

"Can I assist you in some way?" Erik asked.

"No, my friend, my dear Peck. No one can assist me." With these words she wandered away.

Erik worried now that Christine may indeed fall ill with her preoccupation, and he blamed himself for the circumstance. He went to her room that night to watch her sleep and to think. The problems posed by his position and hers seemed momentarily insurmountable – an unfamiliar difficulty for a man unused to insurmountable problems. He had originally thought to be satisfied with the sight and sound of Christine, and found, now that he had also gained her friendship, that he was not. He wanted more and could think of no way to accomplish this. He gazed around the moonlit room as if searching its shadowy corners for the solution he desired – and from long habit expected – to come to mind.

When his eyes returned to Christine, it seemed her open eyes glistened in the darkness toward him. He marveled at the illusion … until she spoke. Erik froze in the darkness, and prayed fervently that Christine spoke only from her dreams.

"Erik," she whispered, sighing. She did not move amongst the bed linens, except perhaps to raise her head slightly and then lower it again. In the low moonlight, she appeared to be looking toward where he sat in the corner chair.

"Erik, I have dreamed you so often, and now you are here. I wish so this were not yet another wayward dream." Again, she sighed deeply, sadly.

After a moment, she said, "Yet, I have much to say to you, and perhaps when I have told you all I know and feel, … perhaps then, you will leave me in peace. Will you stay for a time and listen?"

Erik did not answer, did not move. He heard his pulse beating in his ears as an underscore to her quiet speech.

Apparently accepting an assent from the stillness of Erik's figure, she reached behind her head and plumped a pillow, the better to raise her head to gaze at her dream apparition, before assuming her speech.

"I was a fool, Erik. A fool. I must confess to you now that you are dead and beyond me completely, that I was too young to recognize and accept what you offered. Too young to make sense of the love you showered upon me day and night." Her voice rose as she spoke, no longer the uncertain whisper with which she first said his name. "I yearn, body and soul, for the ecstasy of singing with you, for truly you were the Angel of Music. I confess now that I have never felt such ecstasy and long so to return to its embrace." Her head turned away from him and distractedly, almost brightly, she added, "I thought I heard you singing with me in the garden not too long ago." She turned her head back to him, and her voice became somber again as she said, "I have not decided if the excitement and pleasure that attended that brief fantasy was worth the torture I have endured since." After a moment, she added, "Oh, but it was. It was."

Even as Christine sniffed, and wiped at her eyes with the sleeve of her nightgown – a sure indication of her pain – Erik felt suffused with a glowing rapture at her words that threatened to close his throat and pricked at his eyes. He wished to rush to her, he wished to speak, but knew he could not. Her arm covered her face as she dabbed again and again at tears he could not see. He thought that, with her arm over her face, he might make his escape unseen, but knew he could not leave without hearing everything she had to say.

As though reading his thoughts, she cried, "Don't go yet!" She brought her sleeve down from her face and sat forward, apparently afraid her dream apparition had abandoned her while she covered her eyes. "Don't go. ... Ah yes, good. I have more to confess."

She settled back again and was quiet for such a long time that Erik might have believed her asleep if not for the continued glossiness that revealed her open eyes. Finally, she continued, voice lowered to a hushed whisper. Erik wondered if she whispered to hide her voice from people outside the room or perhaps to hide her own words from herself.

"I love you, Erik. I love you."

The tears threatening Erik's eyes now broke free and coursed down his face in warm rivulets, reminding him vividly of Christine's tears upon his face on the night of her parting from the Opera House. He did not move to wipe them, but allowed them to

146

fall to his shirt. He was so moved with joy at these longed-for words that he felt a crushing in his heart, in his chest.

"I love you, Erik. I was afraid, and so young, and Raoul was so safe. I thought I loved him, and perhaps I did. I have wondered of late if I loved Raoul then or merely loved the safety and escape he seemed to offer me in my weakness and fear." She paused, as if lost in thought.

"You know, Raoul accused me of loving you. At the time, I thought him ridiculous in his jealousy, but perhaps he was not so ridiculous. Perhaps he saw in me what I only now have come to admit." Voice lowered to a barely audible whisper again, she said, "I love you, Erik. I love you."

She paused for a long time and then adjusted her body on the bed, although her eyes never left the shadowy corner where Erik sat, weeping, fulfilled, nearly bursting with joy.

"Ah, Erik," she said with another deep sigh. "Would that I had been fool enough to marry you instead of fool enough to run away. Either way, I am a fool, and only now discovering the worse foolishness of the two." Another sigh, and Christine pushed her head deeper into her pillow, apparently seeking comfort, but still never closing her eyes. "I have made my confession. You can go now, back to wherever dreams bloom. But I pray you will stay." Her eyes finally closed.

After a long interval, when Erik thought she might sleep, her eyes opened again. "You are still here," she said and uttered a satisfied sigh. "I love you," she whispered, and this time her eyes did not close.

Erik sat and sat, limbs beginning to ache with the trembling tension within him. He waited for sleep to come to Christine. His mind reeled with the possibilities now open to him. But still her eyes did not close.

CHAPTER 20
NO DREAM

As Christine lay in the darkened room, eyes laboring to remain on the ghost of Erik, on his familiar eyes that glowed faintly from the corner, she felt free of the pain in her heart that had plagued her days. The weight of her confession removed from her chest, she almost felt she could float from the bed. She fantasized floating into the arms of the ghost-Erik, where he would hold her and sing to her and return her to the Heavenly spaces she knew existed because of his song. Their song. She would sing with him.

"I love you," she whispered again, as she had from time to time, renewing her entire confession with those three words.

She wondered if she had conjured the ghost from its resting place with the need of her confession, her need of him. She defied the ghost-Erik to leave by defying sleep. Like a child, she imagined that, if she could keep him there until dawn, they could walk the garden together, in daylight as never before. Her mind was a chaos of impossibilities.

"Erik," she murmured. "Erik."

As she watched, undaunted in her determination to retain this ghostly image, the eyes suddenly moved higher in the corner. They approached where she lay until, emerging from the deep shadows of the darkened corner, she could make out the body beneath the eyes, the outline of the head in which the dim, glowing eyes were set. The illusion of the man was perfect, although she still could not make out his face. Even in her mind's eye, she could not recall Erik's frightening face.

She watched as the specter floated closer. "Erik," she murmured. "Yes, come to me. I love you."

Closer came the apparition, and closer, until the image hovered at the side of her bed. She slowly reached out. She knew she would feel nothing – she had never heard of a material ghost – but she was drawn, nonetheless. The ghost's hand glowed white in the soft light of the moon from the window as it raised from where it rested at his side and moved toward her own outstretched fingers. His hand stopped its movement toward hers, their fingertips nearly touching. Christine did not move her hand further. She was afraid of banishing the ghost image.

"Erik," she said again, her eyes moving from their two outstretched hands to the slightly reflective eyes of the ghost's face and then back to the hands.

The ghost closed the distance between the fingers and took her hand. "Christine," said the familiar voice.

The hand in hers was a bit cold but very real, and this fact along with the palpable reality of the voice sent a cold shock of terror through Christine. She dashed back across the bed, clutching at her bed linens, even as she let loose a piercing scream.

The ghost did not move, and Christine screamed again, eyes wide now in her panic, eyes attempting to discern the reality of the figure that stood beside her bed.

Erik – *could it be Erik?* – rushed back to the shadowed corner from which he had emerged and to which she had freely and sincerely confessed her love.

And now that my dream has come true, I spurn him?

"Wait, Erik!" she said, sitting forward in her bed, even as she heard the clamoring of footsteps in the hall outside her door. Her screams had summoned Raoul.

The door to her room slammed open and rebounded, and Raoul, clad only in a nightshirt, stood blinking into the darkness, a single guttering candle in hand.

"Christine?" he asked, panting, voice rough. She did not answer. Her eyes strained to see the dark corner in the low light.

"Christine?" Raoul asked again, coming into the room and sitting uneasily on the edge of her bed. "Are you ill?"

"I … I am. …" Christine stammered, eyes darting here and there over the whole room for the figure she knew must be there, the figure that had proved its reality with a simple touch. "I am fine. It was a nightmare. That is all. A nightmare."

Raoul huffed out a breath and said, "Such a nightmare as that I hope never to have. Your scream nearly brought down the house!" He turned up her lantern and placed the candle on her bedstand. He reached for her hand and held it, warm fingers engulfing hers.

Erik's hand was so cool.

Raoul said, "Are you quite sure you are recovered? Do you need anything?" Glancing around the room, and running his hand through his sleep-tousled hair, he said, "I will bring you a glass of milk."

"No! No," Christine answered, and again her eyes searched the now lit but otherwise empty room. "I am fine. I need no milk. I need sleep. I apologize for waking you." With Raoul now stalled in the act of rising, his eyes searching Christine's face, she added, "Truly. I am fine." She wanted nothing more than for Raoul to leave her room.

Raoul's hand still clasping Christine's, he said, "Do you wish me to stay with you?" His face was full of concern.

"No, to bed with you, Raoul. You are kind, but I am fine. Please." She leaned toward him and received a kiss. With a final caress to her arm, Raoul extinguished her lantern, rose and took the candle to the door.

"Good sleep, my dear," he said. "And no more nightmares." He smiled sleepily at her as he closed the door.

Christine waited in the darkness until she heard the muffled sound of Raoul's own door close, and then she rose from her bed. She crept toward the dark corner where Erik had sat through the evening. If it was Erik. Perhaps she had finally and truly lost her mind?

"Erik?" she whispered. She moved forward until she bumped her shin against the chair. "Erik? Are you there?"

She moved in virtual blindness, eyes no longer accustomed to the dark after the brightness of the lantern, hands groping before her.

"Erik? Erik, I am sorry. Please come back." As her fingers brushed the wall beside the chair, she whispered, "Have I gone mad?" She turned and, reaching low to avoid hitting the chair again, she whispered again, "Erik?"

"I am here," came a warm, low voice to her side.

Christine clapped her hands to her mouth to stifle a small squeak. "Erik? Is it truly you?"

"It is I, Christine."

"My God in Heaven, how is it possi ..." she began as she tried to move toward the voice, question cut off as she hit her foot on the chair leg.

A strong, cool hand took her arm, as the warm voice said, "Let me help you." Another hand closed on her waist, and she was guided to her bed, where the hands released her. Seated, her eyes searched the darkness until they found two dimly glowing eyes.

"Here, let me. ..." Christine said, as she lit the lantern on her bedstand and turned it to its lowest level. She raised her eyes up the body of the man standing two paces from her – trim black pants, full black shirt opened at the collar – until her eyes reached the face. She suppressed the shudder that threatened as her dim memory of Erik's face was sharpened by the reality of his unmasked features. Neither she nor Erik smiled in the awkward tension of the unimaginable moment.

With the intrusion of sudden thought, Christine's eyes moved to the door of her room, and she rose, crossed the floor as silent and fast as a mouse, and turned the key in the lock. She returned to her seat on the edge of her bed, aware each moment of the man who had not moved from the position in which the lantern light had trapped him. She raised her eyes to his.

"Erik. Erik, how is it possible?" As she spoke, she kept her eyes upon his face, forcing herself to become familiar with its lines and distortions.

"How is it possible?" he repeated. A small smile twisted his face. "You ask this question of the famed Opera Ghost?" Despite the strangeness of the circumstance, and the still pounding beat of her heart, she found herself returning the smile.

Erik dropped his eyes from her face, and with the first indication of nervous tension, he clasped his hands together before him and said, "I am not ready to believe it *is* possible." He raised his eyes to hers – normal enough in the light of the lantern, she noted, although large and round – and once again they were filled with the sad longing and pleading she recalled from their last night in the Opera House.

Faced with the reality of the man standing before her, the words were more difficult to say, but she would not risk his leaving through her own lack of courage.

"Erik, I meant every word. I have been tortured without you, without your song." She paused and swallowed past a knot of fear in her throat. Looking at her own hands wrung together in her lap, she said, "Erik, I love you."

When she lifted her eyes to his again, she saw his tears, and the sight immediately drew her own from her eyes.

"Your mask," she said, one hand rising toward his face.

"I only wear it during the day," he answered, and again a small smile twitched at the edge of his mouth. "The better to observe you."

"You have seen me?" she asked. Her mind's eye searched through recollections of the streets of London, of the dinners she attended, trying to recall a masked figure.

"Almost every day," he said, and now his smile grew to its full proportions. Perfect teeth glistened beneath his thin lips. She noticed for the first time that his smile reached his eyes, although his misformed nostrils did not change shape. Looking at Erik's face through the eyes of love instead of fear, his features were not so deformed as to leave him appearing inhuman. She could not even recall the full extent of her revulsion in the Opera House.

"Every day?" she asked, only belatedly hearing his statement through her distracted thoughts.

Erik turned from her. His body bent and seemed to shrink into itself. In a voice quavering with the tremors of age, and with the thick accent of a Londoner, he said, "I would rather you sang."

"Peck!" she said, her voice loud with pleased surprise, for she recognized the transformation instantly, and then she clapped her hands to her mouth. After moving to the door to listen for whether she had roused Raoul with her shout, she came back to the bed, and said, "Peck?" She giggled lightly. "So, you see, I loved you even in your aspect of the aged gardener," she said. She felt pride, as though this somehow confirmed her sincerity in claiming to love him.

After a moment during which they gazed into each other's eyes, Christine found the will to speak. "What now?" she asked. "What shall we do?"

Erik paused in answering her. His eyes blazed as he said, "I love you, Christine, as I always have. Now you say you love me." A breath. "I am complete." He turned away from her, presenting his back to her as he continued. "But regardless of love, I remain the hideous monst …"

Christine was up and at his side before he could finish his sentence. "Erik." Her hand pulled at his arm, trying to turn him toward her. "Erik," she said again, and when her efforts could not move him, "Erik, look at me."

As though fighting with himself, with a tentative motion, Erik turned to face her. Their eyes met and he centered and lifted his chin and took on the prideful stance she had seen on him so often in the Opera House. In a flash, she recalled this black, red-buttoned shirt as one he had worn there, once seeming so ominous, now seeming the affectation of a pained person wearing his anguish.

Christine raised a hand to Erik's hollow cheek. His skin was cool and smooth and soft, like the skin of a baby. She felt no repulsion. He tensed at her touch, as if he expected her to draw her hand back in horror. She caressed the hollow of his cheek with the backs of her fingers as she said again, "Erik. I love you."

These words, coupled with her touch, seemed to break something in him, and he again turned his back. He sobbed into his hands, as he whispered, "Christine, oh Christine."

Stepping toward him, she wrapped her arms around him and pressed her head to the loose black shirt at his back. The soft sounds of his sobs and the lurching of his chest under her arms drew tears from her again. She had caused him this pain. She moved around to the front of the stricken man, never releasing her arms, until she stood against him, face now pressed to his chest. After a long hesitation, his arms came around her, and he lowered his face to the top of her head.

They held each other, first standing and then sitting, until neither was crying any longer.

Erik released her, and bringing a hand hesitantly to her tear-tracked face, said, "You must sleep." He stood.

The protest that came to Christine's mind was stifled by a yawn. "Yes, we must both sleep. Of course, now that you have reappeared in my life, we have tomorrow." She smiled and was pleased when Erik returned the smile.

"I will see you in the garden," Erik said, with the voice of Peck.

"You will," Christine answered and lowered her head. Knowing her face was pinking with the audacity of her next question, she said, "and will you come to my room again in the night?"

When Erik did not answer, Christine rose and put her arms around him. Hiding her face against his chest, she said, "I will not let you go at all unless you promise to come again. Promise me."

"I will come," Erik said. Moving slowly as though afraid of what her reaction might be, he brought his mouth to her forehead and kissed her there. Christine smiled and then, just as tentatively, raised herself to her toes, closed her eyes, and pressed her mouth to his thin lips. When she lowered her heels to the floor and opened her eyes, she saw Erik's eyes were still closed. He raised his fingers to his mouth and opened his eyes in slow starts. After one panting breath, he smiled.

With a quick step toward her bedstead, he put out the lantern, leaving the room in blackness. "Good night, my love," he said from across the room.

"Good night, my love," she answered, still standing near her bed. "Until tomorrow."

There was no answer from the darkness. Erik was gone.

CHAPTER 21
ERIK AND CHRISTINE

Christine came early to the garden and, with an impatience that filled Erik's heart, did not wander the paths, but came searching for him. He stood as she came rushing toward him, skirts flying behind her as she moved.

"Erik!" she cried and raised her arms as though to rush into his own.

"Madame," he answered and stepped back and to one side to avoid her embrace. He bowed to her in emphasis of their respective positions.

"Madame?" she repeated, and laughed, attempting once more to step into his arms. Again, he turned away.

"Erik, what is it?" she asked, confounded. "Why do you turn from me? Why do you address me so?"

"I shall address you as Madame whenever you forget you are the lady of this house, and I am merely the old gardener." He spoke at low volume and did not speak with Peck's voice, but with his own.

"Nonsense!" she said. For a long moment, she seemed to be studying his mask, eyes roving over the details of the wrinkled old face.

"I must tend to the far bushes, Madame." He spoke in Peck's quavering voice, "if you wish to walk with me." He turned and moved farther from the house.

He turned again and watched as Christine looked back to the house, eyes glancing from window to window before she followed. He was pleased she finally seemed to be considering his statement. They both walked at a sedate pace, as was their custom when they walked together. Christine did not reach to take his arm as he feared she might and wished she could.

Once farther from the house and safely ensconced behind a barrier of high bushes, she spoke. "Erik, this is ridiculous."

"Hardly ridiculous. I will not see you ruined," he answered, his voice his own.

"But what shall we do? I love you, you say you love me, and yet we will continue this mad charade?" She took his hand and peered into his eyes, as though attempting to penetrate the mask and truly see him.

"Yes, we will continue. There may come a time, a place, a way for us to be together as we wish, but until then. ..."

"Until then, I must what? Pretend you are simply the gardener?" She looked down at the hand she clasped in her own and, pulling it toward her face, turned and examined both sides. "This hand is your own," she said. "I never noticed."

Erik laughed. "The trick to good theater, as you know, is merely providing enough to create the illusion."

Christine pulled his hand to her mouth and kissed it. The shock of her lips against his skin made him shudder.

Despite a sudden overwhelming desire to take Christine into his arms, Erik pulled his hand from her grasp and said, "And yes, until then, I am simply the gardener. You must treat me as such."

"But ..." she began, looking for all the world as if she would stamp her foot in a temper.

"Christine, after all my efforts and all my waiting, your impatience is rather amusing," he chided.

The furrows that had creased her brow thus far smoothed, and she lowered her head. "Yes, and unfair," she said. "I apologize." After another moment, during which Erik plucked dead blossoms from the bush before him, she said, "But what shall we do?"

"Be patient," he answered, with a smile.

"But can we not run away? You kidnapped me once, if you will recall," she said with a sly smile. "Could you not do so again?"

"You are a married woman now, Christine. Do you imagine I would have behaved as I did in the Opera House had you been married?"

"I never thought of it," she answered.

Erik moved down the hedge with his work. She moved toward him, then said with firmness, "You shall be Peck. And I shall be the lady of the house."

Erik nodded.

"So tell me, dear Peck, of your adventures since last we were together. How did the Persian come to write Raoul of your death, and how did you come to be a gardener in London?"

With caution, Erik obliged her, enjoying the surprised expression on her face as he told of his time in Korsnäsborg and her admiration of his maneuvers culminating in becoming the gardener at her home. He did not explain that he owned the house or the financial aspects of his various maneuvers. He did not provide every detail of his visitations to her for fear his liberties would shock her in the newness of their relationship. He vowed he would tell her all, someday.

He sent her away when it seemed she intended to stay the entire day by his side. Christine obediently bid him farewell without argument, but only after exacting a promise that he would come to her that night.

"I will come," he answered quietly.

Clearly, Christine did not understand he intended to continue his visits to the house with or without her invitation, but it pleased him that she insisted.

That evening, after the house quieted, Erik crept through the passages toward her bedchamber wondering if he should find

Christine asleep, as usual. He slipped into her room and lowered himself into the chair in the corner.

Several minutes later, she whispered into the darkness, "Erik?"

"I am here," he answered.

The lantern flared at her bedside, and she rushed toward him, then stopped as though hitting a barrier.

"Your mask! Why are you wearing it? You will never wear that mask again — at least not when we are alone." She held her hand out with obvious demand until he removed the mask. She gazed at his face without apparent fear before she put the mask on the chair behind him. She straightened and threw herself into his arms. "I've been calling your name every few minutes for what seemed hours," she cried. "I thought you wouldn't come."

Erik chuckled at her youthful enthusiasm and released her, eyes moving to her door.

"I've locked it already," she said, following his glance. She moved to the lantern on the bedstand and turned down the flame. "There, is that better?" Her eyes searched his face without the slightest indication of revulsion, and he marveled that what he once wished might be possible, seemed so.

Christine came again into his arms, and this time raised her face to his expectantly. When he did not move beyond embracing her, she raised one hand to the back of his head and pulled his face to hers, and for the second time in as many days, she kissed him, her warm lips touching his for a moment. He thrilled at the sensation of her full mouth against his, and his breath caught in a small gasp.

"Now you must kiss me," she said, her sweet, warm breath mingling with his as it had during the evening he secretly stilled her nightmare.

When still he did not move to kiss her, she again pulled his face toward hers and kissed him, this time taking more time, lips parting against his mouth, soft tongue entering his mouth to touch his own. Piercing desire enflamed him, and panting, Erik released her and stepped back and away from her.

"Erik, what is it?" she asked, in a small uncertain voice. "Have I ...? Am I ...?" she asked, her arms still extended toward him.

"Christine, you are the embodiment of all I desire in the world," he answered, hoping to quell her evident self-doubt, "but I ..." Before he could finish, Christine was in his arms, and he could not stop himself bending to meet her mouth, could not think of anything but their mingled lips and taste and breath.

When at last they broke, both panting in sharp breaths, Erik determined he must leave at once. Although he prided himself on his self-control, he did not believe he could maintain it in the face of his kindled desire. He resolved he would not hurt Christine through his own uncontrolled desire. But Christine took his hand, and drawing him toward the bed, said, "Erik, come. Hold me."

"Christine, beloved," he said, bewildered, as they approached the bed, "I could not desire you more, but you are a married woman, and your husband is scant steps down the hall. I would do you ill to treat you as a wanton, and I would not have our love sullied in this way. Someday, perhaps, if my hopes are realized, we ..."

Christine stopped his words with a finger to his lips. "Hush, love," she said. She released his hand, walked to her dresser, and removing a small box from the back of a drawer, she drew out a ring – the ring Erik had given her in the Opera House. She removed Raoul's ring from her finger and replaced it with the ring from the box.

"I am not another man's wife, Erik. I am your wife. I accepted your proposal and your ring first." She kissed the ring and moved again into Erik's arms. Clear eyes gazing into his, she said, "Come to me as my husband and my love. This shall be our wedding night. Raoul is but the mask I wear."

Erik stood with the warmth of Christine pressed against him and fought with himself against the emotional – and completely illogical – plea she presented. But she was wearing his ring. She was standing in his arms, no fear, no hesitation, love shining in her eyes. When she pressed herself against him more closely, rubbing her body against his as she rose to her toes and raised her chin to receive his kiss, all further thought of fighting his desire left his mind. He succumbed to her with the openness and passion that must be given a demanding angel.

He did not leave her bed until dawn.

**

The weeks that followed contained a magic Erik had never thought possible. As Peck, he spent his days with Christine, and they talked of books and art and Sweden and their respective pasts, and any number of matters both trivial and weighty. When they felt they could, they sang together in the garden, though not at full volume.

As Erik, he spent evenings in Christine's bedchamber, experiencing an ecstasy of a different kind, although he did not do as Christine demanded and spend every night in her room. He reminded her of the dangers of discovery by Raoul, and she unhappily relented under his self-evident arguments.

One reckless day, they took luncheon in the gardener's cottage and feasted only upon each other, but the danger of curious or observant servants kept them from repeating such a meeting.

Each time Raoul traveled, they took the opportunity to dismiss the servants for just one day and sang together both inside the house and out, reliving the ecstasy of their time in the Opera House and spending day and evening as the married couple they fancied themselves to be, with a freedom from the need to be silent and careful they could enjoy at no other time.

Despite Erik's contentment – absolute joy! – in the arms of and with the friendship of his angel, he continued to ponder possibilities for their escape and for a life together without the convolutions of deception. Erik fully understood the inherent dangers of their situation.

These dangers were brought to the fore by an unexpected letter received by Christine in late July. She came to the garden with the letter in hand and a stricken look upon her face.

"Peck," she said, as she approached him almost breathlessly – for it had become their habit to maintain the pose of gardener and lady at all times in the garden – "Peck!" She waved the letter in the space between them.

"Yes, Christine, what is it?" he answered, remaining on his knees.

"It is the Persian!" she whispered.

"The Persian?" he asked, startled at this sudden intrusion of his past into their happy lives. He rose and, wiping hands on his pants, began walking to the hedge at the back of the garden, near his cottage, to which they sometimes repaired for privacy. "What of the Persian?"

"I never told you – I had forgotten – but I wrote to the Persian shortly before you revealed yourself to me. I was in such agony over you, and I asked that he give me some ease about your burial arrangements." Tears glittered in her blue eyes as she said, "I am so sorry, I am so sorry!"

Erik's mind raced as he realized Christine's letter had undone his deception of the Persian.

"What does he say?" he asked, mind jumping to the possible dangers posed by the knowledgeable daroga.

"He is here, in London. He wishes to come see us – Raoul and me!" she cried. She was visibly trembling, letter rattling in her fingers. "What shall we do?"

"Christine," he said, uncharacteristically taking her into his arms in the privacy of the tall hedge in the hopes of calming her. "You must meet with the Persian. We cannot know how to proceed until you hear what he has to say." He released her and said, "Do not worry. I will not allow harm to come to you."

"But to you!" she said and brought her handkerchief to her eyes to dab at the tears that had risen again.

"I have avoided the bloodhound thus far, dear Christine. You needn't worry. Now, dry your tears," he said as he began leading her back toward the house. When he reached the spot where he had been working, he lowered himself to his knees and whispered, "Erik will come to you tonight. We will discuss this further." When Christine did not leave him, he said, "Go now, and calm yourself. You are my strong, strong bride, and all will be well."

"I love you, Erik," she said, and with a deep breath that seemed to return some of her self-control, she left him to his work and his reeling mind.

CHAPTER 22
THE PERSIAN

Christine was not much comforted by speaking with Erik about the Persian, if only for the reason that there was not much to be said. Until they knew why the Persian wished to meet with Raoul and Christine, no plans could be made. It was thus a nervous Christine who met the Persian at the door when he arrived two days later.

"Madame de Chagny," said the tall, dark-skinned figure as he bowed over her hand. To Christine, he did not seem much changed from her days in the Opera House, with his mysterious, curved jade eyes and his round, flat-topped astrakhan cap.

"Monsieur," she answered in a demure although somewhat shaky voice.

"I have come in response to your most gracious letter," he said, as he stood again and removed his cap.

"Please!" Christine said, as she glanced over her shoulder toward the drawing room where Raoul waited. "Make no mention of my letter to my husband, I beg you." When she noted the mix of confusion and analytic calculation that crossed his face, she

169

continued, "Raoul has many mixed emotions regarding Erik, not the least of which is an unrelenting and undeserved jealousy, and I would not have him knowing I wrote to you of Erik. You understand, I hope."

Again the Persian bowed and with a small smile said, "Your reference to warring obligations should have told me as much. I understand, Madame, and will do as you wish."

With quiet thanks uttered, Christine led the Persian to the drawing room.

Raoul appeared quite happy to see the dark man and rose with an enthusiastic eagerness.

"My dear friend," he said, as he clapped the man on the back and led him to a chair. The friendship forged of their near-fatal shared adventures in the bowels of the Opera House was evident in the instant camaraderie of the two men. Christine took biscuits and tea from the maid as she entered and placed them between the two men. After pouring out the cups, she loitered as they exchanged pleasantries, unsure whether she was expected to leave the two alone together. To her immense relief, the Persian solved the dilemma for her.

"Please, Madame, join us. What news I have is for the two of you."

With a quiet exhalation of relief, Christine sat in a chair across from the two men. She did not pour herself tea for fear the cup would clatter against the saucer from the nervous tension bounding through her. Erik had told her he would observe the meeting if he could, but she had no way of knowing if he had managed to slip into the house. The thought that he might, at this moment, be very close to her was both exciting and comforting – but not enough so to relieve her tension at the Persian's presence.

"I will tell you the purpose of my trip to London without further ado. I fear I cannot increase the pleasantness of my news with any wordy introduction." Here, the Persian's face regained its oft-seen seriousness as he glanced between Christine and Raoul. "The Opera Ghost, known to us as Erik, is not dead," he said.

"What?" said Raoul with a small laugh. Christine covered her mouth with her hands. This knowledge in the Persian was what she and Erik feared.

"That is ridiculous," continued Raoul when the Persian did not respond further. "I had the letter by your own hand that explained the monster was dead – assuring us so. How can this be? Or was the letter not your own?" Raoul sat forward in his chair, and his building irritation was evident in his unhappy features. "Explain yourself, man."

"I wrote the letter, of course," the Persian answered. "I was certain of my statements at the time I wrote to you, but I was deceived. I am just as certain now that Erik did not perish when and as I thought, and given the man, I am certain he is alive today."

To Raoul's demanding questions, the Persian explained Erik's visit to him just before his purported death, and the promises exacted, gracefully avoiding a full description of how much Christine had figured in Erik's explanation that he was dying.

He told of his search for the burial site in the lair under the Opera House. He also explained that "for reasons of his own" – Christine was quite relieved the Persian did not explain those reasons – he had recently come to believe he had been deceived. He related his newest visit to Erik's home under the Opera House and the fact that the grave, when investigated, revealed no body.

Raoul's rage grew as the Persian spoke, and by the time the Persian had completed his account, Raoul was no longer in his chair, but pacing with energy about the room, making unkind epithets against "the villainous blackguard" and "murderous wretch." Despite her defensiveness, Christine had to admit to herself that Raoul had good reason to dislike Erik. Especially now, although he did not know it. She pressed her lips together to prevent any of her defenses of Erik escaping her lips.

After pouring himself a half-glass of scotch – the Persian declined to join him – and calming himself somewhat, Raoul asked the Persian the reason for his visit.

"Surely you did not discomfit yourself with this long journey merely to tell us the monster is back at his tricks in the Opera House," Raoul said, regaining his seat. His eyes flashed to Christine.

"Unfortunately, no," answered the Persian, and again he peered between Raoul and Christine, his gaze lingering long on Christine. Noticing again the curious and analytical nature of the look he directed toward her, she realized she had perhaps not reacted with the same horror and fear she had displayed when last she had faced Erik.

"Oh dear," she said, somewhat belatedly, bringing her hands to her mouth in a show of distress. "Can the news you bring possibly be worse than what you have already told us?"

The Persian continued to peer at her with veiled eyes. "Indeed," he said. Standing, and moving behind Christine to place his hands upon the back of her chair – Christine assumed he meant to provide a feeling of protection, although she only felt threatened by his place behind her – the Persian faced Raoul and said, "I believe Erik has left Paris. I believe, furthermore, that he is now in London."

As Christine could have predicted, Raoul leapt to his feet and continued his rage, arms waving as he paced about the room.

Christine lowered her head in a show of dread and, with a trembling voice, asked, "Dear Sir, tell me, if you can, why you believe Erik to be in London?"

"Yes!" roared Raoul. "Why should the beast be here? Do you have proof? Evidence?"

The Persian spoke again from his position behind Christine. He said, "I have no evidence, no. But I believe Erik is in London because *you* are in London." After a pause during which Raoul did nothing more than to open his mouth in surprise or agitation, the Persian said, "I believe your lives may be in danger."

Christine turned in her chair to peer up into the man's jade eyes. "But he released us," she said. "Why should he seek us out now? After all this time?"

"To have you back in his clutches again!" Raoul roared, pacing toward Christine. She shrank back at the volume and violence of his shout.

"But I ..." she began, unsure of what she would say – for indeed she was "back in his clutches," and happy to be so. Even in the tension of the moment, her body flushed as she recalled the physical ecstasy that Erik gave her with his own body, which ecstasy she never knew possible even after all her time with Raoul.

"I shall kill the monster this time. I should have done so before," Raoul continued, as he paced back to his chair, his fist smacking into his open palm. Returning to Christine, he threw himself to his knees before her, took her hands, and said, "You are *mine*, Christine, *mine*, and he shall not have you." He dropped his head to her hands.

Tears pricked in Christine's eyes at the thought of her Erik dead. Dead because of her love and Raoul's jealousy. Raoul's jealous requirement to possess her despite his lack of love for her.

Or perhaps he does love me, in the only way he can. He simply does not understand love as Erik does. As I now do.

"My dear sir," came the quiet, calm voice of the Persian. "Calm yourself, please."

Raoul lifted his head to look past Christine to the Persian. "I love Christine," he said.

174

"Sir, I do not doubt your love for Christine, but neither do I doubt the love Erik holds for this charming lady. Let us consider the facts before vowing murder. It has been nearly two years since the deception Erik practiced against me, and no harm has come to either of you. I promise you, should the man have desired to locate you, he would have done so with no great effort. If he desired immediately to harm you – either of you – he would have made the attempt before now."

"So you do not believe he is a danger after all?" asked Christine, turning again to look up at the Persian with what she knew was pleading in her eyes. Hopefully, the Persian would understand the pleading to be a bid for her life, and not what it was: an entreaty for Erik's freedom and safety.

"I cannot assume that, and neither can you. No one can fathom the mind of a genius such as Erik has proved himself to be. No one can predict his aggressions – neither why, nor how, nor when. I can say I know him to be remorseless and concerned solely with his own whims and desires. I dread the moment those whims lead him to you."

You don't know him! Christine wanted to shout the words. Instead, she merely buried her face in her hands and wept, saying over and over, "No … No …"

Her tearful response seemed to strike both men with the same protective instinct. Raoul stood and drew her into his arms, as the Persian stepped around the chair to her side, and murmured, "There, there, dear lady. There, there."

175

"Christine, you know I would never let harm come to you," Raoul said, proffering his handkerchief and pulling her again to his chest.

"Certainly not," added the Persian. "In fact, this is the very reason for my journey to London, Madame. Precisely the reason. I come to offer my services."

"Your services?" Raoul asked, and Christine managed to stop her tears to hear the Persian out.

"Indeed. I have some substantial talent in police work, and more significantly, I have knowledge of that devious master and his methods. It is my intention, therefore, to take a flat in the vicinity of your lovely home," and here he gestured in a vague way around the room, "and to engage in certain activities of detection."

Raoul lowered Christine to her chair with an absent pat to her shoulder and returned to his chair. "Go on," he said to the Persian.

The Persian also returned to his chair and said, "Either Erik is not in London, in which case you have no reason to fear, or he is here for the very reason I have suggested, and he will be near. I shall seek him out, if I can. I will speak reason to him. If you would find this helpful."

"Yes, of course," answered Raoul, and Christine, hoping for some clue as to the Persian's methods, asked, "But where shall you look? What shall you do?"

"Well, Erik cannot be in the bowels of this house – this is not the Opera House with its convenient foundations and underground lake, after all."

"No, I am to understand this house has been standing for a century," Raoul said.

"And he cannot afford to be seen on the grounds," the Persian continued. "He would certainly be recognized, masked or otherwise, would he not?" Here the Persian looked to Christine.

"Of course. And I am usually at home and throughout the gardens," she answered in hopeful tones. "I would imagine that he would avoid the possibility of my recognizing him. If he is, in fact, seeking us out," she added.

"True, but he will not be far. Whatever plans he is making, he will not be far." The Persian's gaze lengthened as though he looked beyond the walls of the room, his face lost in thought.

"Can I do anything to assist you?" Raoul asked. "While I have not the funds of a vicomte at my disposal, I am enjoying some small success here in London. Do you need funds? Is there anything else we might do?"

"Information and caution is all I ask of you," responded the Persian. "It would be most helpful to understand your routine – where you are engaged, where you go when you are not in the house, your habits."

"My habits are quite simple," said Christine. "I am afraid I am not the socialite my husband might wish," and here she smiled at Raoul. "Unless I am in the company of Raoul, I remain here."

"Ah, then I shall focus on you, Monsieur Chagny," the Persian said.

Christine had to suppress a small laugh when she thought of Raoul's "habits" and wondered how forthcoming Raoul planned to be with the detective. It was none of her concern, and she was sure the Persian would be discreet, even if he learned all.

The Persian made an appointment to meet with Raoul the following day at the shipping offices and excused himself. Christine could not wait for the night to come, and Erik with it.

CHAPTER 23
ERIK WRITES A LETTER

Erik heard and saw the whole of the Persian's meeting with Raoul and Christine. He was astounded by the tenacity of the Persian, and the apparent obsession the Persian maintained with regard to himself. To some small degree, Erik was as mystified with the thinking and the motivations of the Persian with regard to Erik. Erik did not understand why the man refused to understand that he was no longer the flippant torturer he had been when amusing the Sultana of Mazenderan – since he certainly had not behaved so since – but perhaps the Persian thought himself familiar with the unchangeability of the criminal mind and attributed such to Erik. Erik knew he did not have a criminal mind – he had the abilities to commit extraordinary crimes, but did not have the apparently inborn urge. Erik merely knew himself to be outside of society, and therefore did not feel the need to restrict himself with its standards of behavior.

As Erik – dressed in the garb and mask of Peck – left the house for the gardens, he smiled at the impotent ravings of Raoul. There was a time when Erik would have responded with a corresponding rage, but Raoul was even less of an entity in his mind now that Erik had earned and won Christine's love.

Of Christine, Erik was most proud. She performed well, compromising nothing and arousing no suspicions. Her questions assisted with the gathering of information, and her tears alleviated any curiosities the Persian may have been developing. Despite this, Erik retired to the gardener's house rather than working in the gardens, thus removing any temptation Christine may feel to visit him there. Today of all days, Raoul would be most vigilant in his protective observation of Christine.

That night, Erik was in Christine's room long before she. He knew she still went to Raoul's bedchamber upon his request – a matter of necessity unpleasant to them both – and clearly, Raoul had needed to confirm his status of husband to Christine after the Persian's visit. Christine entered her own bedchamber weeping. She locked the door, nearly dropping her lantern before she could put it down, and rushed to Erik, tears gaining force as her fingers gripped and dug into his back.

"Was he cruel?" Erik asked, a certain roughness burring his rich voice.

"No, no. Life is cruel!" Christine clutched at Erik with desperation.

Erik tightened his arms around her in turn as he inhaled the delicious smell of her washed hair that hung, still wet, against his shirt.

"Hush, angel," he crooned and then hummed Christine's favorite lullaby – a tune of his own creation. She calmed quickly in his arms, and after a moment, offered her face for a kiss, which he delivered after wiping her tears away with his thumbs. Christine pulled him to the bed, and they sat upon it, facing each other, legs curled under themselves like children conspiring in whispers after bedtime.

Christine took his hands in hers and said, "What shall we do about the Persian? Oh, Erik! I am so worried."

With a small growl, Erik said, "The Persian angers me. He does not know when to leave well enough alone."

"He thinks the worst of you, Erik," she said with despair. "Did you hear? Were you there?"

"I was there," he said, with another growl. He smiled and, with a hand to her face, said, "You were wonderful, my dear."

"I was so scared!" she whispered.

"Hush, love. I know." His smile faded, and he pounded one fist into the palm of his other hand. "Damn him. He does not keep his nose to his own business."

Christine leaned forward and let her head fall into Erik's lap. The wetness of her damp hair began to soak through his pants. He did not mind the dampness, but knew also Christine was unaware of the passion she was raising in him, which passion she would not be comfortable sharing with Erik so soon after leaving Raoul's bed. He pulled Christine's head up and kissed her. After giving a satisfied sigh, Christine sat back again and smiled. Then her smile faded, and her forehead creased with worry again.

"Erik, I am scared for you. For us. What shall we do?" she asked.

After ruminating, Erik said, "I could always kill the Persian."

"What? No! Erik, you are not what he says. Do not become the monster he believes you are." Her forehead was furrowed with indignation at Erik's flippant, but nonetheless logical, suggestion. He could not suppress the low laugh that escaped, and the laugh sounded sinister even to Erik, given the necessary lowness of its tone.

"No," said Christine, her face clearing, her calmness returning. "We must think of something." She took on an attitude of contemplation, elbow resting on one knee, fist clenched under her chin.

"Listen," she continued. "The Persian did not believe you could be in the house," she smiled, as she plucked at his shirt with one finger, "nor did he believe you could be on the grounds. Certainly, he will not look further to the house or the gardener. We can continue as always. Let him search London as carefully as he cares to."

"The daroga is not stupid," said Erik. "He has some good skill. He is also as relentless as the bloodhound. He will not stop until he has reason to believe you are safe from me. This was the entire reason for my earlier deception."

"I am so sorry, Erik. This is my fault. If only I had not written the letter." She rocked forward and clung to him, and he kissed her on her neck, again breathing in the delicious scent of her.

"My love, I cannot condemn you for an action taken in ignorance and motivated by love," he said.

Christine twisted in his arms until she was seated with her back to his chest and pulled his arms around her. "Oh, Erik. If only there was some way to let him know neither Raoul nor I are in any danger from you. If only I could just *tell* him." She turned her head up to peer at him from the corner of her eye. "Do you think he would believe me if I told all? If I swore him to secrecy and told all?"

"No, dearest," Erik said. "You mustn't compromise yourself. You, my wife, are and will remain a shining pillar of innocence." Erik kissed at her ear and said, "But, perhaps I can tell him."

"How do you mean?" she asked, twisting out of his arms to face him again. "How can you tell him? Will he not try to kill you or imprison you?"

"He said he simply wished to talk reason with me. Perhaps I can reason with him. I can write to him. In fact, I believe I shall. He has experience enough over the years to know I am true to my word. I will not implicate you, my love, but I will assure him of your safety."

"Will he believe you? Will he leave us?" she asked, hands gripping his in her hope for such a simple solution.

"No, likely not," Erik answered. "But I shall try to be persuasive." His mouth twisted in a small smile that he hoped concealed the secret irony.

Christine gazed with hope into his eyes. She said, "Hold me, Erik. I need you so." She pulled him toward her as she lay back to put her head on the pillow. He held her until she slept, and then he crept from the room.

In the morning, Erik began the process of discovering where the Persian was lodging. Wearing the mask he had invented in Paris for his marriage to Christine, his "Don Juan" mask as he called it, he spent some time tracking the Persian. He learned several things. The Persian did not have the ready contacts in London that he relied upon in Paris, nor the knowledge of the streets and byways that Erik had acquired when searching for this house. Because of this lack, the Persian was not being at all circumspect in his search for Erik, but was asking any and all who might be able to answer questions regarding a mysterious masked man. This gained the Persian nothing, as Erik had only worn his two life-like masks in the city – his Don Juan and his gardener masks – and thus no one made report of a "masked" man.

The Persian published an advertisement in the newspaper addressed to Erik and suggesting a meeting regarding "R de C." The Persian went to the appointed spot at the appointed time, and while there did not appear to be any police in evidence, Erik did not chance meeting with the man. The daroga repeated this advertisement twice more with no better results.

The detective also spent considerable time following Raoul through his many travels about the city, apparently trying to determine if perhaps Erik was shadowing Raoul. He only discovered Raoul's appetite for amusement, and his constant presence impinged on Raoul's indiscretions.

Despite the utter lack of evidence that Erik was in London, the Persian's search only became more diligent, expanding to inquiries at banks, railways, and passenger boat docks.

Seeing that the daroga gave no signs of giving up the search, Erik composed his intended letter, writing in the red ink that had long been his trademark. He could not insinuate that he became aware of the Persian through Christine, so he opened the letter by saying he had "caught the trail" of the Persian in one of Raoul's favorite downtown clubs. This by itself should send the Persian into another fruitless hunt of Raoul's frequented lairs. Erik laughed at the frustration Raoul would undoubtedly feel at this continued restriction of his "entertainments." The letter next warned of dire consequences to the Persian if he did not stop his ridiculous search and return to Paris:

> *I swear to you upon my soul that neither*
> *Christine nor her husband are in any*
> *danger from me, but the same does not*
> *apply to you if you continue to irritate me,*
> *old friend. I saved you alive not once, but*

twice — once for Christine, and once for the
pleasure of taking the more difficult course.
Do not try my patience further. You have
not the lives of a cat, and I remain — at
least in your eyes, which think they know
me best — an unrepentant murderer. For
your sake, daroga, this time, take the hint.
Go back to Paris.

After receiving the letter, the Persian stopped all attempts to follow Raoul or to continue his investigations. However, he did not make arrangements to leave London.

The threat did not work, Erik thought with a sigh.

For both the sake of Christine and his own private resolution, he did not wish to kill the Persian. But the danger in his circumstance was rising. And he could not leave Christine. Erik resolved to take any action necessary, but having won his love, he could not leave Christine.

CHAPTER 24
DIRE WARNING

Suffused in the glow of their passionate lovemaking, Christine lay in Erik's arms, the windows open to the warm August night, curtains pulled open to remove any impediment to the movement of the stagnant air. The bright moon shone through the window illuminating their intertwined bodies. Erik's pale skin glowed white in the moonlight.

Christine ran her hand slowly over Erik's well-formed and nearly hairless chest, as her foot moved up and down his exquisitely shaped and also nearly hairless leg. Her eyes drank him in.

"You look a god in this light – like a marble statue in your perfection," she whispered.

"I have always been strong, despite being thin," Erik responded.

"Not just strong. Perfect," Christine said, raising her head from her glance down his body to kiss him. She paused when she saw the pained look in his eyes.

"Clearly not perfect," he said. "I suppose my creator became bored once he reached my shoulders."

"Perfect," Christine murmured as she kissed him. Dissatisfied with his unenthusiastic response to her kiss, she said, "You must forget I ever showed apprehension at the sight of your face. I certainly have forgotten it. I love you and find you perfect. Now kiss me properly, or I shall cry."

Erik obliged with passion, and Christine settled back to her pillow with a satisfied sigh. "I could do this forever quite contentedly, if not for the fact that we must steal each moment we have," she delivered a playful punch to his shoulder, "and that you are less willing to come to me since the Persian's visit. Have you devised no plan for us?" she asked.

"None as yet," Erik answered. "The Persian is still in London. Completely outside of the danger of Raoul discovering us …"

"God forbid!" Christine whispered.

"… The Persian presents a danger. He is biding his time. I cannot guess at his motives or plan," Erik finished.

"Surely he does not still worry you. He has not called for nearly a month, and Raoul says he does not seem to be doing anything. He is quite disappointed with the Persian's efforts. Raoul, at least, does not believe you are in London." Christine wriggled against Erik and laughed at the irony of Raoul's certainty while Erik lay just down the hall wrapped in her arms. "He would send the Persian away in anger for speaking of you at all, but for the fact that he did not summon him in the first place."

"The Persian presents a danger. Believe this," Erik answered.

As if conjured by their midnight conversation, the Persian called on Christine the following day, while Raoul was away. Christine came in from the garden where she had been reading to the gardener. As she left the garden, Erik cautioned her against nervousness or distance, saying that these would only arouse the Persian's suspicions. Christine greeted the tall man with a warm smile.

"I am so glad you could visit again," she said, although the ruse of warm relaxation tested her acting abilities. "Raoul is not here," she said, leading him from the foyer to the more intimate sitting room, "but may I offer you refreshment?"

"Thank you, no, Madame," the Persian responded as he sat in the chair she indicated. He seemed positively dour in contrast to Christine's counterfeit gaiety.

"Have you come with information about your investigation? Raoul does not believe your quarry to be in London. Have you come to the same conclusion?" she asked, pouring herself a tall glass of lemonade. Foolish hope rose in her as she considered that the Persian might have come to tell her he was returning to Paris. Her hope was quickly dashed.

"Alas, no, Madame," the Persian responded. "But before I continue, tell me, have you any information for me? Have you seen anyone who could be Erik?"

"My goodness, no!" she answered. "Of course, I rarely leave the grounds, so how could I?"

"That is probably best," the Persian said as he uncharacteristically fumbled with his hat in his lap, head bent forward as he watched his hands.

"My dear sir," Christine said, leaning forward with a concerned look upon her face. "You do not appear well. Have you something unpleasant to tell me? Why is it best that I remain in my home?"

The dark man's exotic eyes rose from his lap to meet her eyes. "While I have not found Erik in London, I have found evidence he is here. The first was in the form of a letter Erik directed to me, and the second ... is most unpleasant."

"You received a letter from Erik?" Christine asked. "Since your arrival in London?" She sat back in her chair and attempted to adopt an expression of concern.

"Yes, Madame," he answered.

"And ...?" She wrung her hands together in her lap, hoping her act convincing.

"He told me to leave London. He warned me of dire consequences if I did not," the Persian answered.

Knowing the contents of the letter, Christine wondered that the Persian did not also explain that Erik had promised no harm would come to Raoul or Christine.

"And your second bit of evidence?" she asked, and a thrill of fear ran through her. She could not imagine what other evidence the Persian may have uncovered or how much of a threat it posed. She said, "Do tell."

In a seeming change of subject, he asked, "Have you seen the newspapers of late?"

"I do not often read the paper," she responded. "I find most of the reporting to be a morbid reflection of this unpleasant city."

"The city has only become more unpleasant," he said. He reached into an inside pocket of his coat and produced a newspaper clipping, which he held out to her.

Christine read quickly of a gruesome murder of a woman and, shuddering, returned the clipping to the Persian. "It is stories such as these that keep me from enjoying the newspaper," she said. "How horrible."

When the Persian said nothing, but folded the clipping and returned it to his pocket, Christine said, "You said you had evidence that Erik … Oh! Surely you are not suggesting Erik committed that atrocity?"

"Mary Ann Nichols," said the Persian, patting the pocket with the clipping. "Two days ago, on August thirty-first, her body was discovered with slashes to the throat and to the abdomen."

Christine shuddered again, and her hand fluttered to her throat. "And you believe this to be the work of Erik?" she said, a small squeak coming to her voice at the conclusion of her question.

"The police are suggesting this killing was performed by the same murderer who killed another woman, Martha Tabram, earlier this month. Both murders were committed by a sharp knife, although the earlier was by stabbing, and this latter by slashing. Both women were attacked in the throat and the abdomen."

Christine sat back in her chair, horrified at the insinuation the Persian was making, but instead of speaking, she waited to hear his conclusion.

"To answer your question, yes, I believe this to be the work of Erik," he said.

"Why on earth …?" she asked, disgusted by the suggestion and fighting to keep from making the defensive argument that lay in her mind, ready to burst forth.

"The initial murder was committed shortly after my arrival here in London. I believe I have frustrated Erik. He indicated as much in his letter."

"But …" started Christine, again fighting against her instinct and desire to come to Erik's defense against the brutal and unfair accusation. "But … Erik never committed any such crime in the Opera House. I cannot imagine how you could think these particular crimes – out of all the crimes committed in the city – are his."

"Not all crimes in this city are fueled by such obvious rage," answered the Persian. "In the Opera House, he had some hope of your loving him. Here, he does not. I believe his frustration at being so near you and yet not having you has merely increased his madness."

"You make no sense," Christine said. "Your accusation is conjecture!"

"Finally," the Persian continued, "the murders occurred not far from here in the Whitechapel District, which is just south of your home, toward the docks. It is an overcrowded and shabby part of town, and Erik could easily hide himself there. I have long believed this is where he has, in fact, hidden himself."

"With the proximity of these crimes to my home, you might just as well come to the conclusion that Raoul has committed the murders. Raoul travels south from here to the London docks regularly!"

"Certainly you are not comparing your husband to the madman who once kidnapped you and imprisoned you and nearly killed the Vicomte," the Persian said. His expression had sharpened into the familiar one of analytic scrutiny.

Christine realized her mistake at once. Her tone and statements had become defensive of Erik despite her determination to contain herself. In an outraged tone – for certainly she was outraged at the Persian's accusations against Erik – she said, "Certainly not! I simply do not understand why you are trying to frighten me. And frighten me you have! My memories of the Opera House are terrifying enough without your suggestions Erik has grown madder still. Do you suggest I am in danger? Do you suggest Erik will murder me now?" Christine breathed heavily in her fear and agitation.

The Persian leaned toward her and, with an apologetic tone and raised hand, said, "My dear lady, I did not mean to frighten you, I hoped only to warn you to caution."

"So you do believe I am in danger?" she asked.

"I have always so believed. I told you this when we last met. There is no predicting the mind of the man."

"Even at his worst, Erik never hurt me. If he is motivated by his desire to have me, as you have suggested, why should he hurt me now?"

"Then he hoped you would love him. Now he cannot have that hope," the dark man answered.

Oh, but I do love him, body and soul! Christine wanted to shout the words, to tell all, to beg the Persian to leave and allow them their secret happiness. She knew Erik would not approve, and such a confession may indeed worsen the situation.

"What do you suggest I do?" she asked, trying to regain her composure. "What do you intend to do?"

"I suggest you remain in your home, as is your wont. This should not be a burden, since it seems your preference. Your servants are always near and could raise an alarm." The Persian straightened in his chair and assumed an air of businesslike attention. "As for what I intend to do, Madame, I intend to continue my rather circumspect search for Erik, concentrating in the Whitechapel District," – Christine felt a rush of relief at this statement – "and I intend to stay in close contact with the police and Scotland Yard in the hopes of gaining information or lending assistance. If you wish, I can request a guard posted around your residence, and if it would put you at ease, perhaps within the residence as well."

Christine nearly gasped with fear at the thought of policemen in and around the house and gardens, but covered the gasp with a small cough and a sip of lemonade. She said, "Neither my husband" – *Erik!* – "nor I would tolerate the intrusion upon our privacy, I am afraid. Naturally, if you obtain additional information that would suggest that necessity, and you convince us of such, we would be most grateful for your assistance." She smiled at the detective and said, "You are most kind in your concern for us. Without your care, neither Raoul nor I might be alive today." She rose and extended her hand to the Persian. "We are forever in your debt."

As the Persian murmured a statement to the effect that he was merely doing his perceived duty, Christine led him to the entrance foyer. With a smile and both hands clasped around the right hand of the Persian, she said, "Please forgive my earlier agitation. I am afraid the discussion of atrocities raised an old, remembered terror in me. However, with the knowledge that you will be continuing your efforts, you have put me greatly at ease. And I will take your advice and confine myself to my home. Thank you again."

As soon as the Persian left, Christine spoke with the cook regarding dinner arrangements and then strolled to the garden with an attitude of quietude and languor. All the while, her mind and body struggled against fear and confusion and the need to speak to Erik about this latest development. The old gardener was nowhere to be found.

CHAPTER 25
ERIK CONFESSES

"Christine," Erik whispered as he entered her bedchamber that night. He knew from times past that, if Christine were sleeping, his gentle whisper would not wake her. If she was awake, his small whisper saved her the effort of calling his name from time to time to discern if he had yet entered her room.

"Erik!" Christine whispered in return, and the lantern flared. With stricken face, she rushed across the room to pull him to her bed. "Where have you been all day? I have been frantic!"

"Christine, you needn't worry about me," he said, and bent to kiss her. She kissed him and in her upset continued to chastise him.

"I searched through the garden for you once the Persian left. Were you able to listen? I've been so worried! I thought he had captured you!"

Erik sighed, sorry he had caused such turmoil in Christine, and explained. "I did not think it wise to attempt to enter the house after the Persian arrived. I did not see or hear, but you, my dear, will tell me everything. I took the opportunity to run a quick errand, knowing the Persian would be busy with you for a time. When I returned, I stayed in my little cottage as a matter of safety. I am sorry you worried."

Christine pressed his hand to her mouth, exhaled, and threw her arms around his neck. "I love you so, Erik," she murmured.

This time, when Erik pulled her into a kiss, she returned it with passion, seeming frantic in her need.

"Now, tell me, wife, what the Persian came to tell you."

"It was horrible! Horrible what he said, what he thinks of you. I can't imagine how he could say such things." She shuddered as she spoke.

"Tell me," Erik urged.

"There have been several murders, gruesome murders, just south of here, and the Persian thinks you are responsible." Her voice rose as she spoke, and her brow furrowed in indignation.

"The Whitechapel murders," Erik said, as though talking to himself. "Yes, I have read of them."

"They are terrible crimes. Why would the Persian think such things of you?" Christine asked, her voice back to a low whisper.

Erik's eyes met hers for a long time, and he sighed. "I will tell you, Christine, why the Persian might think such things, even if the telling costs me your love. I would rather no secrets between us."

"Nothing could change my love for you!" she said, throwing her arms about his neck.

"First, you must listen. Then you can determine the truth of that statement." Erik pulled himself away from Christine and settled with a small distance between them.

Slow and difficult though he found the task and with a sickness in his stomach that his explanation may forever lose Christine to him, he told of his time in Persia. He described with sufficient detail, first his time "amusing" the young Sultana in Mazenderan by concocting means of torture for her pleasure and during that time, how he came to know the Persian, and then his life after that in Constantinople, and his profession as an assassin in those places. Christine listened wide-eyed with only an occasional interjection of dismay. As Erik finished, he said, "This is why the Persian thinks me capable of such things. I was never known to commit atrocities such as these recent murders, but you have now heard me confess to committing others." Erik hung his head as he said, "If you wish me to go, if you cannot love such a monster, I will understand and forgive you." Keeping his head down, afraid of looking into her eyes and seeing her rejection of him there, he added desolately, "I hope that someday you can forgive me."

Christine was still and silent before reaching out to take his hands in her own. "Erik, I admit to surprise and a certain level of discomfort at your confession. But these acts of torture you performed were at the behest of others. In truth, your employers were the truly evil creatures."

"I do not find myself blameless, Christine. But, after a time, the tortures came to sicken me, and I swore to turn away from such acts, forever. I wish you to believe that." He did not explain that the tedium and ease with which he committed the acts came to separate him even more from the humanity that had rejected him and threatened to make him truly a monster. Now that his dreams of love and acceptance had come true, he had no wish to return to the half-life he once led.

"I do believe that, Erik. I do, because they do not seem acts that could be committed by the man I love, the man who sits before me today."

Erik raised his eyes to hers and read the forgiveness and sincerity in her face. His relief and profound love nearly brought tears to his eyes. He wanted nothing more than to close the space between them and to crush Christine to him in thanks, but he would not press his physical self upon her after the terrible things he had confessed. If she was sincere – and he had difficulty believing she could be so forgiving – she would come to him. He would not force the situation in his desperate hope.

After another agonizing moment of silent, mutual study, Christine smiled tentatively, raised her arms, said, "Come to me, my love."

Erik moved into her embrace, and for long minutes, they held each other, while Erik thanked the Fates for Christine's love and trust and marveled that such a thing was possible.

After a time, Christine said, "Tell me what you know of these murders. I found the Persian's conclusion that you were the killer to be built of little more than moonbeams and spider's web, and my newfound knowledge of your past does not change that perception. Yet now the Persian searches for you with even greater will."

"You have yet to tell me of your discussion with the Persian," Erik reminded. "First, you must tell me what passed between the two of you."

Christine explained her conversation with the Persian, often correcting herself or searching for a word, as though she was making every attempt to render the conversation verbatim.

"The fact that he is planning to search the Whitechapel District for you and is working with the police on the incorrect assumption that you are the criminal is helpful, is it not? It will mean he is less focused upon us here," Christine concluded.

"Clearly, he is focused upon you, Christine. But yes, I suppose the false trail is helpful," Erik answered. His mind was racing with plans to turn the Persian's misconception to his advantage.

"Do you know any more of the murders than the Persian explained?" Christine asked. "I still find his reasoning unsound."

"I do not know much more than he told. Only that, while the crimes were against known ... ah ... ladies of the night, there did not appear to be any carnal violation of the women. As the Persian indicated, the crimes appear motivated by rage, rather than lust." Erik shrugged. "Perhaps the Persian thinks me incapable or uninterested."

Christine laughed at this statement and kissed and stroked Erik until his passion began to rise. "Clearly the Persian does not know everything," she said, with a breathless giggle. Erik, relieved by this return to affection so quickly after his confession, clutched Christine to him, again thanking the Fates.

"Of course," said Christine, "using a lack of … violation … as a clue, the murderer could just as well be a woman. Although, of course, no woman could commit such an act."

Erik, thinking of what he had told her of the Sultana, did not raise his eyes as he said, "Do not be too certain of that, Christine."

Christine's response was a small, choking whisper. "Oh. No. Of course."

Erik struggled to change the subject. "The police are looking for asylum escapees, for they are in agreement with the Persian that the murderer is a lunatic, but they may be wrong in this," Erik said.

"But clearly the murders are committed by a madman!" Christine responded.

"Yes, a madman … but perhaps not by a person so mad as to be unable to function in society. Asylum inhabitants tend to be people who do not think clearly." His speech slowed as his mind whirled ahead of his words. "Yet this murderer has hidden his crimes in the dead of the night and has avoided witnesses and capture. Hmm."

"Erik, what are you thinking?" Christine asked, putting both hands on his shoulders and shaking him from his reverie. "You are worrying me! You can't be thinking of …" Her voice trailed off as his eyes met hers.

"I am merely thinking, Christine. I may be able to turn this situation to our advantage. I must think," he answered.

"Think, yes, think all you wish. Please do not do anything foolish!" The concern reflected in her eyes and in the accompanying crease between her brows brought a smile to Erik's face, and he leaned toward her and kissed the crease away.

"I will not be foolish, Christine," he said.

Much later, as Erik rose to leave, Christine whispered into the dark, "Do you think I am in danger, Erik? The Persian's descriptions of the crimes and their proximity, his concern for my life – it haunts me. Even when I know him to be wrong about the identity of the killer."

Erik returned to her and kissed her. "I would never let you come to harm," he said.

"But with a madman on the loose –" she began, and Erik shushed her and kissed her again, stopping her words.

"I would kill him before I let him harm you," Erik said. "I love you so much, Christine, that I would break my vow and kill for you." Christine stiffened in his arms, and he realized he had again intruded upon the fragile peace she had achieved after his confession. "Please, Christine. I do not mean I would kill at your request, my love, not only because you could never conceive of such wanton cruelty, but also for the sake of my vow. I mean only I would never let anyone take your life – and certainly not this madman."

He waited until he felt Christine relax in his arms. She hugged him tightly and said, "I understand. I feel safe with the knowledge that you will protect me. But, please, no more talk of killing. Or of the murders. It is all too ghastly."

"Agreed. No more. Tomorrow we will sing and talk of love, and we will spend the day in frivolity."

"And the night?" Christine asked, and Erik could envision the coy smile on her face that must accompany this question.

"My greedy little wife," he said with a chuckle, kissing her again. "We shall see."

CHAPTER 26
A MOMENT OF DOUBT

The following afternoon Christine met Raoul as he arrived home, and she waited while the butler helped him to remove his rain-soaked overcoat.

"My darling," he said, as he came to her and kissed her on the cheek. "Repulsive weather, my apologies," he said, as he brought out a handkerchief and wiped at his wet face.

"I'm afraid you've missed dinner," she said, taking his arm as he walked to the sitting room. "I didn't know how late you would be."

"I've eaten," he answered, striding to the fire that had been lit against the dampness that penetrated the old stone mansion even in summer. He rubbed his hands together before the fire and then turned his back to the flames. Smiling at Christine, he said, "Come here, my dear. I hope I haven't been neglecting you. Work has been rather busy."

Christine came into his arms, and he kissed the top of her head as he held her. Face pressed to his shoulder, she could smell an exotic perfume she knew was not her own. She could not condemn Raoul – she had not even before Erik had come into her life – but certainly now, she did not even feel the stabbing hint of betrayal. As she had told Erik, her marriage to and life with Raoul was merely the mask she wore in polite society. It was her life with Erik that was her reality.

"Work has been busy?" she asked, prompting him to the conversation she knew necessary.

"Yes, we've added another shipping line, thanks in part to my connections. And then, of course, the necessary dinners and the negotiations," he said.

"I understand," she said. "You are doing well. I am proud." Stepping away from him, she said, "Would you like a brandy, to warm you?"

"I'll get it," he answered, moving away from the fire toward the small liquor cabinet. "But," he said, throwing a glance at her over his shoulder, "you have not been alone."

Christine felt the uncomfortable thrill of guilt and fear of discovery rush through her as she asked, keeping her voice as light and level as she could, "Whatever do you mean?"

"I understand the Persian has visited you," Raoul answered.

"Ah, yes, the Persian," Christine relaxed her posture somewhat and moved to Raoul, pouring herself a small glass of the warming liquor. "I can hardly call him good company. He came merely to frighten me, to tell me he still believes Erik to be in London and now to be perpetrating horrific crimes."

"He is ridiculous," answered Raoul. "I have been through Whitechapel – there are perfectly respectable portions of the district, I assure you," he added when he saw Christine's sudden attention. "But, there are also the most unsavory sections, and the people there are equally unsavory. Immigrants, and load upon load of the starving. I would not put it past any of the filthy foreigners to commit such crimes. And yet, the Persian insists upon taunting us with the memory of a dead monster."

"You believe Erik is dead?" Christine asked.

"Dead or elsewhere. If he were truly in London, we would know it by now. He would be up to his old tricks, pathetically trying to win you, despite his vileness. Christine, how could he resist you?" Raoul pulled Christine into his perfumed shoulder again with a smile, saying, "I certainly cannot."

She returned his smile and allowed him to kiss her. They both sat and after several minutes, Christine interrupted his reading of the paper to ask, "With the addition of this new shipping line, will there be a requirement that you travel?" She said the words with the tone of trepidation, but hoped for the answer that he would be leaving again.

"It has been suggested, but the Persian has requested I not leave the city at this time. The 'dangers' of leaving you alone and all that nonsense." Raoul's eyes flashed from the paper to Christine, and he added, "Not that I would even consider leaving if I shared his worries, of course." His eyes returned to the paper, and he said, "But I fear the Persian would smother you with his protectiveness if I were to leave, and I would not plague you with him." He read a moment more and said, "Besides, he assures me the blackguard will soon be apprehended, and I have work enough for the time being to keep me busy."

"You can do me no greater kindness than staying, Raoul," Christine said. "I am coming to detest the company of the obsessed detective. And of course, I would not do without you, unless it were necessary."

Raoul folded his paper, rose, and crossed the carpet to Christine, taking her hand. "My dear, you know I must travel, on occasion. …," he said, and she interrupted, "Yes, I know. It is quite all right. I am with my husband in my heart even when you are gone."

"Thank you, my dear," he said and kissed her hand before pressing it to his heart. "I am tired. I am going to retire."

Christine remained in the sitting room listening to the rain against the windows as the fire drew down. She reminded herself to bring a towel to her room before retiring, for Erik, if he came, would be wet.

It was not a week before the Persian came to see her again. She was tempted to send him away, for she did not want to meet with him and hear any more of his outrageous accusations against Erik. However, she also knew she must listen to him to determine if he had any information or suspicions about Erik's true whereabouts. She sighed as she went to greet him. She determined she would not greet him with the same gaiety as she had at his last visit.

"Sir," she said, as he bowed solicitously over her hand. "Have you come with more unpleasantness with which to frighten me?" She smiled to take the sting from her statement, saying, "I have just had luncheon. I do not believe my stomach can survive another scare just now."

Apparently feeling somewhat chastened, the man did not launch into the frightful subject that was certainly the purpose to his visit. Christine chatted quite affably with the man regarding the weather, the gardens, and the book with which she was engaged. As they talked, she enjoyed the exotic aroma of the clove cigarettes he favored and was reminded of the genteel manners of the mysterious man as she had known him in Paris. Eventually, however, she knew he would come to the purpose of his visit, and she determined to prompt him to it.

"You have been most gracious in granting me this afternoon of your pleasurable company. Shall I ring for tea? Or do you have a reason for your visit that would make it best to forego refreshment?"

The Persian rose, bowed to Christine, and resumed his seat. "Erik," he said.

"Ah yes, Erik," she responded, and her mouth bent downward. "You have additional 'evidence'?" she asked. "Have you received another letter?"

"No, Madame, nothing so innocuous." After a nervous pause, during which the Persian moved a hand to an inside pocket and back out, empty, he said, "There has been another murder."

"But surely …," she started, but he interrupted.

"This murder was farther north, closer to your home," he said quickly, and Christine shuddered at the thought.

"Near here?" she asked, and she felt her pulse quicken, finding the Persian's concern contagious.

"Not near, no. It was still within the Whitechapel District, but it was committed farther north. Closer to your home."

"A woman, again, I suppose?"

"Annie Chapman, yes. A very similar crime to the previous, with slashes to throat and abdomen." The Persian coughed into his hand. He did not speak further, as if in apology for the news or perhaps giving Christine the time to digest the information.

She found she was frightened, quite apart from any performance she might feel necessary for the Persian. "And you believe Erik is again responsible?" she asked, surprised to hear her voice trembling through the question.

"The police believe the murderer to be the same man, yes, and as you know, I believe the murderer to be Erik," he answered.

"But why Erik? I don't understand," she said. "He never …"

"No, not in Paris," he interrupted. "But I know somewhat more of Erik's past than you, dear lady, and I am aware of what atrocities he is capable. I would not burden you with the knowledge, but believe me when I say I am certain of the matter."

"I see," Christine answered, rising from her chair. As she paced about the room, nerves rising, she recalled what she now knew about Erik's past. Her thoughts circled about the question of whether she should trust her own current knowledge of Erik and belief in his goodness, or trust the knowledge of the Persian.

He spoke into the silence. "Again, I point out these murders began shortly after my arrival in London. I believe I have awakened in him the ancient anger he is helpless to release in other than bloodshed." The Persian spoke quite fervently, and a gleam of determination came into his magnificent eyes, as if envisioning the moment Erik was in his clutches.

"And you believe I am in danger," she said. It was not a question, but a confirmation of his beliefs.

"I do," the Persian answered.

Christine crossed the room to the yawning fireplace, now dark and cold, and stared into its depths.

Is it possible Erik must release his pent rage in this way? she asked herself. She felt a thrill of the old fear. Then she conjured images of Erik in the guise of the gentle gardener, Erik glowing naked in her arms, Erik's eyes gazing into her own before they closed as he kissed her … and she knew for a certainty.

No. He is happy. The Persian cannot banish Erik's past from his mind, and I cannot banish Erik's present from mine. Erik may have done wrong, but he is not the same man as the monster the Persian seeks. I know Erik better than this man does, for all his prior knowledge.

This realization sunk through Christine with a feeling of such rightness, that she exhaled twice in relief. She turned, giving a timorous smile, and said, "I am quite myself now. I apologize."

The Persian rose and crossed the short distance to stand before her. "No, it is I who must apologize, dear lady, for upsetting you again. I simply felt you should know."

Christine smiled again, saying, "You must go now. Thank you for a lovely afternoon."

The Persian bowed his head in acceptance, although his face bore indications of confusion. He said, "Is there anything that I can do to …"

"No. Nothing at all, thank you. I am quite safe here, I am certain," she answered, and she led him from the room.

She would find Erik, she would tell him of the Persian's visit, but she knew – knew! – she would never doubt Erik again, for even an instant. Gone were the days of her weakness and fear.

CHAPTER 27
ERIK'S PLAN

Erik listened as Christine related the business of the Persian's latest visit, making every attempt to push down the fury that rose in him. He was not angry about the Persian's accusations. Let the Persian think what he wished of Erik – Erik had never cared about the opinions of others. He was angry about the ridiculous persistence with which the man bothered Christine and endangered their precarious, clandestine lives together.

"I must do something," Erik growled in his frustration.

Behind him, Christine rubbed his shoulders and leaned forward to kiss the sharp cheekbone above his sunken cheek. "You must love me, and above all, you must be careful," she answered.

"I will be careful," he responded, keeping back the whole of his thoughts: *I will carefully wring the man's neck!* Erik had no intention of harming the daroga, irritated though he was, but also knew he did not want Christine wondering at the seriousness of his exaggerated – and, to him, somewhat humorous – internal comment.

"I must venture into the city, Christine," Erik said, rolling his head from side to side as she massaged his neck.

"Where will you go? What will you do?" she asked. Erik could not detect any suspicion in her tone, only curiosity.

"Do you trust me, Christine?" he asked, more to comfort himself as to her lack of suspicion than because he had doubts as to her answer.

She threw her arms about him, showering kisses across his shoulders and back, saying, "Of course I trust you!"

"I shall need to be gone from the house at various times, day and night," he continued.

"How horrible!" she cried. "For what purpose, my love?"

"I intend to conduct my own investigation. Perhaps if I assist the inestimable daroga, he will desist in his search for me. Certainly, the capture of the murderer will assist others of the hapless public as well."

"Oh, Erik!" Christine said, as she moved around to face him, and now her tone was full of concern. "You said you would be careful!"

Erik's rich, low laughter did nothing to reduce the expression of panicked anxiety on her face. Holding her chin with his hand and her eyes with his own, he said, "I will be careful. You forget to whom you speak. I am but a ghost, remember?"

"I could not live without you," she said, clutching at him, "without your song, without your love."

214

"You will not have to, I assure you," he answered. He kissed her and said, "It is settled, then."

When he stood to leave, she said, "Where are you going? It is early still."

"I go tonight. I will be back by morning."

"No! Not tonight. Tonight you shall be mine. Tomorrow is soon enough to start," she said as she pulled him back to her bed.

"Tomorrow, then," he said smiling, as he joined her. He had no ability to resist her desire for his company when he had spent so long believing she could never love him. As comfortable as they were with each other, Erik never lost his awe and appreciation that it was possible.

In the morning, Erik set out for Whitechapel. In his guise as Peck, but in the shabbiest of his clothing, he did not think to have any trouble negotiating even the worst areas of the district. He did not carry a weapon – especially not a knife – for if he was picked up as a suspect, he did not want to provide any excuse for detention. He did carry a length of rope that could be used in the manner of the Punjab lasso, if needed. He made certain to carry papers indicating his residence and employer.

His initial attempts at investigation found him speaking only to local residents of the district. Later, through middlemen and other sources, he would discover what the police and Scotland Yard knew, if anything. If he could, he would have spoken to the Persian himself – undoubtedly the daroga knew much through his liaison with the authorities – but the man was convinced he knew the identity of the killer and would not treat with Erik other than to have him arrested.

Erik personally spoke to several of the "witnesses," including the victims' landlords and close associates. He spoke to them under the guise of being a newspaper reporter – he discovered that many residents of the district did not trust the police, so he could not use this ruse. He learned nothing of great value. None of the "witnesses" had seen the murders committed. He heard tales of the occasional "suspicious character," but in the flotsam of the immigrant population, many of the residents were indeed criminals and thus behaved in suspicious ways. He examined the sites of the murders – or at least those sites where the bodies were found – again, to no avail.

One pattern began to emerge, however – the pattern of a complete lack of available clues. This simply reinforced Erik's original thesis that the murderer was no crazed asylum escapee. Such a person was just as likely to commit the crimes in broad daylight, or if wise enough to kill under the cover of darkness, without due caution to possible witnesses. However, the murderer – thus far – had eluded all attempts at capture, despite the efforts of the police, Scotland Yard, and various neighborhood committees committed to the search.

Unlike the police investigations, Erik did not look to the people and places frequented by the customers of the fallen women, for the simple reason that he had no belief these people would have the medical knowledge apparently necessary for the last of the three murders: The uterus of the unfortunate Annie Chapman had been methodically removed. As such, Erik turned away from the residents of the district and looked to medically trained professionals – men and women (for Christine's point was well, if flippantly, made) – who might have reason to know the district. Erik spoke to many prostitutes to determine which medical professionals they might have contact with.

One night, after several such interviews, as Erik was walking north through a quiet portion of the district in search of a cab in which to return home, he was stopped by two bobbies walking their beat. The men pulled their clubs from their belts as they called to him, although the action seemed more a demonstration of authority than a menacing threat.

"Ho there!" said the shorter, stouter of the two. His walrus mustache waggled as he spoke.

"Yes, officers?" Erik answered, "How can I be of assistance?" He made his speech as clear and in as refined an accent as that of any lord. Erik did not wish to be detained as a "suspicious character." Good as his mask was, he did not have complete faith it would survive a thorough search.

""'Ow can I be of assistance,' 'e says," responded the taller, but equally stout partner. "'E's a smart one, eh?"

Erik did not respond, other than to nod to the men in the manner of a small abortive bow.

"Look here, what's your name?" the first man asked, removing a small notebook from his pocket as though to take down the information.

"Erik Smythe," Erik responded, "although my wife calls me Peck." For some reason, this brought a short chuckle from the taller man.

"Smythe, eh?" said the short man, glancing up from his notebook without writing. "What are you doing here at this time of night, *Mister* Smythe? Can you tell me that?" The man leaned toward Erik and sniffed, as if to determine whether Erik had been drinking.

"Good sir, I am returning to the home of my employer, the Vicomte de Chagny," Erik responded. Removing a small card from his pocket containing Raoul's coat of arms, name, and address, he presented it to the mustachioed man, and said, "Is there a problem, officer?" He spoke evenly, although he did feel a small spark of fear at the complications that might arise if Raoul were contacted about the suspicious character of his employee.

"Vicomte, eh?" responded the short man, eyeing the small card as though nearsighted. Handing it to his companion, he said, "Well, I suppose that's all right, then. Run along. It's not safe to be on the streets this time of night."

"You're right batty, you are," added the taller man, returning the card to Erik, "fine-talking gent as yourself in these parts."

"Certainly, gentlemen, thank you," Erik said with a small bow. He left the men as they continued along their beat, but resolved to pay closer attention to any suspects he might uncover who could cow the local police with claims of gentility. These men had neither written down his name nor taken the card!

Later that night, Erik went to Christine's room as much for his own need for comfort as to comfort her. He was frustrated at his lack of progress. When he found her asleep, he could not bring himself simply to watch her sleep. He crawled into her bed beside her, wondering if she would mistake him, perhaps, for Raoul in the muzziness of her slumber.

She rolled toward him and murmured, "Erik. I so hoped you would come." It occurred to Erik that if the man now next to her had been Raoul, she would not have a pleasant awakening, but he was warmed by his name on her lips all the same.

"I love you," she said, as she draped her limbs across him and nuzzled into his shoulder. Erik did not answer aloud, as he hoped she might return to sleep and relieve him of the slight guilt he felt at awakening her.

"I want to see Peck tomorrow," she continued, sleep blurring her words. "You don't have to go out again tomorrow, do you? I miss you."

"I will see you tomorrow," he answered.

And with that, Christine fell to sleep. She did not wake when he left her before morning, refreshed and newly confident he would soon succeed where the police had not.

CHAPTER 28
LETTERS

For several weeks, all was quiet. There were no more murders in Whitechapel, or at least none that could be attributed to the notorious slashing murderer. Christine's life approached its old normalcy, although Erik continued his investigation and often left her alone for hours during the day or night. The only pleasure she derived from his absences was his greater willingness to come to her at night. Of course, she worried most on the nights when he did not come at all, for this suggested to her vivid imagination that he was spending the dark hours in danger. She did not often sleep on those nights, terrified of discovering he had been arrested, or worse, killed in some midnight foray.

As the weeks passed, Raoul's patience with the Persian's injunction against traveling wore thin and, citing the needs of the added shipping line, Raoul ventured abroad once more. He did allow the Persian to persuade him to keep the trip to a mere fortnight rather than the month-long journey he had at first planned. Christine was hard-pressed not to show her enthusiasm over Raoul's imminent departure.

Once Raoul was gone, she dismissed the servants for a day, as they had come to expect during Raoul's absences. She often wondered what the servants thought of the enigmatic dismissals, but as none asked her purpose, she did not venture any explanation.

Once again, as they had not done in months, she and Erik were free to make use of the house and most ecstatically, to sing. When Erik sang for her, Christine was transported. When they sang together, she felt she had discovered Heaven, her bliss was so complete. Happiest of all, Erik did not even suggest leaving her for his mysterious investigations that day or night. They remained in each other's sight or touch for the entire wonderful twenty-four hours. Christine even suggested she could dismiss the servants again upon their arrival the following morning – thus prolonging their ecstasy for another day – but Erik would not allow her to deviate from the accustomed pattern.

Not many days later, a post arrived from the Persian. It contained a short, polite note requesting another meeting with Christine, along with a newspaper clipping regarding the double murder of two women, Elizabeth Stride and Catherine Eddowes, in the Whitechapel district. The article stated that the murders had occurred on the night during which Erik and Christine had been alone together in the house.

Christine paced in agitation about the garden where Erik worked. "I could present the perfect alibi to that meddlesome detective, although it would contain several lewd references,"

Christine said. Erik did not answer, and Christine understood his disapproval of her proposed confession through his lack of response.

"Well, I will refuse to see him," she said. "Unless, of course, you think I must?" She stopped in her pacing to look at Erik.

"No," Erik answered. "I do not say you must do anything you would find unpleasant." With his usual self-control, he maintained the thick accent of Peck as he spoke.

Christine sat for some time, attempting to calm herself, but then rose, saying, "I cannot have peace until I have disposed of this matter. I go now to write my response." She touched the persona of the old gardener on the shoulder and turned toward the house. "Do you have anything you wish me to relay to the Persian?"

Erik lowered his voice to near a whisper. "No, dear. I believe I am getting close to discovering the identity of the murderer. I have several viable suspects, but I do not wish to reveal this to the Persian as of yet."

Christine's reply was full of the anger she felt toward the Persian, both for frightening her with his vivid stories and for suspecting Erik as the perpetrator. She wrote:

> *Your worries and accusations are*
> *meaningless. Do you truly suspect that in*
> *all this cesspool which is London, Erik is*
> *the only one capable of these deeds? You*
> *trouble me unnecessarily. Should I wish to*

know more of these horrific murders, I should merely read the daily paper. I cannot believe I am in danger despite your warnings, and I will hear no more of this matter.

On re-reading the letter, Christine felt somewhat ashamed for expressing herself so harshly, but she determined to send the letter regardless. She did soften the letter with thanks at the end: *I send thanks for your concern over my welfare. However, please do not call, for I will not see you.*

She received a reply from the Persian the following day, which simply renewed her frustration. Again, the response included a polite note requesting a meeting, along with a newspaper clipping. This time the clipping was the reprint of a letter, purportedly sent by the murderer to the news service, published in the hopes that someone in the city could identify the handwriting. The letter was written in red ink.

Christine crumpled both the note and the clipping and dashed off a short reply, which said simply: *I will not see you.*

The following day, Christine was sitting disconsolate and alone in the garden – Erik had gone again – and humming to herself when the maid, Missy, announced that a police inspector had come calling. Christine thought perhaps this visit was due to some request on the part of the Persian. Annoyed as she was, she did not feel she could refuse to see the inspector. She went to the drawing room and asked that the inspector be shown in. When

Missy showed the Persian into the room – his only disguise being the lack of his astrakhan hat – Christine rose in a fury.

"What is the meaning of this?" she demanded.

"Dear lady, forgive me," he said, bowing. Missy fluttered at the elbow of the tall man, and Christine took pity on the poor girl, sighing and waving her away.

The Persian spoke without delay. "I come to remind you that the Opera Ghost wrote all his letters in red ink," he said. His sense of urgency suggested he was afraid of being removed from the house at any moment. The butler, Edwards, stepped into the room. The Persian glanced at the butler and stepped toward Christine, holding out a newspaper page showing two letters, both written in red ink. Christine did not take the paper from his hands, but instead, after waving Edwards away, turned her back on him.

"Sir, may I remind you that Erik cannot possibly be the only person to use red ink? If such were the case, it would not be abundantly available at the stationer's shop."

"And I tell you I believe Erik to have penned these letters," he persisted. After a moment, Christine turned to face him. Again, he held the paper out to Christine, shaking it once in his insistence.

With a huff of frustration and a slight roll of her eyes, Christine took the paper and read the letters. Then, she sat, motioning toward a chair for the Persian. He hesitated before seating himself, and Christine was ashamed to see the extent of the discomfort she had caused him. With all the patience she could muster, she said, "Have you read these letters?"

"Of course, Madame," he responded.

"And have you had occasion to read any of the letters Erik has written? Oh yes, of course you have, for he wrote you himself after your arrival in London," she continued.

"Yes, Madame. I have read that letter and others besides," he said.

"Can you find any similarity between the literacy or penmanship in a comparison between these vile letters," she shook the paper at the Persian, "and Erik's?"

"Erik's penmanship is notoriously bad," he answered.

"Yes, I suppose I must grant that. But not this bad, and certainly, Erik's letters are far more literate. I know. I had reason to read several during my time in the Opera House." She looked to the paper and read aloud, with an appalling attempt at an English accent, sarcasm dripping from her words, "Sor, I send you 'alf the kidne I took from one women prasarved it for you. T'other piece I fried and ate, it was very nise. ..." She raised her eyes to the Persian.

For the first time, the Persian seemed uncertain. Christine took advantage of the moment by holding the newspaper toward him. He rose, took the paper and, returning to his seat, he slowly reread the letters.

"Well ...," he said, "I must admit to ..."

Christine did not let him finish. She said, "You see, without your prejudices – and you must admit I have reason enough for prejudices of my own – I am quite the rational detective. You

225

accuse the wrong man!" she said. Surprised at the volume she had attained by her final sentence, she took several calming breaths.

"I accuse a madman," the Persian responded, the uncertainty still evident in the set of his mouth.

"Yes, granted, the murderer is a madman, but not the man you imagine. Now, do you not think you would do better to find the true monster and, while so doing, leave me in peace?"

"Madame," he said, and stood with a small duck of his chin. Christine reveled in her triumph and imagined relating her victory to Erik when he came tonight. If he came tonight. After another moment during which the Persian looked at the newspaper again, he said, "Please excuse me, but may I suggest the penmanship might be deliberately changed? That the illiteracy may be deliberately affected?"

Christine passed from the quiet contemplation of her victory to a frustration that nearly led to her stomping like a child. Instead, she straightened her posture. In a voice of ice, she said, "Yours is an obsession which matches the obsessions of which you accuse Erik. At the time when I saved your life in the dungeons of the Opera House, I recall Erik speaking well of your prowess. I feel certain he would be disappointed by you now."

The Persian neither moved while she spoke nor responded when she had finished, but the uncertainty was gone from his face. His mouth took on hard lines of determination.

"Please go now," she said. "I have seen you against my will and heard you out, but I must quite honestly tell you that I feel as plagued and haunted by you as I once did by Erik. I ask you to bother me no further with the matter of the Whitechapel murders. Please."

He bowed stiffly and then just as stiffly said, "Madame, as you suggest, I owe you my life. As such, I shall continue to do my duty, unpleasant as my personage is to you. You may have need to thank me for my diligence someday."

With that final statement, the tall, dark man, somewhat slump-shouldered and clearly abashed, turned and left the room. In her frustration, Christine could not find it in herself to pity the man.

CHAPTER 29
SEPARATION

Erik felt certain one of the suspects he was tracking was the murderer. Thus far, he had tracked two doctors who worked within the Whitechapel District, who – besides performing the perfectly respectable functions of surgery and dispensing of medicines to the ill – also regularly performed illicit abortions for ladies of the night. One of these two doctors often traveled to the homes of these women to perform the necessary operation.

Yet another suspect was a midwife who, while performing her functions for any and all who called upon her, was dourly disapproving of the fallen ladies who sometimes called for her and who often asked her to take the baby when she left. There were also two doctor's assistants, one of whom lectured that women, like Eve, were the root of all evil. The second was recently separated from his wife after discovering how she was earning money while he worked. None of these people would be questioned if found moving through the Whitechapel District at night, even if dressed in bloody clothing.

The final suspect, and the most difficult to discover, was a doctor who, for reasons Erik had yet to fathom, came to the Whitechapel District with the weekend cattle boats and spent time in the dark bars of the district, doing nothing more than drinking, brooding, and watching the transactions between the working women and their customers. Although the doctor never approached any of the women, Erik added this man to his list of suspects because the visits were curious and the timing of the cattle boats corresponded with the previous murders. The good doctor's credentials and motives were never questioned by police or local residents because he was known to doctor the royals. As such, he was beyond suspicion in the eyes of the local police or Scotland Yard. Erik was not foolish enough to believe rank or class would keep a man from committing atrocities – they would merely protect him from the consequences.

With six suspects, Erik had difficulty in tracking the movements of all, but he spent many sleepless nights attempting the task. He no longer came to the district during daylight hours. If his constitution were not such that he could function with very little sleep, he might not have seen Christine at night at all.

Erik returned to his residence early one morning to find Christine already in the garden. Tired as he was, he went to her, drawn to her, unable to escape her attraction.

"Peck, you are exhausted," she said. "You must get some sleep, even if it is not to be in my bed."

Erik was tired enough to hear chastisement in her words, but when he looked at her face, he saw only a suggestive smile of invitation.

"I am close, my love," he murmured.

"You still need sleep," she answered.

"Yes," he said and sank to a nearby stone bench, rubbing at his eyes with his knuckles, careful not to dislodge the edges of his mask where it bordered his eyes.

"The Persian came to me again, despite my wishes," she said, sitting beside him. "His conviction of your guilt and his persistence are unflagging."

Erik felt frustration and anger boiling through his blood, and though he knew it to be fueled by his exhaustion, he could not keep the angry words from bursting from him. "I shall dispense of him once and for all. His obsession with me becomes rabid!"

Christine placed a hand on his arm and said, as if speaking to a child, "You are tired, my love." When he merely growled in response, she said, "Do not become the monster the Persian accuses you of being through pique. You are not that man, and I know you are not."

"I must sleep," Erik said. He could not bring himself to assure Christine the Persian was safe from his vengeance, because at the moment he was not altogether sure the wretched man was safe. Rationally, however, he understood that sleep would return him to a quieter frame of mind.

"Please, love, sleep," she said. When Erik rose, she smiled at him, and her eyes were full of love and understanding. He wished he could curl into her arms for the few hours he would need. Instead, he made his way to the gardener's cottage and his bed.

When he returned to the garden that afternoon, he was rested and no longer angry. He did not weed for long before Christine joined him. She sang as she approached him, and he joined her, both singing at low volume. The ecstasy of their song healed the remainder of his exhaustion and frustration.

When she stopped singing, he paused from his weeding to pull a letter from his pocket. Christine took it from him and read the letter he had written to the Persian.

She said, "You say here you will dispense of the murderer. Do you think you can? Do you mean to kill him?"

"I mean to have the man arrested. And yes, I believe I can do this," he answered.

"You ask the Persian to leave if the murderer is apprehended," she continued. "Do you believe he will go? Will capture of the actual killer satisfy the man?" she asked.

"It should," he answered. "What reason will he have for remaining if you have not come to harm and the murderer is proved to be another man?" Erik stabbed a forked rod into the ground near the roots of a weed and dislodged the bothersome plant. "Surely he wishes to return to his life in Paris. Certainly *I* wish it."

Christine read further and then began to read aloud: "'I spare you alive despite your irritating persistence only to show I am not the monster you believe me to be.' Now, why would you threaten him again?"

"It is not a threat but a paradox. If I am the monster, I should have killed him by now. If I have not and do not, then I am not. He must see this and see the truth," Erik answered.

"He must see nothing, my love. You've no idea his obsession with you. He will not see reason. I know, I have tried to reason with him." She explained their latest conversation regarding the published letters. "You provide him with a new letter to compare to the published letters of the killer, but still I do not think he will see reason."

Erik sighed before answering, "You may be right, but I shall try." He worked for some time without speaking until Christine said, "You work every day to make the garden perfect, to make it our Heaven on Earth. You needn't work so hard. You will be working hard again tonight, I'll wager."

"I will not be working in the garden for some time, Christine." He felt the weight of the words settle upon him. The thought of days, perhaps weeks, without Christine near at hand was nearly unbearable, only made bearable by the thought of his return and the return to peace in their lives.

"I dare not believe I understand you," she said, and he could hear the tears in her voice. He stopped his work and looked up at Christine just as the first of her tears tumbled down her cheek.

"I must leave for a short time. I must go and complete this business." He wanted nothing more than to reach up and wipe the tears from her face, but knew it was too intimate a gesture if the servants were watching. He also knew he would leave dirt smudges on the smooth young cheeks. "You will say I asked for leave to tend to an ailing family member." When the tears continued to fall, he said, "I will return to you, I swear it, Christine."

"And if you do not?" she asked, a small choked hiccough following her words.

If I do not, you will have given me something I never thought to have before I died, he thought, but did not say. *Love, and with it, peace.* Instead, he said, "I will return to you, Christine."

Christine wept for another minute before she said, "When do you go?"

"Tomorrow," he answered.

"And tonight? Do you go out again tonight?" she asked.

"No, Christine. Not tonight. Tonight I will spend with you, dearest. I will draw from you all the comfort and love I will need over the days I will not be here."

"Days?" she asked, her hope obvious in her tone.

"Until my task is complete," he answered, refusing to leave her with such a hopeful impression. "And it cannot be complete until the murderer attempts to strike again. No one knows when this will be. It may even be that my observance thwarts the beast."

He watched as despair settled Christine's shoulders. He felt the same weight on his own, but refused to let her see for fear she would take his own bent attitude as a lack of surety that the job would be done – and safely done. And soon.

She stayed with him in the garden, talking of nonsense for the rest of the day, although their conversation was tinctured with sadness. She only went into the house when the carriage came bringing Raoul back from his travels. Erik did not envy the act she would have to perform to convince Raoul she was pleased with his return.

The night was spent less with lovemaking than with whispered words of love, and loving caresses. In the morning, he packed what few things he needed for his venture and left the grounds before Christine could come to the garden. He knew the farewells they might make in the daylight would be too painful.

His first task was to speak with his informants within the police and Scotland Yard establishments to determine if they had any additional helpful information. Predictably, they did not. His second task was to find an amicable landlord. He found a landlady willing to take him on indefinitely and, with a certain monetary incentive – including six months' advance rent – to report to any who asked that the tenant had been in residence for over a year already. This would provide a mild stumbling block to the Persian should he be attempting to track the whereabouts of any new tenants – not that Erik thought that could be done in the crowded conditions of the poorer sections of the district.

The small apartment had a back entrance as well as a front, and the back entrance led into a small fenced yard with an opening to an alley. He constructed a hidden compartment in one wall in which he would hide whichever mask he was not wearing. He only ever left the front entrance as Peck and only ever left the back entrance as Don Juan.

Then he began the arduous task of attempting to track all six suspects at once. Once, he saw the Persian questioning passersby on the street, and although the Persian glanced in his direction, he did not appear to recognize Erik or to have any suspicions about the character he represented as a poorly dressed Peck. Erik smiled to himself and pushed his hands into his pockets as he continued walking, pushing down the instant desire to engage in some mischief with the misguided detective. As enjoyable as such mischief might be, he kept his mind to his task and recalled his desire to finish with this business and return to Christine.

After a week had passed, Erik found he could no longer focus on his task, for his mind was seized on the beautiful Christine. That night, after discovering that each of his suspects had retired for the night – not that this ruled out the possibility that they would rise again and go into the evening, but merely lessened it – Erik returned to Christine's residence, if only to watch her sleep. As he sat in her room, listening to her soft breathing and the occasional sibilant hiss of her body moving against the sheets, he imagined reaching out to her, touching her, speaking with her. He knew, however, that this would only make his departure more difficult and their time apart more painful. He left after only an hour to return to his task in Whitechapel.

CHAPTER 30
CHRISTINE AND RAOUL

Christine was despondent. She could not say her days were less full without the conversation of Peck or the love of Erik. Her tasks and behavior during each day remained as they had been since coming to London. She still chatted in a friendly manner with the two maids or the butler or the cook, as circumstances required their attention. She still spent time reading, writing letters to acquaintances, or mending those things she preferred not to leave to the less capable hands of the servants. She ate, walked, and sang in the garden, and she conversed with Raoul in the evenings. And yet, she felt empty without the sharing of each of these things with Erik.

The mere fact of missing Erik would have brought her misery enough, if she did not also worry she might never see him again. Against her own custom, she began to read the daily paper – sometimes the morning edition as well as the evening – searching for the dire news of a dead man matching Erik's description. She imagined conversations in which she pleaded with her dear father and with Mamma Valérius to watch over Erik. She did not feel the need to explain her love and need for him, for if they were watching over her, and she thought they must be, they already knew of her happiness and hopefully excused her indiscretions in the name of love.

Unhappily, her despondence gained the attention of Raoul.

"Dress, my love," he said, as he arrived home early one evening, smiling and full of energy, as usual.

Christine plucked at her skirt. In a manner she hoped would appear playful, she answered, "Either I have lost my senses, or I stand before you fully clothed." She moved to him with a sad smile and kissed his cheek. "You are home early enough for dinner, Raoul. I shall inform Cook."

"No, tonight we dine abroad," he answered as he flashed a large smile.

"Raoul," she protested, but he took her arm and began leading her up the stairs toward the bedchambers.

"No arguments tonight. I have been neglecting you, and you have been neglecting yourself. The shine has left your eyes, and the apple blossom of your cheeks has gone to winter." He paused before the door to his bedchamber, saying, "Dress, Christine. It will cheer you up. I will take you to dine … and to the theater, if you wish it." This last phrase was said with a forced gaiety that dashed Christine's hopes of avoiding the evening.

Clearly, she had allowed her melancholy to affect her more than she knew, and Raoul was determined to cheer her. She sighed as he pulled her into his arms, wishing she could explain that his plan to cheer her would only make the evening more excruciating for her.

"Come now, Christine," he said in response to her sigh. "It will be good for you. Go now," he said, pushing her toward her own bedchamber, "make yourself beautiful, and I will show you off."

She smiled at him as she knew she must and moved to her bedchamber to dress. Peggy chattered, happiness apparent, as she worked Christine's golden hair into a tumbling mass of curls and baubles, and helped her rouge her cheeks. She made clear that she was in agreement with Raoul that this was just what she needed. As Christine examined herself before the mirror, she thought herself an overdone pastry, but Raoul crowed as she met him in the hallway.

Much to Christine's surprise, no one joined them for dinner. She had expected Raoul to make a true production of the evening, full with friends and business associates, and insipid conversations of which she would understand little having no real acquaintance with the people who spoke. Instead, while Raoul had procured a table for dinner in the middle of the lavish restaurant where they could be observed by the whole of the place, it was a table set only for two. Christine was simultaneously pleased with the intimacy of a dinner for two and distressed with the requirement of carrying her end of the conversation for the evening. She put a good face on the evening, and she even found herself smiling at Raoul's lively repartee.

"Dessert for my sweet?" he asked as the dinner dishes were being cleared.

"I couldn't fit in another morsel," she answered.

"Port," Raoul ordered, and with only a glance at Christine, amended, "Two."

"A pleasant evening, Raoul," Christine said as the waiter moved to obey the request.

"Just the two of us," Raoul said. Taking her hand, and raising an eyebrow, he said, "I thought we could benefit from a night spent as newlyweds."

Christine did not understand his reference, and she covered her confused silence by sipping at the port when it arrived. Raoul winked at her and settled back expansively – he was very masculine, Christine had to admit – as he drank his port.

"Are we for the theater?" he asked, leaning toward Christine as he finished his drink.

"I think not, Raoul," she answered and then, guilty that she could not appreciate his efforts on her behalf, she said, "unless you truly wish to go."

"I wish to do nothing except enjoy my Christine this evening. Is there some other entertainment with which I might entice you? I am yours tonight, my dear, as you are mine." The happy, mischievous glint in his eyes again confused Christine, but also convinced her that tonight of all nights she would not disappoint him if she told him her true desires.

"I am pleasantly sated with the meal. I would be most comfortable if we were to return home for the evening." Feeling that she sounded as though she was dismissing Raoul, she added, "Perhaps for another drink before bed?"

"And so shall it be!" said Raoul, standing and moving her chair back for her. Leading her from the center of the dining room, he took her arm and leaned in close to whisper, "I am happy to see the light has returned to your eyes."

Has it? she thought, and her mind turned to Erik and the reason the light had left her eyes.

Once in the carriage, Raoul took her in his arms and kissed her with passion – more passion than she could recall from him in some time. She wondered if the lack of passion between them was due to her own withdrawal or his. Without doubt, both. Uncharitably, she thought about the fact that there were other ladies upon whom he lavished his passion. Recognizing the unfairness of the thought, she determined to return his passion, as she should. Once they broke, Raoul seemed pleased and eager, and after a long look into her eyes, swept her into another kiss, just as long and just as ardent.

Once back to the house and relieved of their outerwear, Raoul dismissed the servants for the night. Christine led the way into the sitting room and poured them each another glass of port. Unlike at dinner where they spoke of Raoul's work and acquaintances, now they spoke of subjects that involved Christine – her books, what she had heard in letters from Sweden, and –

without the level of importance Christine assigned the matter – the missing gardener. Raoul's only comment on the gardener was that he hoped the old man would return soon, as he was certainly the best gardener in England outside the palace grounds.

"Yes, I hope for his quick return as well," she said and sipped her port to cover the slight tremor in her voice.

Before either could finish their port, Christine rose and said, "The meal was wonderful, Raoul. Thank you. It was a most pleasant evening."

Catching her hand and gazing into her eyes, he said, "We should do this more regularly."

"Yes," she answered, and she found she would not be sorry if her evenings with Raoul were without the crowds with which he almost always surrounded himself.

He stood and bowed low over her hand, pausing to place a slow kiss upon it. Without releasing her hand, he raised his head and said, "I know what you need, Christine. You must trust me."

Confused again, she said, "Thank you again, Raoul. And now, the meal and the port call me to bed. If you can excuse me."

"I'll be up in a moment," he answered, smiling with tenderness. "I wish to finish my drink – t'would be a shame to let such a fine port go to waste."

"You can finish mine, if you wish," she answered, returning his smile.

Christine took longer to prepare for bed than usual, the maid having gone for the evening and the complexity of her coif presenting no small problem. She hummed a sad tune to herself and thought of Erik – and the fact that he would not come to her this evening. She had just settled into bed and was readying to turn off the lantern when her doorknob first turned and then rattled against the lock she now customarily turned.

"Christine?" She heard Raoul through the door, then a knock. She lay frozen, not knowing how to respond. Raoul never came to her room, but made rather formal requests to be joined in his own.

"Christine?" and another knock.

"Yes, just a moment, Raoul," she answered, rising from her bed to open the door.

"Ah, Christine," he said as she opened the door. He took her into his arms. As he kissed her, he backed her two steps into the room.

"Yes, Raoul?" she answered, rather breathless as she broke from the kiss.

Ducking his chin and peering at her from under his brows, he took her hand and led her to her bed. She thought to pull away from him, a panic overwhelming her at the idea of lying with him in this bed. This was her room! Hers and Erik's! His entry here was a violation!

Raoul sat on the bed, holding tight to the hand with which he had pulled her across the room. Taking her other hand in his and turning her to face him, he said, "You must trust me, Christine. I told you I know what you need."

She stood still before him and managed not to pull her hands from his. She did not speak. Her mind was a turmoil.

"You are still melancholy from the loss of our child. I had thought for a time you were overcoming your grief, but I see now this is not the case. Lie with me, Christine. I will give you another." He pulled on her arms bringing her face close to his, then kissed her tenderly. "I will make you a son."

The pain brought on by the memory of her lost daughter stabbed Christine, and she thought angrily, *A son! A son! All you care about is a son!* The depth of the anguish overcame her anger, and tears sprang to her eyes.

"Yes, I can see your pain," he said. He tried to pull her to the bed with him, but again, Christine rebelled at the thought of Raoul sharing Erik's bed with her and held her stance. Her mind circled, panic-stricken between her duty to Raoul and her love of Erik, her duty to Raoul and her love of Erik. The separation between the two was easier to maintain when divided into the two bedchambers.

"Let us go to your room, Raoul," she said, and she pulled against Raoul's hands as if to lift him from his position. "Undoubtedly, you would sleep better there." Her strength was nothing compared to his, and he pulled her toward him. When she raised her knee to the edge of the bed to avoid being pulled face down on to the surface, he released her and lay on his side, head propped on one elbow. He patted the bed with the other hand.

"Your bed seems comfortable enough," he said, smiling. He lay further back and beckoned to her with his hand. She nearly shuddered thinking of the bare act Raoul requested of her as compared to the passion and pleasure Erik brought to her.

An image sprang to mind of Erik watching from the darkness as she lay with Raoul. Her mind raced to find a way to move him to his own room, but she found nothing. Her mind also raced to try to recall the last time she lay with him, wondering if she dared refuse him this night. It had been only once since his return from his travels, and she could not recall how recently before then. Christine reached a decision.

With a forced smile and a hand stretched to his face, Christine crawled onto the bed and came into his arms. It was her duty to allow Raoul access to his wife. And Erik's bed or not, she could not reject Raoul tonight. He was here to give her a son. In thinking through her trips to his bed, and belatedly and more importantly, her natural cycles, she knew he might be too late. If her natural cycles were any indication, she was already with child.

CHAPTER 31
A DISCOVERY

It was late, and Erik was tired as he followed the doctor southwest on Whitechapel Road. While Erik had managed several hours' sleep in the afternoon, those few hours were the longest stretch of sleep he had enjoyed in the past several days. All the rest of his time had been taken up with tracking the movements and patterns of the five suspects – now six suspects, as the mysterious doctor of the royals had arrived this afternoon. With the patchy nature of his current sleep cycle, Erik was beginning to feel the effects of prolonged fatigue. His movements were slower and less assured, his thoughts more muzzy.

After ascertaining that the doctor of the royals was quietly ensconced in the pub he frequented for his glowering staring matches with the locals, Erik decided to check on the local physician, Dr. Jones. Dr. Jones was not abed, as he had been when last Erik checked on him; instead, he was just leaving his residence with his black bag in hand. Erik guessed the man was headed out for another late night visit to a prostitute for the purpose of performing an abortion.

246

Erik fought against the instinct to duck or otherwise react when the doctor stopped at the corner of Whitechapel Road and Commercial Street to peer around at the lone late-night cab and the several pedestrians. Erik thought this behavior strange for the doctor, as he had often tailed the doctor to his late-night appointments without noticing such cautious behavior. The man usually walked with the assured confidence of his profession and his right to be about his duties.

As Erik followed the doctor up Commercial Street, he took even greater precaution than usual to keep to the shadows created by the various pillars, arches, and awnings along the street. Again, under the gas lamp at the corner of Commercial and Dorset streets, the doctor paused to look around before walking into the darkness of the narrow street just beyond the brightly lighted Britannia Pub on the corner.

Erik was helped in his endeavors to follow the doctor down Dorset Street when a group of drunken revelers emerged from the pub and, with loud laughs and hollers, broke into two smaller groups, one of which went in the direction of the doctor. Again, the doctor looked over his shoulder at those in the street behind him, and Erik felt the prickle of gooseflesh as he realized his mission might soon be over. The doctor's behavior this night was uncharacteristic and suspicious.

Erik rounded the corner of Dorset Street and Miller's Court just in time to see the doctor enter a doorway in a small, shabby, white-bricked building. Clearly, the doctor was expected. This brought Erik a simultaneous feeling of relief and impatience. Before deciding to leave to return to his vigil at the royal doctor's pub, Erik sneaked to the lighted window at the corner of the building to relieve his mind as to the doctor's purpose.

The illuminated scene was as Erik expected. A woman stood speaking with the doctor. The doctor spoke and gestured to the bed. He bent and placed his black bag on the floor near the bed and then stood and, as a model of politeness, turned his back to the woman. The woman followed his invitation, first removing her clothing and, after folding them, placing them on a chair near the bed. She lay on the bed on her back. Her head rested on a pillow and her hands moved in somewhat nervous motions over her stomach. Her legs were pressed together.

With a tired sigh, Erik turned to make his way back to the pub where he had left the enigmatic royal doctor. Glancing back over his shoulder, he saw the moment when the light in the window was extinguished.

In that instant, Erik knew there would be no operation performed in the darkened room. Spinning and running back the few steps to the building, Erik did not hesitate to crash through the door to the small apartment. The lantern had not, in fact, been extinguished, but merely turned low. In the short moment during which Erik registered this fact, he also knew he was too late.

The gruesome tableau was burned into his eyes like the black image of the sun gazed at midday. The woman, he knew, was already dead, although choked gurgling sounds emitted from her slashed throat and the arm nearest him twitched, fingers spasming weakly. The line where the scalpel had been drawn across her throat was black in the low light and growing wider as dark blood seeped from it. The doctor was at the side of the bed, one knee raised as if he meant to straddle the prone figure.

In the short interval in which Erik paused to take in the scene, the doctor snarled and, drawing back his upper lip from his teeth like an animal, leapt at Erik. The doctor's speed was astounding. Erik spun to avoid the cutting blade of the brandished scalpel, and then continued his spin to bring both fists, clasped together like a club, against the doctor's back. The doctor grunted against the blow and fell against the open door, closing it with a loud bang as he dropped to the ground. Erik leapt upon the man, hoping to disable him while he remained grounded and stunned.

The doctor was not stunned. Before Erik could close with the man, he saw the scalpel again flash out toward him. In his surprise, Erik reached for the scalpel as he fell toward the man. He felt the ice-water pain of the sharp blade cutting his hand before his momentum carried him with a shocking thump on to the man and the scalpel. He felt the rich new scalding pain of the scalpel entering his abdomen.

For a moment, there was no further movement, as Erik groaned and the doctor panted. Drawing all of his considerable strength to bear, Erik pushed at the doctor and made an effort to leap to his feet. He did not want to give the doctor any time to root around his innards with the scalpel. Erik realized his attempted leap was, in fact, more a stumble to his feet, and he stumbled again as he tried to back away from the man. He pressed his hands against the wound in the side of his abdomen.

The doctor moved with a preternatural speed as he rose to his feet and again charged Erik. Even while moving in defense of himself, Erik wondered whether the apparent speed and strength of the doctor was natural to the man or the result of his own exhaustion. The doctor lunged with the scalpel. This time, Erik was able to block the blood-blackened blade from piercing him, but the weight of the doctor's charge smashed Erik against the window through which he had previously peered. The crashing sound of shattering glass seemed dim in Erik's ears, as if heard through cotton swabbing.

Erik did not hesitate, but bounded from the window toward the doctor. He caught the doctor's right wrist in his left hand and wrenched the arm to the side, moving the scalpel away from his own body and twisting the arm out and to the side of the doctor. The bloody gash on the palm of his hand burned, but he did not loosen his grip. Erik brought his open hand in a chopping motion to the side of the doctor's neck, as he simultaneously kicked at the doctor's knee. His balance thus compromised, he did not dislocate the doctor's knee as he intended, but the knee buckled as the doctor's head snapped to the side.

Still Erik did not release the wrist that held the weapon despite the pain in his hand. Instead, wincing, he wrenched the wrist again. The doctor dropped the scalpel, and Erik breathed a grunt of relief as he heard the dim tinkling sound of the metal striking the bare floor.

The doctor recovered his stance and struck at Erik with his free hand – the left hand, which should have been the weaker arm and hand. Erik marveled at the man's strength and stamina. He ducked the blow and delivered one of his own, straight into the doctor's face. He felt the satisfying crunch of the doctor's nose breaking under his fist. He pulled back his fist to strike the man again, but before he could deliver the blow, he felt a crashing impact connect with the side of his own head. The only thought in his mind as he fell in what seemed timeless slowness to the floor was that he must not let go of the doctor's wrist.

***

Erik awoke in the dim room. He did not move any part of his body except for his eyes. He lay on his side and, even in the small room, the expanse of the floor seemed long and wide in perspective. He could see the bed and the edge of a white, blood-spattered knee at the edge. He could see the chair with the woman's undergarments still neat and folded upon it. He could not see the doctor. Erik closed his eyes again and listened. He could hear nothing moving inside the apartment.

He made to rise, but a searing pain in his abdomen brought him again to the floor. As he brought his hands to the pained area, he looked down to see his shirt soaked with blood. There was a small puddle of blood on the floor under the wound. He remained on the floor panting for a moment.

Knowing he must quit the murder site, he clutched at his side and managed to gain his knees. After another burst of panting, he pressed up to his feet. The pain in his side lessened in some measure as he straightened. He inspected his abdomen with his fingers and eyes and made the determination that none of his organs had been pierced. He would likely heal. He shuffled to the bed and looked down at the dead woman.

She had been completely ravaged. Clearly, the doctor had been greatly enraged when he had set upon the task of finishing his gruesome ritual of gutting the woman. The abdomen was completely eviscerated – the carnage between chest and spread thighs in no way resembling something human.

Erik looked upon the scene with disgust. It seemed that, with Christine's love and friendship, he could not look upon such sights with his old detachment, although he still felt a flickering sense of curiosity. What was the purpose? What was the doctor thinking as he acted out his rage? Noticing the bedclothes were disarranged in the extreme and slashed, Erik tore several pieces loose. Folding one into a wadded bandage, he pressed it to his abdomen. He used a longer piece of cloth to tie the bandage into place. Then, he wrapped his hand, although on inspection, the bleeding had long since stopped.

After completing the ministrations to his wounds, Erik looked around the small room, seeking anything the doctor might have left. Nothing. Erik wondered why the doctor had not finished him off. Perhaps the doctor thought him dead. Or perhaps he thought to have Erik found with the body and thus be accused as the murderer. With this thought, Erik reached with care into the pockets of his coat and was not surprised when his fingers closed on the handle of a scalpel.

Even in his pain, Erik could appreciate the doctor's ingenuity, and a low chuckle escaped his lips. He turned off the still low-burning lantern and shuffled to the door in the darkness. He paused to button his coat over his bloody shirt before he opened the door and slipped into the dark street.

The doctor must surely think Erik a passerby, a lover, a customer, or perhaps a landlord. The doctor could not know Erik had been tracking him for some time. The doctor could not know Erik knew where he lived. Erik knew where he must go.

But not tonight. Tonight, he was much weakened, and the doctor had already proved his prodigious strength and speed. Not tonight. But later.

With slow and careful strides, Erik made his way to Commercial Street and found a sleeping cabby. He awakened the man and gave the man the address of Raoul and Christine's house. His house. He gritted his teeth at the pain that came with climbing into the cab and the lurching progress down the streets to home. He paid the man a handsome sum for his assistance in disembarking the cab. As he crossed the fog-smeared grounds to the gardener's cottage, the November sun was pinking the dawn sky.

CHAPTER 32
PLEASURE AND PAIN

Christine moved her breakfast tray from her lap to her nightstand and smoothed the morning edition of the paper over her lap. She forced herself to read through the entire paper, as usual, praying she did not find anything that might relate to Erik. She found nothing. The lack of information did not quell the unease she felt at Erik's long absence.

Climbing from the bed, she wandered the room in preparation for dressing. She stopped at the window and looked out at the garden. She nearly screamed in delight and dismay when she saw the familiar figure of Peck moving about the garden, apparently surveying the work he must accomplish to bring the garden back to its formerly pristine condition. For a long moment, she stood at the window, hands pressed upon the glass, smiling.

She called for Peggy and began dressing herself. She forced herself to calmness rather than give the maid any reason to wonder at her strange excitement. Even so, Peggy commented that she must have gotten a restful night's sleep.

Christine forced herself to walk leisurely into the garden and to move through it as she might always do. She almost could not keep herself from running the last few paces as she approached Peck, and throwing herself into his arms. She could not contain the tears of happiness that flowed down her cheeks and chin as she spoke.

"God has answered my prayers," she said as she came up behind the kneeling man.

She watched as the gardener's head bowed, perhaps in answering prayer, and then came up again. He looked over his shoulder toward where she was standing and said, "Christine, my love." His eyes seemed filled with pain. His breath came in pants.

"Oh, Erik!" she whispered, and her hands came up to her smiling mouth. She did not wipe at her tears.

"Peck," he said with another pant.

"Peck, then," she said, with some impatience. "I love you," she whispered, horrified that she could show such impatience at the instant of Erik's return to her.

"And I, you," he answered in a whisper as quiet as hers.

"Can you come sit with me a moment?" she asked, and she gestured to a stone bench not far away. She did not look to the bench. She could not take her eyes off the man before her.

"I can," he answered.

Instead of turning toward the bench, Christine watched every movement, eyes drinking in the figure of the man she had longed for every hour of his absence. When she saw that he moved in slow increments, as if in great pain, she could no longer maintain her distance. She rushed to him, and helping him rise, she said, "Eri … Peck! What is wrong?"

"The bench," he answered, and this time she noted his panting breaths. She supported his arm as he walked toward the bench. Her eyes danced over his figure as they walked together.

"Your hand," she said, eyes fixing on the soiled wrapping. "Are you hurt?"

"Hurt, yes," he said, as he settled to the bench. She gasped at his answer and pulled his hand across his body toward her. He winced at the motion and sucked in his breath.

Christine released his hand, and her hands flew to her mouth. Her worry was now approaching panic. "What is it? You must tell me," she cried.

Erik inhaled through his nose and exhaled sharply through his mouth, three times in succession before he answered. "I have found the murderer," he said. "Unfortunately, I was unable to stop him."

"He has hurt you?" she asked. Her hands came down from her mouth and she began to reach toward him with both hands before clasping them into her lap. Her fingers writhed against each other like a battle of garden snakes, and the coolness of the stone bench began to seep through her skirts, chilling her. Another thought occurred to her. "I didn't see anything in the paper about another murder."

"Then the body has not yet been found," Erik answered.

Christine noted he had not answered her first question, so she repeated it. "You must tell me. Has he hurt you?"

After releasing a sigh, he said simply, "Yes." At her gasp, he continued. "It is not bad. I will survive. You mustn't worry, Christine."

"Worry? I mustn't worry?" she said, and she could hear the panic in her voice. "Where? Where are you hurt? I will fetch a doctor."

Her terror only mounted when he replied, "I would appreciate the assistance of a doctor."

"Erik!" She nearly shouted the word.

"Peck," he answered and chuckled. The chuckle was cut off and again he winced.

"Let me help you to your house," she said, as she rose from the bench.

"I can walk. ..." he started, but she gathered all her authority into her voice and said, "I will help you!"

She helped him to his small cottage and to the bed. She felt a calmness wash over her as she became determined to help in any way needed. "Show me where you are hurt," she said, pleased to hear the quiet decisiveness in her tone.

She began unbuttoning Erik's shirt as she saw his fingers fumble with the first button. When she tried to remove the bandage on his abdomen, his hands moved to stop her.

"I must see. I must know what to tell the doctor." Her eyes locked with his. After a moment, Erik released her hands. She unwrapped the bandage and sucked in a breath as she peeled the bandage from the wound. She replaced the bandage. Standing, she said, "Do not move from this bed. I will call the doctor at once."

Once back to the house, she sent Missy to fetch the doctor and asked the cook to heat water. She gathered clean linens and returned to the kitchen for the pot of heated water and a clean bowl.

With barely a glance at the cook, she said, "Bring soup to the gardener right away." She did not stay to hear Cook's answer.

The doctor did not stay long. While Erik floated in and out of consciousness, the doctor stitched the wound and confirmed to Christine's overwhelming relief that he did not believe the wound to be immediately fatal. He did, however, warn that the wound could become septic, which in the end could still bring death. As he left, he marveled at the exceptional physical condition of the old man. Christine ushered the man out, thanking him repeatedly and praising his efforts. Then she returned to Erik's bedside.

When Erik returned to consciousness, Christine explained that the doctor had questioned her regarding the wound and she had given the excuse that Erik had fallen on his own pruning shears.

"I do not know that he was completely convinced, but he certainly seemed unwilling to doubt me to the extent of reporting your injury to the police," she said.

Erik patted her hand with soft strokes and said, "You have done well, wife. Thank you." He pressed a weak smiled at her, then said, "If you can spare a servant, hot water and a ginger and oregano oil poultice will keep the thing from going septic."

"I will bring it myself," she answered.

"Christine, you should not...," he began, but she interrupted.

"Nonsense. You are my gardener. The maid has already seen that you are injured when she came with the soup. No one will question my concern. In fact, it is completely within my character to assist you," she said.

"Yes," he answered. "It is your character. You are unfailingly kind." He closed his eyes.

Christine leaned forward and kissed his eyelids, first one, then the other. "I love you, Erik."

"I love you, Christine," he answered, eyes still closed.

"Tell me what happened," she said.

"I interrupted the man," he answered, and his eyes opened in a slow blink. "I was unable to do anything to stop him and unable to affect his arrest."

"The Persian will believe. ..."

"Undoubtedly," he answered. "But I have a plan." After a deep sigh, he said, "I must leave you again for a brief time."

"Not before you are healed," Christine answered. She felt ready to tie him to his bed, if need be, but his lack of argument showed in his failure to move. He closed his eyes again. He lay without moving for so long, she thought he slept.

"Talk to me, Christine," he said. "Tell me how you've been."

"Besides frantic with worry and longing for you?" she asked. She smiled when he chuckled, and she felt her own smile fade when he winced in pain.

"Yes, besides that."

Christine wondered whether she ought to give him the news that had nearly burst from her the moment she had approached him in the garden. Before she could finish contemplating, the words flew from her lips.

"I believe I am with child," she said. His eyes opened in a flash, and before he could say anything, she said, "I believe it is your child, Erik. I pray it is your child."

His eyes searched her face and then squeezed closed again, revealing pain. She wondered if the pain was from his wound or from the news she had given with such abruptness.

She took his uninjured hand in hers. "So, you see. You must be careful from now on, and you must stay with me."

His eyes opened again, and she could still see the pain behind them. "I don't know that I am capable of giving you a child," he said. And then, even closer to a whisper, he said, "And I don't know that you would want a child such as I might give you." He turned his head to face the wall. Christine now understood his pained eyes.

"You seem capable in every other respect," she said, and she hoped he could hear the smile in her voice, "so I do not understand why you could not give me a child. And I could not love any child more than your own." She squeezed his hand to give emphasis to her words.

"It is something I have never even dared to wish," he said, still facing the wall. He turned his head to look at Christine again – his eyes filled with the warmth of love and the unbandaged slice of pain – and her eyes filled inexplicably with tears. "To be loved for myself, yes. To live a normal life, and to have a wife, yes. A wife I could take out on Sundays. Yes. All these things. But I never thought to be a father. I never thought to have a family."

Pain lancing through her, Christine recalled Erik's plea to her before she left him in the Opera House. The plea for a normal life and a wife. She waited to speak until the lump had left her throat. "Would such a thing make you unhappy, Erik?" She dreaded his answer, but determined to wait for it.

"Never, my love," he answered, and this time, it was he who squeezed her hand. His eyes sank in sadness again, and he said, "But it is Raoul's child. You will see."

Christine did not answer because she felt certain she knew the father of her child. The certainty ran through her like a flame, starting from her belly where the child grew and traveling with warmth to the tips of her fingers and toes.

"I will get you more soup," she said.

"I must sleep, Christine," he said. Again his eyes closed.

"Sleep then," she said. She stayed with him until his hand loosened around hers and she was sure he slept, and then she went back to the main house.

***

The next fortnight saw Christine as an almost constant fixture at the gardener's house. As she predicted, no hint of suspicion attached to her behavior or his wound. Raoul even escorted her to the see the gardener one late afternoon. Christine turned the lamp down to assure that Raoul could not well see the old gardener. Raoul did not stay long. He stood in obvious discomfort in the doorway and spoke to the old man.

"I bring you well wishes," said Raoul.

"Thank you, kind sir," Erik answered, his accent thicker than usual.

"You have always done a marvelous job," continued Raoul.

"Again, I thank you," Erik answered.

After a short silence, Raoul said, "Is there anything I can do to assist you?"

"No, thank you, kind sir," Erik answered.

"Ah. Then I leave you in the capable hands of my wife." Raoul leaned close to Christine and said, "Do not be long, darling."

"Just the soup," she answered with a smile. Raoul patted her cheek and left. Christine was pleased Raoul had not insisted the other servants assume care of the old man, nor prohibited her from assisting as she might. Raoul was rather gracious in his own way.

Happily, Erik's recovery seemed to be progressing quickly. Unhappily, Christine knew this meant he would leave her again soon to finish his business.

CHAPTER 33
IN WHITECHAPEL

Erik was desperate to be on his way. He felt ready to go within days of the physician's visit. He did not, however, have the heart to leave Christine when she so clearly did not believe he had recovered enough for whatever confrontation was to come.

Erik did not want a confrontation with the doctor. But he lacked the evidence necessary to have the doctor arrested and charged with the murders. It was certain his own testimony to the effect that he had witnessed the murder would not prevail. His wounds might add weight to his testimony, but without other evidence, the doctor need only deny the testimony as the ravings of a lunatic. Erik was not even sure the doctor had not arranged an alibi for the evening in question.

He needed more information. To gather that information, he needed to leave his small cottage and Christine's worried ministrations.

He wisely did not press Christine to allow him to go; nor did he urge her that he was well enough to do so. Instead, he resumed his work in the garden, careful not to push himself in any way that might lead to a revealing wince of pain. He bided his time, and Christine seemed happy to have him assume his regular activities. It seemed to him that Christine denied to herself he ever meant to leave her again. Of a certainty, they never spoke of it after that first day. After a fortnight of recovery, he even resumed his visits to her bedroom in the night, and she welcomed him with open arms – although she remained careful of his wound.

After three weeks, he could wait no longer. "Christine," he said, when she joined him in the garden one morning. "It seems Peck must pay another visit to his ailing brother."

Christine's welcoming smile evaporated upon the instant.

"Christine, you know I must," he said.

"I …" She seemed to be searching for words, for any argument that might make him stay. "I have warned the Persian away," she said. "Why must you endanger yourself when…"

"The Persian will not leave us alone until this matter is finished," he said. "He may, at some point, discover my whereabouts." He watched Christine as several emotions moved across her face. "There will also be more murders if the monster is not stopped. Would you wish that on any more unfortunate women?" In the past, this would have bothered Erik less than the idea that the Persian would not leave, as he had been accustomed to disregarding the lives of people from whom he considered himself completely separated, but now the idea of additional murders did distress him. He could picture with vivid exactness the eviscerated woman among her bloody bedclothes. He knew for a certainty the idea would bother Christine.

As he expected she would, she dropped her head in defeat.

"You know I am well recovered," he said.

"What will you do?" she asked.

"I will merely try to find evidence that will lead to a conclusion of this matter," he answered. He was not altogether certain of how he would gather this evidence, but now that he knew the identity of the killer, he thought his job would be accomplished with relative ease.

"Tomorrow?" she asked.

"Tomorrow," he answered.

"Is there anything you need? Can I assist you in any way?" she asked.

"Love me," he answered. "Wait for me."

"Without question!" she answered. He could tell from her posture she was fighting to keep from rushing to him in her fervor. He stood and moved farther from her along the hedge, and he was pleased to note he felt no twinge of pain in his abdomen at the movement.

***

Like the last time he left Christine, he left at sunrise with his small bag of belongings. He was distressed to discover that his landlady, upon finding he no longer occupied his apartment, had re-rented the dwelling, thus accepting double payment for the unit.

She proved unwilling to evict the current tenants, insinuating he had no proof of having paid for six months in advance.

Rather than make an issue of the matter – although he had a signed receipt for the advance rent – he located other lodgings under a similar arrangement to the first. When the tenants were out of his original apartment one afternoon, he entered and recovered the hidden mask.

Then he began his work. He trailed the doctor day and night, sleeping only when he knew the doctor slept. He did not use his guise as Peck for fear the man would recognize him. He witnessed numerous office calls, sick calls, and in one case, an abortion. The doctor always appeared kind and courteous with his patients. He came to know the man's eating habits (relatively unvaried and tending toward the bland), drinking habits (not excessive), and treatment of his wife (kind but distant).

From watching outside the man's residence, Erik came to know his regular movements in his home. Still, he observed nothing that would constitute evidence. Through an informant, he questioned the doctor's wife about her husband's whereabouts on the evening of November 8. She referred to a diary before she answered that he had slept beside her all night. Upon learning of the diary, Erik acquired it and discovered that the same diary testified to the doctor's having been "home all the evening" on the nights of two of the other murders. Erik began to despair that he would need to interrupt another murder to catch the man.

One evening, quite late, Erik observed the doctor leaving his darkened home, again carrying his black bag. Erik followed the man, as usual. This time, however, he pulled a length of strong rope from his pocket and, hands working behind his back, began fashioning the rope into the Punjab lasso he could use with such effectiveness. Far in front of him, the doctor turned down a small alley between buildings that was arched over with bricks suspended between the buildings on either side. Erik paused at the entrance to the black alley to listen for footsteps against the brick. He heard nothing.

Just as he moved to step into the alley, he heard a shuffling movement just inside the arched opening. He froze.

"Who goes there?" he called into the darkness.

"Why are you following me?" came the deep-throated answer. Squinting into the darkness of the alley, Erik's eyes caught the glint of wan light chasing down the edge of a scalpel. He stepped back a pace without answering. He kept the hand with the Punjab lasso behind his back.

"Why are you following me?" This time, there was a hint of a growl in the otherwise smooth voice of the doctor. Erik again had the impression of an animal and wondered at the change that had come over the usually well mannered doctor.

"I know where you are going and what you plan to do," Erik answered.

"What am I to do?" the doctor asked, and an incongruously high-pitched giggle punctuated the end of the question. The doctor took a step toward Erik, legs and extended weapon hand coming into the pallid light of the street. The rest of the body remained in the shadows.

"I was there at Miller Court," Erik said. He did not move from his position.

"You!" came the growled answer, and the doctor took another small step forward, as if to peer at Erik more closely. He was now fully into the dim light, and Erik noted a changed savage expression on the doctor's face. The slight cant in the doctor's broken nose was evident in the shadows, and the eyes seemed mere pits under the brows. Although Erik's appearance did not match his appearance at the last murder scene, the doctor said, "I wondered what became of you." The doctor stepped back into the darkness of the alley.

Erik waited, unmoving, eyes focused on the somewhat lesser darkness of the doctor in the black, black background of the alley. A sick smell of decay wafted over him as he waited for the doctor's next statement.

Without the warning of any sound, the doctor lunged out of the alley, scalpel brandished, again pointed toward Erik's abdomen. Erik did not hesitate. The Punjab lasso swung out with a long-practiced movement as Erik darted to the side of the lunging man and his gleaming weapon. With a jerk, the lasso tightened about the doctor's neck and the scalpel fell, ringing, to the brick. With another jerk, Erik yanked the man back into the dark alley, hearing the unmistakable sound of a snapping spine. Erik lowered the man to the ground.

Erik stood his ground, breathing in short, even breaths, and pondered his situation. The damnable doctor was good and well gotten rid of, but this did not give the satisfaction he wanted. Still, he had no evidence this man was the murderer. More to the point, he could not abandon the body, for the Persian would identify the unique ligature marks about the man's neck and finally have good reason to continue his search for Erik.

Damn the mess.

Erik did not brood, however. He lifted the man from where he lay in the alley and threw the man's arm about his own shoulder. With the other arm, he supported the dead man as he half-walked, half-dragged the man along with him, as though supporting a drunken friend.

He felt an unwelcome stab of pain in his own abdomen as he supported the weight. Ignoring the pain, he moved toward his own apartment, thankful his apartment was not far, and also thankful – as the doctor had always been – for the darkness of the streets. He drew no attention as he went and soon had the man in his apartment. He left the doctor on the floor just inside the door and returned to the black alley to retrieve the doctor's bag.

By the following morning, his plans were complete, and he began making the necessary arrangements to travel. He obtained a large travel trunk and booked passage across the channel to France.

Once there, he traveled by train to Paris, arriving early in the evening.

Paris! Erik had forgotten how much he loved the city, especially as it was now, shining with myriad lights and glowing with the promise of freedom — for it was only in the covering darkness of night that Erik had ever traveled the city with any sense of freedom. Even with the anchor weight of a monster's body in the trunk he traveled with, even while wishing for Christine at his side, Erik felt himself come alive at the sights and sounds of his adopted home city. He drank the city in through the open window of the carriage as the driver took him to his intended destination.

As the carriage approached the Opera House — his abandoned home — Erik felt his excitement muffle in a sudden rise of melancholy. He thought to ask the driver to stop, but stifled the urge as both blissful and painful memories battled to produce a lump in his throat. The carriage driver seemed uncertain as Erik indicated the darkened spot he wished to debark on the nearby Rue Scribe, but Erik explained that a friend would be meeting him soon.

Upon accepting the fare along with a lavish tip, the driver unloaded the heavy trunk near the obscure gated entrance Erik indicated. Erik waited until the driver turned the corner before tripping the misleadingly rusty lock and dragging the trunk into the dark, humid space beyond.

"Ah. Home." Despite the difficulty — and intermittent pain — Erik, dragging the trunk, unerringly made his way through the darkness away from this secret entrance toward the dark lake under the Opera House. His small boat remained moored at the shore, and it was only upon reaching it that he dared to light a torch for the remainder of his journey. He sang in a low voice as he crossed the lake, trunk before him in the small boat, but unseen through the memories that fogged his vision.

Christine, a mere chorus girl, when first he heard her beautiful voice …

Christine, believing him the Angel of Music, disciple to his lessons …

Christine, horrified at seeing his features, leaving in the arms of another man …

That was another life. I must return to my Christine. After all that, my *Christine.*

After completing his business, Erik did as he had never done when he lived in the bowels of the Opera House: he purchased a ticket to the performance to be held that evening. Box 5 was unavailable, but he allowed Madame Giry to escort him to Box 2 with all the same rigid dignity she had always shown.

He left partway through the performance, for it did not hold the same enjoyment for him as it once did. Carlotta still reigned on the stage, and he had even less tolerance of her strutting and squawking than ever before. He boarded a morning train back to the channel in rather high spirits. He laughed at his own cleverness as he composed a letter to the Persian in his mind. He slept, after thinking pleasant thoughts that each chug and clamber of the train wheels against the track brought him closer to Christine.

Upon his return to London, Erik packed or disposed of the items in his Whitechapel apartment. He waited until night to return to his home and Christine. Later that night, he entered Christine's bedroom and softly touched her sleeping face. He whispered her name.

"Erik!" she whispered, waking. She threw her arms about his neck and, nearly pulling him bodily from the floor, showered his face with kisses. It was only then that she released him in concern.

"I am so sorry! Did I hurt you?"

He chuckled and kissed her. "No, my love."

"Is it finished? Are you home to stay?" she asked.

"Yes. Home to stay." He kissed her again.

"Come to bed," she said, pulling at his clothes in the darkness.

"Christine, I should ..."

"You are not leaving me tonight," she said, relentless in her efforts to remove his shirt.

He succumbed to her less-than-gentle persuasion. In the morning, he wrote his letter to the Persian. First, he explained he had apprehended the murderer and that the murders were now finished. Then, with great enjoyment, he explained where the body of the murderer could be found.

*There is now a murderous horror buried in
the grave outside my home in the basement
of the Opera House. You should be
pleased with this fitting end. Leave me to
my happiness, and believe me when I tell
you again that neither Raoul nor Christine
is in danger from me. Be warned. Be gone.
At this moment, your meddling is the only
cause of my rage, which you seem to believe,
I delight to give vent.*

Erik laughed with relaxed enjoyment as he posted the letter.
He determined not to focus on what actions he might take if the
Persian did not relent and return to Paris.

CHAPTER 34
A FAREWELL

On the morning following Erik's reappearance, Raoul informed Christine he would be going on another trip – this time a rather lengthy one, including visits to various countries across Europe. He could not guess at the time of his return, but he indicated he knew it would be several months. Despite Christine's immediate joy at the relative freedom this would provide her to enjoy Erik's company – especially since Erik had now returned to her – she was also struck with a sudden uneasiness.

When she responded to the announcement with a visible level of upset, Raoul, with his usual graciousness, asked her if she wished to accompany him. Knowing she would not leave Erik, she was adamant in her desire to stay in London. Raoul did not seem confused at her desire to stay in the city she claimed to detest. Instead, he seemed relieved at her response and did not press her further.

In truth, Christine *was* disturbed at the timing and predicted length of his journey. Not because she would miss Raoul or needed him near her – she did not believe she would miss him at all – but

275

because she had not yet told him she was with child. If he were gone for too many months, he would return to discover a child in her arms, and the surprise may not be a welcome one.

In the short time before he left, she worried over whether it would be more proper to inform Raoul of her condition before his leaving. In the end, she decided against telling him. After all, she had lost her first child and may lose this one as well. Better that he not worry over her while he was gone.

Yet, somehow, she felt guilty over this decision. She stood in his rooms, feeling helpless as she watched him pack his many travel trunks with the careful assistance of his valet.

"You seem quite upset at my leaving, Christine," he said, stopping in the middle of folding his trousers to approach her across the room. He took her in his arms and kissed the top of her head. "I find it rather charming that you will miss me so."

Head pressed against his chest, Christine merely murmured a noncommittal, "Hmm."

"You will be fine, won't you?" he asked.

"Of course," she responded.

"I will be sure to write you and to send you exotic gifts as I travel," he said, still holding her against him. "Nothing will be too good for my wife."

"You are too kind, Raoul."

"Nonsense," he responded. He released her and returned to his packing, on occasion directing Edwards to collect some item.

After another moment in the room, hands pressed to her stomach where she knew a child grew, she left the room. Still plagued with a vague sense of guilt, she wandered the lower rooms of the house, restless. She did not allow herself to go to the garden where Erik worked.

She grew even more agitated when the afternoon post brought another letter from the Persian requesting to pay her a visit. "I have respected your wishes to be left unmolested, Madame," the letter read, "but have something of the utmost importance to discuss with you. I assure you with all sincerity I will bring you no horrific tale of murder to disturb you this time."

Christine could not imagine what the Persian wished to discuss with her. She knew from Erik's brief statements the night before that the murderer was now dead. Erik had assured her the killing was done in self-defense and that he had only just avoided another – possibly more dangerous – attack from the scalpel. Christine, while running her fingers across the still healing scar on Erik's abdomen, did not dare to doubt him. In fact, surprisingly and quite against her usual nature, she found herself protective of Erik to the point of being thankful for the death of the evil man, even if it was at the hands of her beloved.

And now, the Persian. Again.

She sighed and sat to write an immediate reply. The Persian could call on her four days hence – after Raoul had gone. She reminded him of his promise not to come with more gruesome details.

That night, after another dutiful visit to Raoul's bedchamber, she sat enfolded in Erik's arms and spoke of the Persian.

"I told him he could come. Was that wrong? I cannot imagine why he wishes to see me again."

"I wrote him another letter. Perhaps he comes to bid you adieu," Erik answered.

"Could it be?" she asked.

"We will not know until he comes," Erik answered. Christine was surprised at the lack of frustration in Erik's calm reply.

"What did you write?" she asked.

"Merely that the murders were finished and where he could find the body of the loathsome man. And that he must now leave London."

Must. The word was not lost on Christine, and she surmised that the letter had contained another threat. She sighed internally and wondered why Erik maintained his habit of threatening the Persian, when she knew Erik did not intend to carry out the threats. But perhaps she was wrong. And perhaps Erik was correct, and the Persian was merely coming to inform her of his departure.

"I have set the appointment for four days hence. Raoul will not be here. Will you listen?" she asked.

"I will. I hope most sincerely the Persian will please us both with what he has to say," Erik answered. Christine heard the implied threat in that statement as well.

"Erik, you mustn't …"

"I will do nothing untoward, my dear. I promise you," he answered. His sincerity confirmed Christine's suspicion that Erik merely threatened the Persian out of habit.

Satisfied, Christine turned the conversation to the other subject that occupied her mind. "I have not told Raoul I am with child," she said.

"Good!" Erik answered. He kissed her and with a smile said, "He might decide to stay – God forbid." He rolled his eyes and kissed her again, this time on her stomach, and she could not help but giggle.

After another moment of thought, she sobered again. "I feel inexplicably guilty for not telling him," she said.

"Your guilt comes from your unaccountable certainty that you do not carry his child. But you will see," he answered. His expression became somber and laden with sadness. He whispered as he turned his face away from her, "He will return to a healthy and beautiful child, as he so desires, and your gift to him will be greater than any he could have asked of you."

His fear of the alternative – that she should bear Erik's child with Erik's own deformities – was evident in both his statement and his tone. She imagined the fear slashing through him as painfully as the doctor's scalpel. She did not share his fear, but knew there was nothing she could say to ease his sadness or his trepidation.

"Erik. Oh, Erik," she said, and she embraced him and held him a long while, as though consoling him.

***

The day came for the Persian's visit. Christine threw open the heavy curtains and waited for him in the sunny drawing room. She called for tea and biscuits when he was escorted into the room.

"With an assurance of no unpleasantness, I thought we might enjoy a small repast. I hope that is appropriate," she said. Despite her nervousness at the reason for the Persian's visit, she managed to smile and to gesture graciously to a small table with two chairs.

The Persian bent in a deep bow, but did not return her smile. "I did not promise no unpleasantness, Madame, merely no horrors. I remain concerned for you, I am afraid."

Although tempted to frown at the dark man, she maintained her smile and said, "I believe small concerns can still be compatible with tea and biscuits. Perhaps even alleviated by them. Please, sit." She swept into a chair and again gestured for the detective to join her.

Apparently determining he was to be granted time for a hearing, the Persian reverted to his normal mannerly custom and bowed over Christine's hand before sitting. He spoke of inconsequential things until the tea and biscuits had arrived and for some time after.

Placing her napkin alongside her plate, Christine poured another cup of tea for them both and said, "And now to business, I suppose." She found, despite her nervousness at what was to come, she rather enjoyed the Persian's gentility and courtesy – when he was not accusing Erik of atrocities or forcing her to look at details of gruesome murders.

The Persian cleared his throat, and with a quiet "May I?" lit one of his pleasant-smelling clove cigarettes.

"I have received another letter from Erik," he began, without further delay.

"Yes?" she answered. She licked and then pursed her lips into an expression of curiosity to keep her mouth from twisting in the small, knowing smile that threatened at the edges of her lips.

"I am afraid that despite assurances, I still believe you are in danger," he said.

Christine stopped herself from uttering an exasperated sigh. Instead she asked, with an expression of innocence, "Oh, has there been another murder? You promised me, Sir, that we would discuss no such thing."

"No, no, dear lady. No murder," he answered.

"Then?" she asked. This time, she allowed a small amount of her impatience to creep into her tone.

"Erik assures me the murders are finished. However, who better to make such assurances than the murderer himself? I believe he tells me this simply to induce me to leave London. So, you see, I still have reason to fear for your safety."

Christine imagined Erik, listening from his post behind one of the walls near her, kindling with frustration. His frustration was easily imagined as her own blossomed within her.

She leaned toward the Persian expressively. "Please, my dear detective," she said. "Please, I beg you. Go home. Return to Paris."

"Do you care so little for your life?" he asked. He seemed puzzled and concerned, as though he feared she had a wish to meet death.

"I have no need to worry for my life," she said. The words rushed from her. "I am happy. Can you not understand that?"

She could see from the sudden, analytical expression that replaced his expression of concern that she had said too much. So be it. She determined to continue, now that the damage had been done.

"Erik is wrongly pecked upon by you, an honorable man, who should at least take note that Erik has not dispensed of you despite numerous threats to do so. Can you not admit there is something almost comical in the repeated but unfulfilled warning? Can you not allow that, in Erik's own terms, he has treated you as a friend?"

The Persian did not answer at once. Without taking his dissecting eyes from Christine, he took a long draw on his cigarette and sat back in his chair.

"You know much," he said.

She said, "Perhaps more than you." She dropped her eyes from his and took a small sip of her lukewarm tea.

"I see," he answered. Christine looked back to the Persian to watch the slight bending of his head, first toward one shoulder and then the other, as he again drew from his cigarette and exhaled with slow deliberation. The elbow of his cigarette hand rested upon the fist of the other arm that was drawn across his chest. He seemed lost in contemplation. His exotic eyes narrowed and squinted through the smoke as though he was trying to see Christine the better.

"What do you see?" Christine asked, as much to answer his last statement as to question his piercing gaze.

"I see you have been in contact with Erik," he said.

"And have not come to harm," she answered, the statement pouncing from her. She paused and said, "And still I feel I can assure you as to my safety and happiness." Both statements were made with the fervent tone of having proved her point.

"I see," he said again, and his eyes dropped from hers. A strange grief seemed to color his downcast features.

Christine reached her hand across the table to cover the dark hand that rested there. His skin felt warm under her cool fingers. With more pleading in her voice than she intended, she said, "Go. Go back to Paris. Go, my dear sir, and begin the remainder of your life without the constant companionship of your obsession. Your *obsession*." She squeezed his hand to emphasize her final word. "Go, I beg you."

When the Persian lifted his face to hers, she saw the glint of added moisture in his jade eyes. "You accuse me," he said. Christine could see that her statement regarding his obsession had cut him deeply.

"I do not accuse you," she answered. "I simply release you." A small smile graced her lips, but she knew her expression was one of pity and consolation, not of happiness.

The Persian nodded, once slowly, and a second time, more decisively, as though he had reached a decision. He stood and drew in a deep breath.

"Thank you for your patience with an old man," he said.

"Not old," she responded. "Honorable."

"I will return to Paris immediately," he said, and then almost below the level of hearing, "and leave you in peace."

Christine felt warm relief flood through her at the statement. Standing, she said, "I call again upon your honor, before you go." When he merely looked his question at her, she said, "I ask you, on your honor, to mention nothing of our discussion here today, to anyone. Ever. Can I count on your honor extending so far?"

"Madame," he said and again bowed over her hand.

He stood from his bow and, walking with stiff limbs, as though chastened almost beyond bearability, he left.

CHAPTER 35
A CHILD IS BORN

The Persian left the city, as promised, and the relief that lifted Erik was palpable as bird's wings. True, other than the one day per month when Christine dismissed the servants, he could not experience the same freedom he had felt in the presence of Mattis the sailor, but he was as happy as he could remember ever being.

With the approaching winter, he did not have as much to do in the garden, and the cooler weather was not often appropriate for Christine to enjoy a stroll with the arduous gardener. Unwilling to relinquish her time with Erik during the day, Christine had taken to walking to the small gardener's cottage for her luncheons. In answer to the gentle circular questioning of her maid, Christine explained that she had struck up a friendship with the lonely old man during the course of ministering to his wounds and had discovered that he, too, had visited Sweden for a time.

Because Christine's melancholy for her home country was well known to the servants, her explanation seemed acceptable. It did not apparently cross the minds of the servants that the young Christine was dallying with the old man.

On one such day, after the solicitous young Missy left their luncheon on the small table in his kitchen, Erik noticed the ring on Christine's hand. It was the day after their monthly freedom from the servants. It was Christine's habit to wear Erik's ring on these rare and wonderful days, and clearly, she had forgotten to remove it.

"My darling Christine," he said, chiding her, "you have forgotten to replace Raoul's ring."

She laughed without worry and looked at her hand. "I know. I chose not to. I am your wife in my heart, Erik, and the servants will not notice."

"That is dangerous, Christine," he answered, with his rare darker tone of disapproval.

"They will not notice, Erik," she answered, although with less glee and certainty in her voice.

"They certainly already have noticed," he answered. "If I know your personal maid at all, she noticed as she was dressing you."

"I don't care," Christine answered, with the impudence of a child. Erik was charmed by Christine's impatience with their situation, and while sharing her wishes and impatience, he never forgot the precariousness of their shared lives.

"Raoul," Erik said, and knew he need not say more. He could see the thoughts flitting across Christine's face as she undoubtedly recalled Raoul's still unrelenting rage if she dared to sing under her breath or even to hum a wordless tune. Word from a servant to Raoul that Christine wore a ring he thought long disposed of would enflame him. She was immediately contrite.

"I am sorry, Erik. I am selfish. I endanger us both for a whim of the heart." Tears sprang to her eyes. She removed the ring and placed it in the deep pocket of her dress. Then she knelt at his feet where he sat and wept onto his knees. Erik stroked her long golden hair and let her cry.

"Oh! These ever-present tears!" she said as she took Erik's handkerchief and wiped at her eyes. "I am plagued with them, warranted or not."

Erik pulled her to his lap despite his uneasiness over what a servant would make of the intimate tableau. "It is the child within you, Christine. You are giddy with happiness or running with tears, all at the whim of a child, and much in the manner of a child. This is natural. This will pass."

Together, they rubbed their hands over the roundness of her burgeoning stomach. Christine brightened and gave him a shy smile, still sniffing.

"At least the sickness has passed," she said.

After a kiss, during which Erik listened for any sounds of approach to the cottage, he helped Christine rise from his lap so she could sit at the table in a more appropriate manner. "I will serve," he said.

"And I will behave," she answered. With a coy tilt to her head, she continued, "Until tonight."

Erik was astounded that Christine's motherly condition had in no way diminished her desire for him — if anything, her condition had increased her hunger. He imagined that, as her stomach grew, her discomfort might lessen her passion. It would not lessen his. To his eyes, Christine became more beautiful and desirable as the days passed.

The blissful winter months passed, and Erik discovered he was correct. As her stomach grew, Christine could only sleep in comfort on her side, and there were many more nights that they merely held each other in the dark of her bedchamber. Even so, she insisted on his presence in her bed every night — an insistence Erik was only too happy to indulge, with Raoul safely absent.

Letters and gifts came from Raoul from time to time informing Christine of his whereabouts. To Christine's relief, he never wrote that she might join him, and he often insisted she not feel the need to return his letters, as he moved too often to guarantee that any such correspondence would reach him. He spoke more of the beauty, sights, and sounds of the places he visited than of his work, and he often explained in great detail the local significance of the gifts that came with the letters.

At first, Christine seemed reluctant to discuss Raoul's letters with Erik. After Erik explained he would rather there were no subjects that could not be shared between the two, Christine began the habit of reading the letters aloud to him. Together, they would discuss the various cities, and Christine always seemed interested in the additional details Erik could provide regarding the differing countries and cultures as he reminisced over his own extensive travels.

Several times, she exacted promises from him that he would take her to some particular place. He indulged in her fantasy of traveling freely with him as his wife, despite the fact that he had become quite convinced the opportunity would never present itself. His dream of taking his wife driving on a Sunday afternoon would never be fulfilled. His current calmness and happiness kept this fact from sitting in mind like a bitter pill on the tongue.

Erik's only fear – and it was a fear that was with him constantly, although he attempted never to let it surface in his conversations with Christine – was fear for the child Christine carried. She remained unrelenting in her certainty that she carried Erik's child, and even her infrequent statements to that effect left him cold with sweat.

He dreamed several times a week of a small, ugly white monster cradled in his arms, while accusing fingers pressed against him from all sides. Had he been a praying man, he would have prayed most that Raoul, unlikable creature that he was, had fathered the child.

The evening finally came when Christine woke him with her groans. "What is it?" he asked, moving her hair back from her face. He lit the lantern. He thought perhaps that she, like he, was suffering from a nightmare, and he would comfort her back to sleep.

"It comes," she said and attempted to smile, although the effect was closer to a grimace.

"It comes," he responded. It was not a question, but a statement of acknowledgement and disbelief at once. For a moment, his nightmare of the monster child returned with full power, blocking his vision of the dim room around him.

"Do you need the maid?" he asked. Peggy and Missy had taken to sleeping in the house against the eventuality of this occurrence. "Can I help you to the door?" Erik arose to begin dressing so he could leave the room to the ladies, although the idea of leaving Christine alone at such a time as this struck him as madness – damn the conventions.

"No, no. Please, come back to bed," she responded, fingers clutched to his wrist with surprising strength.

"She will need time to fetch the midwife!" he said, voice rising in volume with his worry.

"Babies do not rush from their mothers," she answered with a small laugh. "Come to bed. I want you to hold me."

It was several minutes later before another small groan escaped her lips. Erik tightened his arms about her and then released her to massage her shoulders. His desire to leap from the bed to personally fetch the maid was overpowering, and only the terrible consequences of such a foolish action kept him beside Christine.

Finally, he could stand it no longer. After another groan, he released Christine. Rising to one elbow, he said, "Enough. You must summon the midwife."

"Yes, it is time," she said. She rolled toward him and held out her hand. He helped her to sit upon the edge of the bed before dressing himself. He helped her to the door of her room and stood supporting her as she unlocked the door and swung it partway open.

He kissed her and, after assuring himself she could stand by herself, he said, "Be brave, my darling."

She smiled and said, "Go, my love."

He moved to the secret doorway that led to the passages of the house as though his legs moved through water. He looked back at her twice during the short-long walk. Christine waited until the secret door was closed before calling to Peggy.

Erik stood at his peephole, intending to remain the night through to assure himself of Christine's safety. He watched as Peggy came. After she helped Christine to her bed again, she left to give instructions to Missy and to summon the midwife. Christine lay alone in the now brightly lit room, and after a short time, she curled up and groaned again. Erik could barely contain an answering groan. Perhaps he did not contain his groan, because a moment later, Christine spoke to the empty room.

"Go, Erik. Go. Come again tomorrow night. Go now."

Only his fear that he had not, in fact, contained his groan, or that he may not be able to remain outside the room through the ordeal, made him leave. As he moved down the dark passageway, he heard Christine again. "Go. Please go." As he crossed the garden to his cottage, he saw the silhouette of Missy moving against her curtains.

The remainder of the night and the next day were interminable. He did not venture out of the gardener's little cottage. He did not sleep. He knew if he slept he would dream.

When night fell, he watched the main house, waiting for the lights to extinguish, feeling that time had stopped. When all the lights in the house had been out for a mere fifteen minutes, he could contain himself no longer. He crept through the passage to Christine's room.

From his peephole, he saw that the lantern was turned low and the room was in partial light. Christine lay upon her side on the bed, a small bundle gathered to her breast. For all his haste to reach her room, he could not now enter it. Christine seemed asleep, peaceful, healthy, and whole. ... but what did she clutch to her breast? Was it man or monster?

It is Raoul's child, he reminded himself. *It is Raoul's child.*

"Erik?" It was only a whisper, and Christine's eyes remained closed. Still Erik could not move. Had she sounded plaintive? Sad? Minutes later, in the same quiet whisper, she called his name again.

He could not deny her. He must match her bravery.

"I am here," he said as he entered her room.

"Lock the door," she said.

He locked the door and moved to her bedside, each step measured and followed by a space of time. She smiled at him through tired eyes.

"Is it …?" He could not ask the question.

"It is a boy," she answered.

"Does he have …?"

"He is beautiful. Perfect and beautiful." She pulled at the bundle of wrappings around the child to reveal a small, round head of dark hair. Erik could not see the face, only the profile of a plump cheek as the baby nuzzled against Christine's bare breast.

"He is beautiful. Come see," she said. She gently used a finger to remove her nipple from the baby's mouth, and Erik heard three distinct suckling sounds from the child. Christine rolled the still sleeping child until he lay on his back.

The child *was* beautiful. Beautiful because it was perfect, all the wrinkled, puffy features as they should be. Erik's knees buckled, and a small breath woofed from him as he looked at the child. He caught himself on the edge of the bed, and as Christine slid away from him, making room, baby clutched against her, he lowered himself to sit. After a moment of gazing at the perfect face of the small child, he raised his eyes to Christine. She smiled and raised a hand to him, gesturing him closer.

"You are a wonder," he said to her. Leaning over the baby, he kissed Christine's smiling lips. He gazed down at the sleeping infant.

"He has your hair," she said. Her hand moved over the child's dark hair.

And, thankfully, Raoul's face, he did not say.

"Do you want to hold him?" she asked. She did not wait for his answer, but began lifting herself to a sitting position as she transferred the small bundle into her arms. "Come, sit with me."

With care, but no longer with fear, Erik moved to sit beside Christine, both of their backs against the heavy wooden headboard. He took the child in his arms. He moved the blanket to reveal a small splayed hand. He put his finger to the small open palm, and the miniature perfect fingers closed around the tip of his finger. Amazed, truly moved, he turned and smiled at Christine. She returned his smile, still looking sleepy. They sat together without words for a long time, Erik holding the child in the full satisfaction that his nightmares had not been realized. It was the first, but not the last time he would hold the child through most of the night.

CHAPTER 36
RAOUL HAS A SON

The child was a month old before Christine took him out of doors. To a person, the women of the household warned Christine it was too soon to take the child out of the house, and he would certainly take ill and die. Christine responded only that the child was too hale to suffer in the mild spring weather. When she informed them she intended to take the child to luncheon with the gardener, she was met with additional objections that the child could well bring illness down upon the old man and bring about his death.

"Nonsense. At the introduction of life into this household, all you can speak about is death. The gardener wants to meet the child." She left Cook and Peggy and Missy in the kitchen shaking their heads and clucking soft admonitions.

In his Peck mask, Erik met her at the door to the small house and gestured for her to enter. Christine was struck with the realization this was the first time Erik wore a mask in the presence of the child. Over all of the evenings of the last month, Erik had only seen the child in the night, in the quiet of her bedchamber.

She was uneasy at placing the boy into the arms of a man whom the boy knew and trusted as well as his mother while that man wore a different face. Erik clearly had no such uneasiness. He took the boy from Christine's arms.

"How is little PP today?" he asked. With accustomed expertise, he cradled the child in one arm and moved into the kitchen to sit. She had named the boy Philippe Petter. She thought Raoul would approve of the boy being named after his brother, the late Comte, and Petter was her own father's given name.

"Petter is fine," she said. "I'm sure you could hear his lusty squalls from across the garden." She called the boy Petter, but Erik insisted Raoul would prefer Philippe and thus only called the boy PP. She watched Petter closely to see if the child reacted badly to the strange old man's face as it hovered above the boy.

"You're to be a singer, then," Erik said, speaking to the baby. The infant rested in Erik's lap, cradled in the indentation between his legs, eyes open wide, arms and hands waving in the air between them. Erik put a finger into the boy's open hand, and the small hand tightened around it. Petter pulled Erik's finger to his mouth. After a moment of suckling, the child sighed his disappointment, closed his eyes, and went to sleep.

"He knows you," Christine said, with some amazement.

"My voice and my smell," Erik answered. He lifted the child to his arms and cradled him against his chest. "I'll have to keep his grasping little fingers away from my mask when he is awake. He'll dislodge it."

Christine was again uneasy at the mention of the mask. As the boy grew, he could come to know the old gardener, but how would he reconcile the appearance of a strange man in her bedchamber at night? All the bright visions of the simplicity of their relationship seemed to crumble in a moment. She and Erik would need to give this careful thought.

Of course, the simplicity of their relationship was dashed for yet another reason. "Erik, I have had another letter from Raoul," she said, as she moved to sit with him at the table. She pulled the letter from her pocket.

"Where is the man now?" he asked. His adoring gaze did not lift from the face of the sleeping infant.

"He writes he will return within the week," she answered. This news brought Erik's eyes up from the baby's face to meet her own.

"Ah."

The mask of the old man obscured any ability for Christine to determine his expression or thoughts. His eyes returned to the boy just as the boy's limbs jerked as though startled in the midst of his slumber.

"What shall I do?" she asked. Her hands wrung together in her lap. She was nervous in the extreme at the thought of presenting Raoul with a child upon his return. She wondered for the hundredth time if she should have tried to get a letter to him with the news, despite never knowing whether the letter would find him. "What shall I do?"

"You shall present Raoul with his son," Erik answered.

"Your son," Christine responded, almost under her breath. She had become more adamant in her insistence that the child was Erik's, but she could not now determine whether it was because she saw a similarity to Erik in the child or simply because she wanted the child to have been fathered by the man she truly loved. She quite honestly thought the shapes of Petter's fingers and toes reflected the lithe slimness of Erik's digits, but at the moment, this seemed a contrived imagination on her part.

Erik did not answer. The matter of the child's paternity was the only source of disagreement between the two. Consumed by her anxiousness regarding Raoul's return, Christine did not want to argue with Erik. She did not press the matter further.

Later, when Missy brought their luncheon, she commented on the sleeping child's comfort in the arms of the old gardener. She did not say – although the judgment was quite obvious on the young girl's face – that she thought the gardener mad for risking illness by actually *holding* the child.

Later, Petter woke and demanded feeding. Christine suggested that she could feed the boy without returning to the house, but Erik was adamant that Christine not perform such a taboo operation in his cottage. He did ask to hold the child again before she left him. As the child began warming up to a true wailing, Erik leaned too close to the grasping hands, and the mask was caught in an instant in the insistent grasp of the little fist. Christine sprang to Erik's assistance.

"Is the mask damaged?" she asked once the boy was in her arms. Again the uneasiness at the subject of the mask rose within her.

"Does it appear torn?" Erik asked. His voice contained a hint of laughter. Before she could answer, he said, "I will examine it once you have gone." He leaned around the squalling child to deliver a chaste kiss to Christine's cheek.

At the door, she turned and said, "We must discuss this, Erik. Your mask. What will the child think?" Flying forward in her imagination to the time when the child could speak, she added, "What will he say?"

Even with the mask, Christine could see the sadness come into Erik's eyes. *Ah*, she thought. *Erik has already given this some thought. And the answer brings him sadness.*

"We have time, Christine," he answered, grief lacing his tone. He opened the door for her and closed it behind her.

His sad eyes haunted Christine's thoughts through the remainder of the day.

***

Raoul arrived at the house three days hence. He swept into the house like leaves before a storm and dropped his valise and coat to the floor of the foyer to sweep Christine into his arms.

"Christine!" He drew her into a lengthy kiss, completely ignoring the blushing Peggy, who fluttered at the display before dashing for his coat and bag and nearly running from the foyer.

Christine had not yet caught her breath from the surprising and enthusiastic kiss before Raoul said, "Oh, let her flit and scurry. I am in my own house, am I not?" He threw his head back and laughed as he released her. He held her hands in his own and examined her at arm's length, as though refamiliarizing himself with her.

"You look as radiant and beautiful as ever," he said, throwing her a broad smile.

"I …" Christine tried to pull her scattered wits together, tried to remember how she must act with the man. "You look fine, as well, Raoul. How are you?" She forced herself to return his smile.

"Fine, fine. Good as ever. Come, let us sit. You must tell me how you've been. You've gotten my letters?" He had her by the elbow and was leading her into the sitting room. He gazed raptly at her as he walked.

"Raoul, I …" Christine stopped, and he turned to her, confusion on his face, although he kept smiling.

"Yes?"

"Raoul, I …" Again, she forced herself to smile, hoping the smile appeared genuine and happy through her nervousness. "I have a surprise for you."

"For me? But you are all the gift I need," he said, turning again toward the sitting room. "Come!" With a glance over his shoulder he said, "My God, but you are even more beautiful than I remember!"

Christine did not move to follow Raoul. She must do this now.

"Come, Raoul. Please. I have a surprise for you, and it will not wait." She smiled again as she gestured toward the stairs. Her hand was shaking with her apprehension.

He raised an eyebrow and glanced sideways up the stairway to the upper rooms with a sly smile lifting one side of his mouth.

"Really," he said. In her anxiety at presenting Raoul with such a surprise, she could not understand the suggestive tone of his one word.

She held her hand out to him. He took her hand and allowed her to lead him upwards. As she approached the open door to her bedchamber, Raoul pulled on her hand and, spinning her into his arms, amorously murmured, "Oh, Christine," before kissing her again.

Now she understood his suggestive tone and lifted eyebrow. "Raoul, please!" she said, in tones rather sharper than she intended, as she pulled away from his embrace.

His look of confusion almost made her laugh, but not quite. She knew she would be sharing his bed soon enough. She loathed the idea after all the months of their separation and their lack of familiarity.

Again, she forced a smile as she said, "Come. See." She led him into the bedchamber and to the high bassinet that held the sleeping child. She could not look at him as she said the words that nearly choked in her throat before she could utter them. "Your son."

She stood looking at the sweet boy, watching as his pink lips made small suckling motions and grew still again. Her stomach began to flutter sickeningly as the time grew with no response from Raoul. When she could wait no longer, she turned to peer cautiously into Raoul's face. She was surprised to see tears standing in his eyes, a small smile turning the corners of his mouth.

"My son," he said. After another moment of gazing at the child, he took Christine in his arms and began dancing her in circles about the room. More loudly, he said, "My son!"

Even through her guilty suspicion – knowledge! – that this was not Raoul's child, she was pleased at his positive reaction to the boy. This time her smile was genuine. "Raoul, you'll wake him," she said, and she was laughed as he pulled her raucously about in another great circle.

He stopped and made a great show of tiptoeing back to the bassinet to peer in. She came to his side. The child still slept.

"Come, come, Christine, you must tell me," he whispered. He pulled her from the room like an excited child. Once outside the room, he pulled the door partway closed and said, "What is his name? Have you named him?"

"Philippe Petter, if that is acceptable to you."

"Ah, Philippe! How appropriate. Again, we will have 'Philippe, Comte de Chagny!'" Raoul nearly skipped down the stairs in his excitement.

Christine stumbled as he spoke, instantly taking in the full import of his statement. Until that moment, she had so much considered the child to be Erik's child she had not stopped to think what Raoul would see – the importance this male child would represent to Raoul.

"Champagne," Raoul called to the passing Peggy as he swept into the sitting room. "We do still have champagne, do we not?" he asked as an aside to Christine. His face was nearly split with a large and glowing smile, and he chuckled as he looked to Christine for the answer.

"Of course," she answered. She was shaking with shock. She had worried Raoul might not appreciate the discovery he was a father, or worse, that he might question the paternity of the child – she was prepared with the timing of the entire affair – but she had not thought his mind would move so rapidly to the matter of the child's inherited title. Of a certainty, hers had not.

"Don't you see, Christine?" he asked. He poured himself a small glass of sherry and took the whole down in a single mouthful, apparently unwilling to wait for the coming champagne. "We may be able to return to Paris!" Then, as though speaking to himself, "Paris is just as beautiful as ever."

"But, Raoul ..." she began.

"Yes, yes, I know. I must write to the estate guardian and ask if the estate has yet been claimed by a prior-born male heir." He paced as he spoke. "I do have two sisters, you remember," he said gaily, as if he doubted they had yet produced an heir. He

303

laughed and rushed to her and began dancing her about the room again, laughing and repeating, "Philippe, Comte de Chagny, Philippe, Comte de Chagny."

Her irritation that Erik had been correct about the name Raoul would choose for the boy seemed petty in the midst of the upheaval in which she found herself, but she could not shake it, nonetheless.

She pulled from him and went to a seat far from where Raoul cavorted. Peggy, when she brought in the champagne, gaped at the still-dancing Raoul as though convinced the man had lost his mind.

"Just bring it here," Christine said. She looked at Raoul and was disgusted at his ridiculous capering. She poured herself a glass of the golden fluid and poured another for Raoul when he stopped to join her.

"I call him Petter," she said and bent her head to sip at the cool liquid. Her eyes did not leave his face as she drank.

"Fine, fine, call him what you will," he said, smiling a broad, face-splitting smile and panting from his exertions.

Shall I call him PP, Raoul? Would that suit you? Anything, so long as you recover your manor in his name? Bitterness filled Christine as she thought of Erik's loving care of the child juxtaposed against Raoul's solely mercenary response. She turned her body in the chair and gave him her shoulder.

After more energetic pacing, Raoul seemed to notice her dark demeanor and came to her with concern in his eyes. "Are you not well, my dear?" he asked.

"I am ill," she responded. She was not lying, as she truly felt sick at her stomach. She put the champagne down as she felt her gorge rise.

"Ill? Oh my. And here I am, in the mood for dancing!" The smile returned to his face and then fell away. "But I must not be so callous. I will help you to bed."

"No, please, Raoul. I am no invalid. I can manage quite well," she said. She swallowed against her stomach. Managing a smile, she said, "You go. Dance, Raoul. I'm sure your friends will … also … be glad of your return. I shall be better tomorrow; you will see."

He hesitated before leaning forward to deliver a brisk kiss to her forehead. "Get some rest, then," he said. She heard him speaking to one of the maids from the hall: "See to your mistress." He was gone in a moment, the closing of the heavy front door causing her to jerk from her frozen position. From the direction of the stairs, she heard Petter's thin wail and thought to match it with her own.

She was not at all sure she would be better tomorrow.

CHAPTER 37
PLANS FOR PARIS

Erik knew Raoul had returned in the late afternoon. For this reason, he was surprised to find Christine in her bed when he arrived at her room that night, instead of sharing Raoul's bed, as he expected. His surprise rose to the level of concern when he heard Christine weeping. He let himself into the room, and after ascertaining the door was locked, he went to her side.

"Did he hurt you?" he asked. He was pleased he managed to keep the growl from his voice as he asked the question.

"No," Christine answered, although she did not lift her hands from her face. Then, "Yes!"

"He hurt you?" he asked again. This time the growl was quite evident.

"No." She sniffled, threw her arms around his neck, and buried her face against his shoulder without allowing him to see her face. "Oh, Erik!"

He tried to extricate himself from her grasp, if only to examine her face for signs of violence, but she clung to him with amazing strength and shook her head against him. He did not want to harm her. He wrapped his arms about her and let her cry.

When her crying lessened under his petting and murmuring – or perhaps simply because she had no more tears – she eased away from him and backed onto the bed, making room for him. She did not raise her head, but kept her loose golden hair forward covering her face. With great care, Erik used a finger to part her hair and lifted her chin into the light. His quick examination of her face did not reveal any bruising or swelling. Or at least no swelling that had not been caused by a long time weeping.

"I look terrible," she said. She wiped at her nose and eyes with the sleeve of her gown like a small child.

"You are always beautiful," he said, running a finger along her cheek. "Now, tell me." This last statement was delivered without the gruffness but with the clear air of a command.

"He doesn't care about Petter. He doesn't love him as you do. You are more a father to Petter than Raoul ever will be, despite your insistence otherwise." New tears gathered in her eyes and slid down her cheeks. Erik wiped them away.

"What did he say? Was he angry?"

"He only cares that the child is a son. A *son*. Do you understand? He intends to claim the title and the manor on behalf of Petter."

Erik paused before answering. When he answered, it was with the gentleness of explaining a harsh reality to a youth. "Christine. Listen to me. This is not a cruelty. He is looking out for

the interests of the child. He is looking out for your interests."
Christine stiffened, and when her eyes snapped up to his, there was
anger in the reddened orbs and a flush rising to her mottled cheeks.
Quickly, he amended, "Yours and his. And Petter's. Do you
understand?"

Christine's briefly erect posture crumpled again, and one
lone tear rolled down her cheek to darken another spot on her
already tear-marked sleeping gown.

"But he doesn't love Petter like you do," she said. Although
she whispered, the statement was nearly a wail.

"He does not know Petter," he answered. He despised that
he was defending Raoul's actions and reactions, but he also could
not deny the logic of his statements.

"You loved Petter the moment you laid eyes upon him,"
she answered.

"I love his mother," Erik said, then internally winced as she
turned a wounded look to him. "I am sure Raoul will come to love
Petter. The boy is perfectly charming – how could he help
himself?" Erik smiled and again lifted Christine's chin until her eyes
met his.

"He wants to go to Paris," Christine said in a small voice.
The question in her eyes seemed to ask if she should consider this a
blessing or a curse.

"Soon?" Erik asked. His immediate thoughts ran to the
only just recently disposed of Persian and the problems the man
might cause upon a return to Paris.

"As soon as he receives confirmation the title has not already been claimed. He has two sisters, you see. The title goes to the first-born male heir." Christine seemed to be reclaiming her composure as she spoke. "He plans to write tomorrow."

"Ah," Erik answered. In addition to the Persian, complication upon complication began rising in his mind. Rather than begin any discussion of those complications with his distraught wife – he thought the word "wife" with fervency – he said, "I must think, Christine. We will discuss this tomorrow. You must sleep."

She inched closer to him on the bed and rested her head on his shoulder. "I don't want to sleep." She tilted her face toward his and gave him a slant-wise kiss.

Erik could not keep himself from a low chuckle. They had not lain together since the baby had come, Erik being far too concerned for her safety. Christine was becoming rather impatient with his reticence. Taking her face between his hands, he kissed her squarely, and said with all seriousness, "Tonight, you must sleep, wife." She sighed and slumped against him, and he felt his claim of "wife" had helped calm her, as well.

"I must get a cool cloth for my face," she said. "Will you wait?"

"Raoul?" he asked, as she moved to the door.

"Dancing," she said. The word dripped with venom.

In the morning, Raoul went to his offices rather later than was his wont. From Erik's vantage at the side yard, Raoul seemed somewhat worse for the wear of the evening.

Christine joined Erik in the garden mid-morning. He was pleased the weather was such that she could resume her walks in the garden, for he was certain Christine would no longer join him for luncheon in his cottage, now that Raoul was returned. Furthermore, if all went as Raoul wished, she would never join him in the garden again. Paris.

"Good morning, Peck," she said as she approached him. He was curious at her shy posture until she raised her face. Her eyes were still swollen from her long weeping in the night, although the redness was gone.

"Good morning, Christine," he answered. His voice was laced with love for her. And sadness. The sadness was his own.

"Have you had time to think?" she asked. "Have you found a way to ease my worries?"

Erik continued weeding as he prepared to answer, although the pain that rushed through him at his planned response nearly crippled him.

"I have thought about nothing but you," he started. "And Petter."

"And?" The hope in her voice cut at him.

"The best solution – the *best* solution, Christine – is for you and Raoul to go to Paris and claim the title for your son."

"Do you think so?" After some consideration, she said, "How will you live there? How will I see you?"

"You shall go without me, Christine." The pain at these final words sharpened in his chest. Another wound from the murderous doctor's scalpel would have seemed sheer joy in comparison.

"Wha-at?" she said. The single word was broken in two, like his heart. He looked up at her, determined to keep the threatening tears from his own eyes, and watched as she blinked twice, in slow succession. Again she said, "What? What did you say?"

"You are a family, Christine," he said. He must say the words quickly, or he would not be able to say them. "You are a family, and your son may be Comte. You have a ... husband" – he thought to choke on the lump in his throat as he forced the word – "and a son and an inheritance. For your own good, for the good of your son, you must go." He hung his head and tried to focus on the rich brown earth before him through the blur that filmed his eyes.

Christine's words came from near his ear as she fell to her knees beside him. The whispered words were harsh with anger, with pain. "Yes! I have a husband. *You* are my husband. How can you speak to me so?"

"Christine!" he answered. He pulled back from her in surprise at her lapse and rose to move away from her, eyes glancing toward the house.

"I don't care what they think. I don't care! I will disgrace myself gladly before I will live a day without you. Not a day!" She rose to her feet as she spoke and moved toward him again.

"Christine," he said, stepping back from her again.

"You will speak to me. If you cannot do it here, let us retire to your quarters." With that statement, she spun on her heel and began walking down the path toward his small cottage. With a sigh, he gathered his tools and followed.

She waited at the door as he approached, and the anger on her face was evident. Her cheeks were flushed with the heat of her passion. He opened the door and followed her in.

"Christine, I ..." Before he could say another word, she flew at him. Her small fists pounded against his chest, one, two, three times before she collapsed to the floor at his feet and, with arms wrapped about his legs, began to weep again.

He bent and loosed her arms and lowered himself to the floor beside her. Her arms flopped away from him, hands resting limply in her lap, palms up, as though all muscle strength had left them. She bent her head and wept disconsolately, large tears dropping directly from her eyes to her skirt.

"Christine, I ..." He felt helpless to console her.

"How could you?" she sobbed, the words coming between panting breaths.

"I thought only of ..."

"How could you imagine I could live without you? Without your love? Without your song? How could you?" She peered up at him from under her brows, and her eyes were full of accusation.

He wrapped his arms around her and pulled her to him. "Christine, I love you." He could think of nothing else to say, and it was truer this day than on each of the days that preceded it.

"Then stay with me!" she cried. "Come to Paris, and we will find a way. Or tell me you cannot go to Paris, and I will stay." She hiccoughed through another sob and said, "But do *not* tell me that I must live without you!"

"Hush," he said, again pulling her close. "Hush." At first, she pushed against him, then her arms came around him and clutched at him with a desperate grip as a fresh spate of sobs and tears tore from her.

He did not have the strength to fight his heart and hers. "I will come to Paris, Christine. I will come. I don't even know if I could have stayed away, even for your and Petter's sake."

She cried for a while more before the tears began to lessen and the sobs faded to heavy breathing.

"You'll stay with me?" she asked.

"Forever, Christine. I was wrong. I was wrong in what I suggested. I can no more live without you than without air."

"I love you, Erik," she said.

"I know," he answered, and this knowledge warmed the cold, cutting pain that he had lived with since late at night when he thought he must give her up. As he continued to hold her, he wondered at the curiosities of love. His love for her made him think he must give her up, and her love for him would not allow that. In the same beautiful way in which their bodies fit together, in which their singing harmonies fit together, their reciprocal love came together to build an indestructible whole.

"Come, I will get a cool cloth for your face," he said. "You cannot return to the house in your condition."

Christine giggled as he rose, and she brought a handkerchief to her face to wipe her eyes and nose as she smiled.

"What is amusing?" he asked.

"The servants," she said, and she giggled again. Her hand came to her mouth. "Raoul behaved rather strangely yesterday afternoon, and little Peggy was mortified at least twice. When she came to my room this morning and saw my face and that I had clearly been crying, she came to her own conclusions about Raoul's behavior with me in the night. She practically ran from my room once I was dressed to gossip with the others, and by now, I am sure they have all decided he is at least a cad, if not worse."

Erik brought a cool, damp cloth from the washbowl. After dabbing at her eyes twice, he gave the cloth to Christine.

"If I come back to the house crying, I promise you, they will not credit the 'dear old gardener' for my tears."

"Even so, we should not remain closed up here," he said.

She rose and placed a hand along the cheek of his mask. "Dear old Peck," she said. "If we go to Paris, I shall miss him."

She left the house and wandered the gardens for another half hour before returning to the main house. Erik stayed in his cottage. He had much to plan.

CHAPTER 38
HARD SOLUTIONS

Raoul kissed Christine on the forehead as he came into the room early in the evening. "Was there anything from Paris in the post?" he asked, as he plucked a canapé from the tray beside her and popped one in his mouth.

"No," Christine answered. She did not look up from her mending. She had toyed with the idea of intercepting any post from Paris, if only to delay Raoul his answer, but Erik was correct that it was Petter's inheritance and she would be wrong to purposefully deny him.

"Mm," Raoul said as he picked up the evening newspaper and settled into a chair. "Any day now." His impatience showed in the manner in which he flicked open the paper. He did not read long before he lowered the paper to his lap again and gazed out the window into the twilit sky. His foot jittered back and forth where it rested on the small stool before him.

"How are you feeling?" he asked.

She knew what he was truly asking. She had not yet taken to his bed since his return, using the baby as an excuse for her inability. She used the word "inability" rather than "unwillingness." She would have felt a twinge of guilt at her failure to do her duty by her husband, except that Erik had only recently agreed to love her again ... and the evidence of perfumes and rouge upon Raoul's clothing showed the man was not lacking in late-night companionship. Certainly, his discretion appeared to be waning since his return.

And she still had not forgiven him for his indifference to the son whose inheritance seemed to fill his every waking thought. He had only seen the child twice since his return from his travels, and both times were merely due to the happenstance that Christine was holding the child when he passed through the room. He did not make any effort to interact with the child other than to call him "dear Philippe" and perhaps to poke at his stomach.

Instead of waiting for her answer, Raoul rose and crossed the carpet to her and lowered himself to one knee. "Christine, I would not dream of harming you. You mean too much to me. You must tell me if you are ready for me." He bent his head and kissed the back of her hand.

His gentleness and understanding, the concern in his eyes, flooded her with guilt. She was being unfair.

Against her own desires, she said, "I ... believe I am better, Raoul."

"Are you? Are you certain?" Again, his brows knit in concern.

"I ... believe so, yes." Christine smiled at him shyly. In fact, she did feel shy of him. It had been nearly a year since he first left on his extended voyage and, therefore, nearly a year since she had shared his bed.

Raoul stood and walked to the window, and his eyes combed the deepening sky. He turned and smiled at her.

"I would wait until you are certain, my dear," he said. He walked to his chair and carefully folded the newspaper. "If you don't mind, I think I'll go out for dinner this evening. Meeting of the directors, you understand." He kissed her forehead again as he left the room.

Christine sat in the chair for some time without continuing with her sewing. Somehow, for all his gentility, she felt Raoul had just slapped her face. After a moment, she decided she probably deserved his rejection of her, and, after all, she was happy enough with the result. She sighed and put away her mending. Petter needed to be fed.

***

When she left her room in the morning, she saw that the door to Raoul's bedchamber was already open, and the bed was made. Clearly, he had risen earlier than she. She took her breakfast in the sunny drawing room. The morning newspaper lay upon the table, still folded. While she no longer read the newspaper since Erik's safe return from Whitechapel, it was unusual that Raoul would not have read the news before leaving the house. She questioned Missy when the girl came to clear the dishes.

"Did Monsieur Chagny simply forget the newspaper this morning, or did we have two delivered?" she asked. It was an idle question, and she did not really concern herself with the answer.

The maid ducked her head and continued clearing the dishes onto the tray.

"Missy?" Christine asked.

"Monsieur Chagny ..." the girl said, her eyes darting from the tray to Christine's face and back, "Monsieur Chagny ..."

"Did not return home last evening. I see," Christine answered. She could see the girl was uncomfortable in the extreme, and Christine knew the proprieties behind keeping the staff separated from such uncomfortable admissions. "Yes, now I remember," Christine continued. "He did mention he might stay at Lord Chadwick's residence last evening, if work kept him late."

"Yes, Madame." The girl's face cleared on the instant, and she bobbed her head twice as she smiled. "Very well, Madame." She hurried from the room with the dishes.

It was the first time Raoul had stayed out all night, and Christine found she did not care.

A strange coach came to the house not long after the breakfast encounter with Missy. Two men, one obviously a police officer, were shown in to where Christine sat at her mending again. Christine placed her sewing aside and rose to greet them.

"How can I help you gentlemen?" she asked as she glided toward them.

"Madame Chagny?" asked the police officer. His hawkish face remained stone-like as she approached him. The round-faced man in the dark suit removed his hat and held it by the brim in both hands before his chest. He appeared rather nervous or embarrassed as he pushed one hand through his unruly black hair.

"Yes," Christine answered, and with a gesture to the maid still standing in the doorway, "It's quite all right, Peggy."

Christine gestured to several chairs and returned to the chair she had abandoned to greet them. The two men moved toward the chairs but did not sit.

"My husband is not here, gentleman, but perhaps I can be of assistance?"

"Madame Chagny," the nervous man said, turning his hat before him in both hands, like a slow pinwheel. "My name is Cadstow, Detective Inspector Cadstow. This is Sergeant Williams."

"Yes, Inspector Cadstow?" she answered. The hairs on her arms and the back of her neck prickled as she thought of the Persian, the Whitechapel murders, and Erik. Had the Persian said something to the police? Was Erik in danger? She could not keep herself from glancing to the window that opened on the back garden. As soon as she realized she had done so, she snapped her eyes back to the round-faced man and waited for the blow to fall.

"Madame Chagny," the man said again. When he did not continue, the Sergeant stepped forward one pace. The man in the suit nodded to the Sergeant, and the Sergeant turned his expressionless face to Christine. She felt the panic rising in her as the man opened his mouth to speak.

"Madame Chagny," the Sergeant said, and Christine noticed that his sharp nose bobbed over his lips as he spoke, "Your husband is dead."

For several moments, Christine could not decipher the strange sounds into understandable words. She looked her confusion between the two men.

"Do you understand, Madame?" the round-faced man asked as he stepped forward to come even with the Sergeant. "Your husband is dead." Apparently, he could deliver the dreaded words, now that the Sergeant had uttered them.

This time, Christine understood the words. "Raoul is dead?" she asked. Even understanding the words, the statement did not make sense to her. Inspector Cadstow nodded, and his slight jowls nodded with him.

"Raoul is dead?" she asked again.

"I'm afraid so, Madame," the Sergeant said.

"How ...? Why?" she asked. She searched within herself for how she felt about this incomprehensible news and could not discern her own feelings. She felt curiously blank.

"Probably a duel," answered the Sergeant, in curt, clipped tones. "Over a woman, most likely," he said. He consulted a notebook that he pulled with efficiency from an inner pocket.

Inspector Cadstow put his fist to his mouth and cleared his throat, while pointedly glaring at the Sergeant. The Sergeant said,

"Ah, yes" and, looking somewhat embarrassed, cleared his own throat and returned the notebook to his pocket.

"A duel?" Christine asked. Her mind seemed thickened with molasses. The repetition of the words did not bring a sense of reality.

A duel? Raoul? A duel? Instead of focusing on the fact of Raoul's death, her mind moved to an inconsequentiality. "Dueling is illegal," she said.

"Ahem, yes, Madame," answered Cadstow. "And perhaps it was not a duel. Unfortunately, we do have one witness to the shooting, and certain other evidence at the scene would suggest a duel."

"Did your husband have gambling debts?" asked the Sergeant in his brisk monotone voice, again retrieving his notebook. "Sometimes these things happen when there are gambling debts."

"Gambling debts?" asked Christine, as Cadstow coughed again into his fist – more loudly this time – and jabbed an elbow into the ribs of the Sergeant. The Sergeant "oofed" lightly and took a step back away from Christine.

Under his breath, the Sergeant said, "Sorry, ma'am."

None of this made any sense to Christine. She returned to the one statement she had grasped. "Raoul is dead? Are you sure? Could there be some mistake?" The idea seemed unreal.

Cadstow's eyes softened with pity, and he took a step toward Christine, hat still firmly gripped between both hands. "I'm afraid not, Madame."

"I ... I ..." Christine was shaking, and she could think of nothing to say.

I ought to be crying, she thought.

"Can I see him?" She was not at all sure she wanted to view the dead Raoul, but she felt she could not believe he was dead without the gruesome confirmation. She recalled him kneeling at her side just last evening, eyes filled with concern. Then the brisk, dismissive kiss to her forehead as he left. She raised her hand to her forehead with the memory.

"It would be best if you could positively identify your husband, Madame," said Cadstow. "We would take you to the coroner's office now, if that is quite convenient."

Convenient? she thought. *Convenient? A man is dead, and they ask me if it is convenient?* From a dark corner of her mind, another thought followed. The thought of Erik and the notion that Raoul's death *was* rather convenient. She pushed the thought down, mortified at finding any benefit in the death of the man who had treated her so well for all this time. She glanced around the room where she sat. *He provided this beautiful house in which I have hidden. And the beautiful garden.* And with an intrusion she found impertinent but inescapable. *And the gardener. The ability to be with Erik.*

She had to move, had to settle this matter, had to occupy herself with other thoughts to escape the guilt that grew within her with every moment. Guilt that she would not truly miss him.

"The other man," she said. "He will be prosecuted?" In her turmoil, she thought the least she could do would be to press for the murderer's punishment.

"Ah, yes. Well." Inspector Cadstow coughed into his fist again, and his eyes flashed to the Sergeant and back. Christine decided his habit of coughing to avoid speaking was quite irritating.

The Sergeant spoke. "The witness was not clear. ..." The Sergeant removed the notebook from his pocket again, consulted it, and with a snap of his wrist replaced it in his jacket. He seemed uncomfortable with her question – the first hint of emotion evinced from the stone-like man.

They will not prosecute a gentleman. Disgust rose from her stomach in a burning mass to her throat. She wondered if these men would have been as lenient with Raoul – a foreigner – had he been lucky enough to win the duel. Her disgust turned inward as she found herself contemplating such thoughts in the wake of Raoul's death, rather than mourning the man.

"I will come now," she said. There was a crispness to her voice, and Christine marveled again at the curious blankness within her.

***

The blankness did not leave her as she trailed the two men toward the draped figure to which they led her. The blankness did

324

not leave her as they drew down the sheet that covered Raoul's face. But as his face came into full view – strangely like a waxworks version of Raoul, Christine thought – her knees betrayed her, and she nearly crumpled to the floor before the tall Sergeant could catch her. She closed her eyes to the still-handsome, yet unearthly paleness of Raoul's face. Through teeth clenched together to prevent a sudden rising gorge, she said, "Yes, that is my husband."

Not my husband. Not my husband. She was unsure whether she was privately claiming Erik as her husband or denying the awful reality of Raoul's death.

Turning from the table and accepting the support of the Sergeant in leading her away, she said, "Tell me what happened. How did this happen?"

Neither man answered her until they had led her from the room. "Would you care to take a seat?" the portly Inspector asked, gesturing to a chair with his ubiquitous hat. The room, despite several desks and the seating area to which she was directed, was empty save for an elderly, uniformed woman at a far filing cabinet.

"No, thank you," she answered, taking a deep breath and recovering her composure. "Tell me what happened."

The two men exchanged glances, and while the Inspector coughed again into his hand, the Sergeant shifted his weight from foot to foot. Finally, the Inspector said, "We know nothing more than we have said, Ma'am."

Christine felt anger rise within her – her first discernible emotion since the announcement of Raoul's death – at the ridiculous statement. Her eyes moved between the two men and then with emphasis to the pocket where the Sergeant kept his notebook. She remembered his various scattered comments – "a duel," "over a woman, most likely," "gambling debts," "the witness," – and thought to accost the man for the notebook that likely contained the information she wanted. Needed.

Needed!

"You must tell me! *You must!*" Her fists pounded the chest of the Sergeant several times before he managed to catch her wrists.

The Inspector dropped his hat in his surprise and in a voice full of indignation said, "Madame, please! Get a hold of yourself!"

Suddenly, the uniformed woman was at her side. "Let me take 'er to the washroom." The Sergeant released Christine's wrists, and Christine, feeling limp, allowed herself to be led away by the matronly woman. After several consoling statements of "there, there," the matron threw a comment over her shoulder at the silent, stunned men. "This 'ere lady 'as just lost her 'usband. 'Ave a 'eart." She tched at the men before returning to the cooing "there, there."

Christine felt the blankness returning as the kindly woman bathed her face with a cool, wet cloth. "Dunno what they told you, but t'was a duel, it was." The words washed over Christine before she realized that this woman was answering the question she had posed to the policemen. She brought her eyes up to meet the sympathetic eyes before her. "I'd want to know if it was my 'usband."

"Go on," Christine said, taking the cloth from the woman's hand.

The woman removed her small uniform cap from her head, revealing dull grey hair pulled into a high, tight bun. "I'm sorry to say it, truly I am, you being 'is wife and all, but t'was a duel over a woman."

Christine ducked her head and said even more quietly, "I knew of my husband's habits."

The woman patted Christine's hand and said, "The man who done it was a duke. I won't say who, but I can tell you, there's an end to it. 'E won't be prosecuted."

"No, I imagine not," Christine answered. Then after a moment, "How do you know all this?"

"Aw, them men. They talks in front o' me as if I didn't have no ears. I 'eard them talking with the witness."

"Go on," said Christine, not certain if she wanted to hear more, but needing to.

The woman shrugged one shoulder toward her ear as if reluctant, but then with eyes lowered to her shoes, said, "The duke surprised his wife, and of course … your 'usband. I suppose the duel was a fair one, as far as duels go. Shot through the 'eart, 'e was."

Christine waited, expecting some emotion to overcome her numbness, but could only stand mute, gazing in the direction of the woman's midsection, but seeing nothing.

"If it 'elps any," the woman continued, raising her head and pulling Christine's chin up until their eyes met, "t'was your family was on 'is mind when 'e died."

"My family?" Christine asked, confused by the words.

"Aye. The witness said his last words was, 'at least I 'ad a son.' That must 'elp you a bit." She pressed her features into a sad, sympathetic smile.

Christine huffed out a broken sigh as a wave of sadness swept aside the numbness. With a final dab of the cool cloth to her forehead, she said, "Thank you. I am quite myself now."

***

When she returned home in the afternoon, she declined having the Inspector and Sergeant accompany her into the house. She still felt empty, scraped bare of all emotions as she moved through the quiet house. From room to room she wandered, hoping something would catch against her attention and reawaken her from her numbness. The servants kept to the edges of the rooms she roamed as though torn between serving her needs and leaving her the privacy her emptiness demanded. She could not bring herself to cry, even for the sake of their expectations.

Just before sending the servants away for the evening, Christine asked for and received the day's post. There was only one letter – from Paris. She wanted to laugh at the irony of its arrival on this day of all days, but she opened it with the same lack of feeling that had plagued her since the policemen first arrived at her door in the morning.

Felicitations and congratulations on the birth of your son, the letter read. *Unfortunately for your son's claim* … Christine did not need to read further. She crumpled the letter and threw it against the wall as the tears that would not come during the day finally burst forth from her. They were not tears for Petter. They were not tears for the title her son would not inherit. They were tears for Raoul. Finally, tears for Raoul.

"I am relieved at least, Raoul, that you did not have to live to see this disappointment," she said through her tears. Her failure of him. Her disappointment of his goals. The last in a long line of disappointments she provided the man. Was she weeping for Raoul or for her own self-condemnation?

And then she could not see or say anything more as her sorrow and weeping came fully upon her. She did not fight Missy or Peggy when they found her on the floor of the sitting room and insisted on helping her to bed. She did not insist they leave her when Peggy brought a pallet into the room to sleep with her. She did not know the instant when she moved from tears and sobbing to sleep. She did not miss Erik beside her, for it was Erik of whom she dreamed all that night.

CHAPTER 39
CHRISTINE MEETS A LORD

As much as the heavy black mourning dresses she wore caused her to overheat in the humid summer months, Christine felt she owed at least that much deference to the memory of Raoul. In the months that had followed Raoul's death, it was only the first night that she wept for him. As much as she felt she wronged his memory with her lack of true concern over his death, she could not bring herself to miss him any more than she ever had. Erik had been her life and her love for too long before Raoul's unfortunate demise to have his absence disturb her now. But she did worry for Petter.

Without Raoul's income, what would become of her? Of Petter? She tried speaking of her concerns to Erik, but he seemed unworried regarding her finances. Of course, she had no real worries as of yet, for it seemed Raoul had some small savings. He also had a modest income still coming for his contributions to the mercantile success of his last voyage. But neither the savings nor the income would last forever. She pondered all this as she watched

Petter struggle to sit up from his position on his stomach where he lay on the blanket at her feet in the shade of the large oak.

She spoke to the nearby Peck from the middle of her thoughts, with no introduction to the subject. "I could do without Missy," she said. "That would present some savings, although I loathe to let her off without warning. I must try to help her gain another situation." Erik did not answer, although he did stop to coo at Petter before moving to his next chore. "It would be rather an irony if I could not continue to pay you as the gardener," she said with a laugh. When Erik turned to smile enigmatically at her, she said, "Although, of course, you know I would let all the help go before I …" She was mortified that in her ponderings over the finances she had insinuated Erik was merely a hired hand.

"My salary is paid by the owner of this estate," he said.

"Oh," Christine answered. Then after a moment, "How ever did you arrange that?"

"I have my ways, Christine. You should know that by now." He had a strange smile upon his face that brought some small level of frustration to Christine. Here she was, struggling to conquer what she had truly never understood – or cared to understand – and Erik did not seem to appreciate her difficulty. Her thoughts circled again to what she should do. Release the servants? Move to another, more affordable house in London? Return to Paris? Return to Sweden?

"Did you ever think to remarry?" he asked. He was no longer looking at her, but the smile on his face wrinkled his mask into the wizened features of an old, old man. He looked to be barely holding back laughter.

At first, Christine was mortified and hurt by his suggestion, but upon noticing his effort not to laugh out loud, she decided he was teasing her.

"I *have* a husband," she whispered loudly, and she threw a small broken twig in his direction. It fell short. He could no longer contain his laughter, and it burst from him in a rich peal.

They sat in silence for a time, she enjoying the slight breeze, and Erik working. Petter had given up his effort to sit and was sleeping on his stomach, one hand under his plump cheek where it rested on the blanket, pink fingertips just visible near his pouting mouth.

"You probably should make an effort to leave the house from time to time," Erik said at last.

"I never have done so," she answered. Inexplicably, perhaps from pity, perhaps from some strange sense of duty, she had received numerous invitations to dinners or other innocuous outings since Raoul's death. "I find I am still uninterested."

"Have you received no invitations of interest?" he asked. She could not understand his curiosity, but because they spoke of anything and everything, she had no objection to discussing the matter.

"No, not really. Oh, I suppose there was one interesting invitation, although from no one with whom I am acquainted. He is the talk of the town – I have heard Missy and Peggy talking of him." Unable to let go of her prior musings, she said, "Perhaps I can seek a position for Missy with him?" She tapped her fingernail against her teeth before she continued. "He is a foreign recluse, new to the area. He is throwing a ball to introduce himself to the gentry, although as a recluse, I don't understand why he would bother. I am certain to have liked him better for his reticence."

"Perhaps you are kindred souls. Perhaps you should accept the invitation."

"And why should I?" she asked. "The ball is a week hence, and I would rather spend the evening with you." Her statement came with a slight tone of petulance, although she spoke most sincerely. She would rather spend every evening with Erik, talking quietly, singing, or reading aloud to each other, but with him.

"Which day? Not Friday, I hope," he said. Again a small smile she could not decipher.

"Yes, Friday. Why?"

"I am afraid an errand calls me away on Friday. I will not be back until late," he answered.

"You and your errands of late! Can you not tell me what demands so much of your attention?" She rose and walked to where Erik worked. She placed a hand on his shoulder, and he rose to stand with her.

"Small matters, Christine, I assure you," he answered. He smiled at her, and she felt something inside her melt. To avoid treating him as anything other than the old gardener, she turned to regain the shade of the oak. After a moment, he said, "I think you should go. You will be able to tell me of all the gossip when you return and perhaps describe something intriguing about this foreigner."

She was irritated with his insistence, but found the vision of gossiping with him late at night in her bed an attractive one. Then a darker thought came to her: Perhaps his persistence that she attend the ball was a reflection of his desire to enliven their relationship with some new matter. Certainly Raoul had always wanted her to be more social.

"I will go," she said, although she felt a sadness creep upon her with the newly budding fear that perhaps Erik was becoming dissatisfied with their relationship. She felt better that night when he joined her in her room and evidenced no such dissatisfaction.

***

Peggy was indecently thrilled with Christine's plans to attend the ball, and as Friday approached, she made every effort to convince Christine to abandon her mourning black for the evening.

"I will do no such thing, Peggy," Christine said, rather more sternly than she had answered the suggestion the numerous other times Peggy had posed it. Peggy's face fell, and Christine took pity on the girl. She patted the young girl's cheek and said, "I do not wish to mortify people on my first night out, or they will not extend another invitation." Peggy's face lit up, and Christine knew at once that Peggy was happily envisioning dressing Christine night after night for different social events.

Friday came and, with Erik already gone on his mysterious errand, Christine allowed herself to be combed and perfumed and trussed by the enthusiastic girl. Even in mourning black, Peggy could not allow Christine to go without the most exquisitely styled hair. After Peggy applied too much cheek and lip rouge, Christine could not help but laugh at the girl's enjoyment as she wiped most of the color from her lips.

"I am a widow, Peggy," she said as she next moved the cloth to first one cheek and then another.

"You are a widow, Madame," Peggy said, and she dipped her head once in reverence to Christine's unfortunate status, and then her head rose again, almost defiantly. "But you needn't look like an *old* widow!"

Christine laughed again in the face of Peggy's youthful outrage and devotion. She deliberately placed her cloth on the dressing table before her and straightened to look into the mirror. Peggy hesitated, not at first recognizing Christine's capitulation. Then she squealed, retrieved the rouge, and began carefully dabbing at Christine's lips again.

"Not too much this time, Madame, I understand," she said.

Christine smiled in response. She only dabbed a little rouge from her lips before she left.

The manor in which the ball was held was quite a distance from the heart of the dismal city, and Christine felt her spirits rising as her carriage moved her into a more graceful countryside peppered with rolling fields, stone walls, and charming vistas. She was thankful her journey began before the daylight completely faded and she could appreciate the scenery. On her return trip later in the night, it would all be blackness, without the street lamps of the city to light her way.

The daylight had almost completely faded before she reached the manor, and she wished she could see the splendor of the place during the day. The manor appeared enormous in the night, but with the brightly lit torches lining the drive and the brightly lit windows, it did not appear the brooding, hulking block of darkness she expected. The edifice, though made of huge stone blocks, almost seemed to dance with airy lightness as she alit from the carriage.

The inside was as beautiful and sumptuous as the façade suggested, but it was here that Christine's usual discomfort returned to her. There were a great many people spilling from room to room under the towering ceilings, and too many seemed to want her attention. As much as she knew she was once an object of pity among the women who knew of Raoul's philandering, she was again an object of pity as his widow.

Even more angering than the pity, Christine overheard one particularly loathsome crusty old woman suggesting – rather loudly – that Christine's unusual interest in this particular ball was for the purpose of garnering the attention of their elusive and mysterious host. Tempted as Christine was to respond to the biting accusation of the bitter, bejeweled old woman, she maintained her poise and simply moved away. She determined if she could keep from meeting the host at all – a feat that seemed quite possible in this gathering – she would do so.

She finally saw the man from across the main salon. Several of the women with whom she was conversing suddenly began tittering and pointing with their fans or handkerchiefs in his direction. Christine was surprised to note the man was far younger than she had assumed – perhaps in his late thirties or early forties. He was speaking solemnly with a much older man and did not seem to notice the stir he caused in the room. There was no announcement made regarding his presence or identity, and Christine watched as he quietly moved from one small group to another, apparently not at all interested in flaunting himself or demanding recognition. She found herself liking the man immediately, although she managed to remain as far from him as ever.

As the evening wore on, Christine began to tire of the same conversations, identically delivered in their infinite variety. She had refused several invitations to dance and now made polite suggestions that she needed to return to her home and her child. As she moved away from the several ladies with whom she spoke – one of the women being the one who had inadvertently revealed Raoul's behavior as Christine hid behind a pillar at another party so long ago – she nearly came into bodily contact with the quiet host of the ball.

"Oh, excuse me," she said immediately, backing away and curtsying to the man. "I didn't see you." When the man merely smiled at her, she said, "You have a lovely home, my lord. Thank you so much for having me." Realizing this man most likely had no idea of who she was, she held out her hand and said, "Madame Vicomte de Chagny."

The man took her hand and bowed over it. In a moment of nervousness, Christine looked around to see if she could detect the odious woman snickering or holding her nose in the air at this meeting. Before she could return her eyes to the man bowing before her, he spoke.

"I am so very glad to have made your acquaintance," he said, and Christine started at the rich voice. This man spoke with Erik's voice, although his was slightly deeper than Erik's speaking voice and completely without Erik's unidentifiable accent. She stared at the man, her hand still in his. "Lord Bastion, at your service," he said.

Christine scrutinized the eyes, the mouth, completely at a loss. She wanted the man to speak again. As she stood, fairly gaping at the man, she realized she had left her hand in his for far too long, and she pulled it back to clasp it to her other.

"I am so pleased you like my home," he said, with a small smile.

Christine felt she was losing her mind. This man could be Erik's brother! The eyes, the mouth, the voice.

"Perhaps you would like to make it your own?" he said quietly, and then, most surprising of all, he winked at her.

In a near panic of confusion, Christine looked from side to side to ensure no one stood close enough to hear their strange exchange. Throwing all caution to the wind, she whispered, "Erik?"

The man threw his head back and laughed, and the laugh was Erik's as well. Christine could feel all the eyes in the room directed at their exchange, but she was determined not to let go of this mystery.

The man stepped closer to her, and with another small wink, removed all uncertainty from her mind. In Peck's thick English accent, he said, "P'haps we can discuss this later, Christine."

Christine's mouth fell open and would have remained so had she not felt the need to speak immediately, before the closing spectators joined them.

"How ...?" she asked.

"I must not neglect my other guests," he said, his accent back to the refined tones with which he had first addressed her, his volume raised from the whispered words he had last spoken in Peck's voice. "Thank you so much for coming, and do not let me keep you." He bowed over her hand again, and as he walked a step or two away from her, arms open to welcome the curious group that approached them, he said over his shoulder, "Perhaps we could meet another time, Madame Chagny?" Christine could hear the whispered gasp his statement of interest inspired in those closest to them.

She forced herself not to rush at Erik – her Erik – and demand an immediate explanation. She forced herself to turn and after retrieving her cloak, enter the carriage and begin the ride home. She was unsure whether to be angry with Erik or thrilled with the spectacle he had created. She giggled as the carriage left the grounds.

But even so, Erik had a lot of explaining to do. She thought she would go mad waiting for him to join her in her bedchamber that night.

CHAPTER 40
ERIK AND CHRISTINE

Erik did not arrive at Christine's room until almost morning, the darkness of the sky that of the deep blackness just before dawn. The moon had set and but for the light of a guttering lantern set at its lowest, Erik would not have been able to discern anything from his peephole.

Christine appeared to be asleep, as he expected, but he also knew if he did not come, she would be disappointed and perhaps even angry. He let himself into the room. As soon as he approached the bedside, she leapt from the bed, startling him back a step.

"Erik!" she cried. He could not at first tell if the cry contained joy or outrage. She threw her arms about his neck, and then both their heads turned toward the bassinet as Petter emitted a small cry. Neither of them moved as they waited to see if Petter's cry would develop into wakefulness or subside. After another moment with no further movement from the bassinet, Christine turned her face back to him. In the darkness, he could make out her features but not her expression.

"We must go where we can talk," she whispered. When Erik hesitated, she said, "Now!" Then she kissed him. Erik smiled as she released him, and he led her down the hall to one of the guest rooms that also gave access to his secret passageways. Once in the room with the door closed and locked, Christine flung herself at him again and kissed him again. She smelled of soap and freshness. He chuckled as he lit the lantern and chuckled again when he saw the expression on Christine's face, for despite the kisses, she looked as though she would slap him.

"You should have slept, my darling," he said. He brought his hand to her cheek.

Her expression immediately softened, and she ducked her head as she said, "I tried not to sleep, waiting for you, but I did sleep from time to time." She seemed embarrassed at the admission. Not to be so easily dissuaded from her goal, she pulled him to the bed and said, "How? What have you done? That was you, wasn't it?"

"So you liked the old boy, did you?" he asked, and he laughed again.

"Erik!" she cried. She pounded the bed with both fists, lifting herself off the bed and back down in a motion that made the bedsprings squeak. He could see that her curiosity and frustration were nearly beyond bearability. He could toy with her no longer, much as he had enjoyed his mischief.

"I merely procured another disguise, my love," he said. With a hand to her face again, and in lower, deeper tones, he said,

"How else to woo and win the hand of the fair widow Chagny? How else to make you my wife?"

He saw tears gather in her eyes and was surprised to find tears in his own. He kissed her again, more tenderly and lingeringly than those kisses she had crushed against him in the few minutes they had been together.

When he released her, she sat in silence for a time, looking at him. He could see her gathering her thoughts and questions, and he waited for her to speak.

"How?" she said. "How could you afford such lavishness, even for one night? How is it I have heard of this Lord Bastion for some many months, only to discover you in his place? Have you kidnapped him? Or did he agree with this impersonation through some strange humor on his part? How, Erik?" The questions rippled from her without breath or pause between them. As she finished, she put her hands on his shoulders and shook him gently. "How?"

"I am Lord Bastion. His house is my house. You must know titles and houses can be purchased, Christine." He watched as his words seemed to bounce behind her eyes and she tried to grasp what he was telling her.

"Bought with what, Erik? I don't understand!" Christine's eyes swam with tears again, but this time not with the happiness he had seen only moments before.

"Christine. Christine, listen to me," he said. He put his hands on her shoulders and held her eyes with his own. "I have told you I worked for sultans." Christine nodded as she toyed with a lock of her hair. "I am a wealthy man, Christine. I am an extremely wealthy man."

Her eyes widened as the realization of the breadth of wealth necessary for the Lord Bastion charade caused her to draw in her breath. She obviously did not feel she could trust her understanding of his explanation.

"Wealthy enough to …" she asked, and gestured toward the window, hand rotating limply at the wrist.

"Yes. Wealthy enough to purchase the manor in which you first met Lord Bastion this evening. Wealthy enough to own any number of such manors."

"But … but … you work here as a gardener," she said.

"I work where I can be with you every day," he answered.

"And the owner of this house knows?" she said.

"I am the owner, Christine."

Her eyes flicked about the room and returned to him. "The passages!" she said. "Of course, why did I never think of that?" She smiled, and the worried creases between her brows eased away.

"You have been worried about your finances and frustrated at my lack of assistance in helping discover a plan for survival. Do you see now? I want to marry you, if you will have me before the eyes of the world. Neither you nor Petter will ever have to worry about finances again. As Lord Bastion, I can marry you. Do you see?"

Christine's smile grew, and she nodded, eyes again welling with tears. But Erik needed to hear the words. He took her hands in his, and softly, deliberately, said, "Will you marry me, Christine?" His memory returned to the first time he had asked her and the disastrous events that followed. Time had certainly changed the circumstances.

The tears spilled over as she threw herself against him, head nodding, chin digging into his shoulder. "Yes, yes, Erik. I will marry you," she said. She pulled away from him again. With eyes still streaming with tears and a beautiful, brilliant smile, she said, "I will be your wife, and we can go out riding on Sundays."

He kissed her then, kissed her, and held her until they fell to the bed together, lips locked together as though they could never be parted. They slept for a brief time until the sounds of the servants moving about the house awakened them. Christine waited until Erik had moved into his hidden passage before unlocking the door and creeping down the hall to her own bedchamber. Erik watched from his peephole into her room as she glanced into the silent bassinet to find Petter awake, attempting to pull one of his feet into his mouth.

"You are a beautiful boy, Petter," she cooed. "Your mummy and daddy love you very much." She lifted Petter from his bassinet and took him into her bed. He fed hungrily as she drifted back to sleep.

Mummy and daddy love you very much. Her words echoed in Erik's mind as he made his way to the gardener's cottage. For the first time, Erik allowed himself to think of Petter as his son. Not merely as a boy he loved as a father would love a son, but as *his* son.

My wife. My son. Peace flowed through him like a warm stream. He slept.

As he had so very long ago, in the basement of the Opera House on the fateful night of Christine's leaving him, Erik dreamed a wedding of his bride and her monster, a wedding song ringing out from them – but this time, he dreamt the monster was simply a man.

A happy man.

***

The next months passed in peace – and humor. Erik divided his time between Peck and Lord Bastion, as did Christine. She continued to spend days in the garden with Erik in the guise of the old man. As Lord Bastion, he called upon her, much to the tittering pleasure of Missy and Peggy. As Lord Bastion, he issued invitations for her to call at his manor.

Erik knew the gentry of London were agog at the attention Lord Bastion lavished upon the young widow, especially in the face of his utter reticence to attend any social events. The story was oft repeated of their first meeting at his introductory ball where she was the first and only person to make him laugh. At least one old maiden had occasion to sniff as she explained with haughty righteousness that she had predicted their liaison.

No one seemed surprised when the announcement came of their marriage engagement. Erik ensured no one was offended by the failure to receive an invitation to the wedding ceremony, since no one received an invitation to the ceremony. Yet, all who attended the introductory ball received an invitation to the subsequent reception ceremony at Lord Bastion's manor. The reception promised to be a grand event.

"I want to invite the Persian," Christine said, as she brushed her hair in the privacy of her bedchamber at night. She turned to look to Erik where he lounged across her bed. He was at ease and in good humor as, between each block's visit to Petter's mouth, he helped the boy stack building blocks.

"Certainly not!" he answered and chuckled, thinking Christine to be making a joke.

"Why not? I think it would be perfectly appropriate," she answered. When Erik brought his eyes to her, she was facing away from him again, looking into the mirror as she brushed and brushed. He drew himself up to a sitting position, making sure not to topple Petter, and then he moved the boy to the center of the bed along with the blocks.

"Christine, you cannot be serious," he said. His sense of ease diminished as he pictured the confrontation with the daroga.

"I am perfectly serious," she said. She placed her brush on the dressing table and turned to face him. "Erik, think of it. I have received only one letter from the Persian since his return to Paris, on the occasion of Raoul's death. You know as well as I that while he made no accusation against you in the letter, he worried you were the perpetrator of his untimely demise. I think an invitation to help us celebrate our union would be the perfect ending to a long and horrid affair, and will finally quell the Persian's fears for my safety." With hands on her knees she leaned toward Erik in the fervency of her argument.

Erik rose to pace the small room. "Christine, I ..."

"He cannot help but see my happiness. Our happiness," she said. She rose from her seat and came to him and, with hands on his chest, rose to her toes to kiss him. Despite his certainty no good could possibly come of Christine's fantasy of resolution, confronted with her kiss and the glow of her happy eyes, his resolve weakened. He sighed.

"The Persian cannot know Lord Bastion and Erik are the same man. Can you not see the difficulties he might bring to bear?" he asked.

"Then I shall not tell him," she answered. "I shall merely invite him to our reception. Your disguise has improved since your first mask, and he will not know you. I barely knew you. He will see I am married again without interference from 'Erik,' and even this will put his mind to rest." She twirled away from Erik, and her light sleeping gown billowed out from her body. With Christine moving between Erik and the lantern light on her dressing table, he could see the silhouette of her slim body through the white fabric. "He probably will not attend, in any case," she said, and she stopped twirling.

The gown settled against her. Erik came to her and drew her against him, hands running down her back to her waist, the gown barely concealing her skin from his fingers. He could not resist her.

"Invite the Persian," he said, and he kissed her.

"Thank you," she whispered against his ear, and a tingle crept from his ear to his neck and chest. She kissed him again, pressing her body against his.

"When will Petter be ready for bed?" he asked, and Christine smiled as her hands explored his body.

***

Christine issued the invitation to the Persian. Erik's unease began to lighten when the time was long past for a response, and no response was forthcoming.

Erik, in the guise of the absent owner, made arrangements for the sale of the house in which Christine lived. Christine helped secure outside positions for the servants with the understanding they would remain in her service until the marriage was accomplished. Erik made all the necessary preparations for the private wedding ceremony, as well as the lavish arrangements for the reception at Lord Bastion's manor. The happy day arrived.

After the small, sweet ceremony, during which both Erik and Christine wept as they made their vows, Erik rode with his new bride to Lord Bastion's manor. No one seemed surprised at the lack of a formal reception line, for the two were notoriously reserved. Many commented on the freshness and beauty of the widow-turned-bride. It seemed to Erik that many found it charming that, even when speaking with their guests, the two had eyes only for each other and did not leave each other's sides. In truth, Erik's eyes did surreptitiously search the guests for the figure of one particular invitee, but when – well into the reception – the Persian still had not made an appearance, Erik relaxed into a singular focus upon his radiant wife.

As a culmination to the reception, an announcement was made calling the guests' attention to the newlyweds. With a cryptic smile, Erik escorted Christine to a small platform, and together they faced the crowd. All the attendees quieted their conversations to a silence strange in so large a group. Erik nodded to the musicians seated to the right of the platform, and the first strains of a lilting song lifted from the side of the couple. As a final culmination of his dreams, he held Christine's hand – thumb running over his old ring with which she insisted he marry her – and together, they sang the wedding song he had long ago composed.

As much as the crowd swooned to their perfect harmonies, so did Erik swoon – it was the perfection he had always dreamed. No one seemed to notice the tears rolling down his masked face, and Erik was proud to see that many attendees also wept at the beauty of the performance. At the end of the performance, even before the crowd could gather its wits to respond, Erik smiled and swept Christine into his arms and carried her away. Christine laughed in his arms as applause followed their exit.

CHAPTER 41
AN UNEXPECTED VISITOR

The servants had been given strict instructions to allow no visitors for three days and not to disturb the couple before noon each day. On the fourth day, at noon, the kindly matron who served as Christine's personal maid knocked at the bedchamber and entered with a breakfast tray loaded with breakfast for two. The woman reminded Christine of dear old Mamma Valérius, and Christine was tempted to call the woman "Mamma."

"Thank you, Sybil," Christine said as she rose from her window seat. She covered her breast before placing a satisfied Petter in the playpen at the base of the window and moving to the table.

"Thank you, Sybil," Erik echoed as he rose from his lounge to join Christine. When the woman did not turn to leave the room, Erik said, voice laced with kindness and patience, "Yes, Sybil?"

"M'Lord," the woman answered and curtseyed. "M'Lord and Lady have a visitor. He came the first day, but James told him you would not see him before today. He has returned." She reached into her pocket and brought forth a card, which she laid upon the table. "What shall I tell him, sir?"

Christine took in the name on the card, then looked to Erik. She tried to smile, but she felt trepidation at Erik's reaction to this visitor.

"I warned you, Christine," Erik said, and her smile faltered. He pondered the card a moment longer and then raised Christine's hand to his lips. Turning to Sybil, Erik said, "Tell the man we would be pleased if he could join us for breakfast. We will be down momentarily." With a glance to the window, Erik continued. "We will take the meal on the patio."

Christine almost sighed her relief at Erik's measured reaction. She was tempted to apologize to Erik or to promise a positive outcome from the meeting, but she knew there was nothing to be said until they determined the caller's mood and reason for this visit.

She matched Erik's silence as they dressed, confident his silence did not derive from anger at her, but from thinking and planning for the confrontation. As they approached the patio where the Persian sat at the table, just finishing a fragrant cigarette and sipping at tea, she took Erik's hand. She swallowed and had to admit to a certain level of anxiety.

As the Persian saw them approaching, he rose from his seat and, with an emotionless face, bowed deeply. Christine stopped beside Erik as he pulled her to a halt some paces from the Persian.

Erik dropped her hand as the Persian straightened and approached Erik.

"My Lord Bastion," said the Persian. "You are Erik." His face remained devoid of any hint of emotion or reaction. His eyes roved over the face of the lord before him.

Christine controlled her urge to gasp aloud, stepped closer to Erik in a sudden overwhelming protective urge, and took his elbow. The Persian turned to face her. He studied her face, his eyes darting between her own. His face softened as he took her hand and bowed over it.

"And you, my lady, are ... happy." He gave Christine a sad, tentative smile before turning and walking back to the chair he had previously occupied. "I would be honored to join you at luncheon," he said, again with a small smile.

Erik brought his hand to Christine's hand, where it clutched his elbow, and he led her to the table. He held the chair for her as she sat. Her eyes darted between the faces of the two men.

"Daroga," Erik said as he sat, confessing all with the one word. "What brings you to my door?" Christine heard the caution with which Erik spoke, but she could detect no threat or animosity.

"I wish the answer to a mystery," the Persian answered.

Christine could contain her curiosity no longer. "How did you recognize him?" she asked.

"One could never mistake that voice raised in song, once heard," the Persian answered. His head dipped toward the table as though reluctant to utter such kind words as he said, "The wedding composition was most moving, and the delivery, perfection."

Erik lowered his chin and said, "I thank you most kindly, daroga." Christine could see that, even with Erik's well-mannered response, he had not yet lost his reserve.

In the silence that followed, Christine poured tea for Erik and herself. Each of the three seemed to be waiting for the other to speak. Christine watched as the Persian toyed with his cigarette case, then said, "Please, help yourself, sir." As he lit a cigarette, Christine continued, forcing the conversation to its unknown conclusion. "What mystery, sir?"

After a hesitation during which the dark man took a drag of his cigarette and exhaled luxuriously, his eyes turned from the garden beyond the patio and he said, "I wish to understand the situation at hand." His eyes moved from Christine to Erik and back to Christine.

Christine looked to Erik, and when he did not respond, she placed her hand atop Erik's and leaned toward the Persian. "The situation at hand is that we are deeply in love and wonderfully, wonderfully happy. I would hope that, out of friendship to me, if not to Erik, you would do nothing to disrupt our happiness."

"And Raoul?" the Persian asked. Christine felt, more than saw, Erik stiffen beside her, but before he could respond, Christine quickly spoke.

"Raoul came to his end by his own foolish actions. A duel." Christine tightened her hand over Erik's as a signal to allow her to finish. "Please do not misunderstand me. Raoul was a kind man to whom I once ran for protection, and neither Erik nor I wished him ill."

Christine did not look to Erik as she said this, because she was not altogether certain the statement was true of him. This distinction did not matter to her now. "But I have come to know the man I ran from and have learned a greater love." Now she looked at Erik, and she knew the sincerity of her love shone from her eyes. "Erik had nothing to do with Raoul's death. I also know your previous accusations against Erik were unfounded. I know this for a fact, sir." When the Persian made no response, Christine thrust forward a final plea. "Please, sir, I beg you, leave us to our happiness."

The Persian extinguished his cigarette and turned to Erik. Even without the question being spoken, Erik answered.

"I love Christine more than life itself. I have loved her for many years now, daroga, as you know. I would never hurt her. Nor anyone, except in defense of myself or my wife." After a pause, he said, "Or my son." The Persian's eyes widened at the addition. Erik lost the stiffness of his posture, and his head dropped before he continued. "I know you have reasons to expect the worst from me, daroga, but as I swore before my escape from Constantinople, I am no longer that man. I have not caused the death of a single soul since that time, excepting of course that of the murderous doctor of Whitechapel, and again I say, I acted in self-defense."

"You did not act to stop certain deaths," the Persian answered, and Erik stiffened again at the implied accusation.

"This does not make me a murderer, daroga. At worst, it makes me indifferent." The statement was delivered with a distinct growl.

The Persian lowered his head for a moment, then raised it to look at Erik squarely. "You are right, Erik," he said. "I have unfairly accused you. I have unfairly pursued you with my own fears and guilt." He held his hand out toward Erik over the table. "Please forgive me."

Erik looked at the extended hand for a some seconds before he took it and shook it once.

"My Lady?" the Persian asked, as he stretched the same hand to Christine. She felt somewhat ridiculous shaking his hand in the manner of a man, but she mirrored Erik's action nonetheless, a small smile twisting the corner of her mouth.

The Persian stood suddenly and said, "I will encroach upon your time and hospitality no longer. Your joy in your union is as obvious to me as was your identity when I heard you sing, Erik. I swear to you both, in reparation for my unseemly suspicions, no living soul will ever know from me the true identity of Lord Bastion or," and here the man turned to Christine, "the events that led you at long last to your husband." He bowed and returned his cigarette case to his jacket in preparation to leave.

"Please, sir," Christine said. "We invited you to join us for our meal, and we would be pleased if you would do so." She held her hand to him in invitation, then looked to Erik.

Erik smiled at her and said under his breath, "You are a wonder, wife." He stood and, gesturing from the Persian to the chair the man had vacated, said, "Please, daroga. Join us, friend."

After a brief hesitation, the tall man smiled, teeth brilliant in his dark face, and seated himself at the table. As soon as Erik was seated, the Persian, glancing from Erik to Christine as he slathered jam on a piece of toast, the now-familiar analytical expression on his face, said, "So, you must tell me about your son." One dark eyebrow lifted, and he cocked his head to one side.

Christine noted the amused glint in the eye of the detective, indicative of a desire to smell out yet another mystery, and felt a flush at the insinuation behind the question.

Erik threw back his head and laughed. It was the laughter of a truly happy man.

EPILOGUE

Lord and Lady Bastion lived another year in the beautiful manor just outside the city of London. Despite numerous requests, they were never heard singing in public again, although the servants of the household could have testified to the rapturous songs that often rang through the bright, open spaces of the stone building. The servants, however, respectful of the privacy of their master and mistress, never spoke of the beautiful music, as each of them found the kindness of the couple as well as their musical performances compensation well worth their silence.

At the conclusion of their year at Lord Bastion's manor, the servants were all released with significant severance payments, and the manor was sold to a wealthy American couple. Two of Lord Bastion's previous servants stayed in service to the new couple for a time, but found their lack of gentility, especially in comparison with their previous employers, too disturbing to tolerate.

No one knew where the Lord and Lady Bastion made their new home, although there were rumors among the London elite that the enigmatic couple had moved to one of the Scandinavian countries. No attempts to discover their whereabouts revealed the existence of any Lord and Lady Bastion.

In truth, Erik and Christine, in the guise of a French duke and his wife, made their home on a quiet portion of the east coast of Sweden, between Stockholm and Korsnäsborg, where they could enjoy the quiet beauty of Christine's homeland, while still having the metropolis of Stockholm close at hand. Erik never once wore a mask after reaching his new home in Sweden, and the few people who came in contact with the couple quickly learned to overlook his malformed visage in their respect for the man. Erik, still called "Lucky" by his friend Mattis, was pleased to renew his friendship with the old sailor and even more pleased by the shrewdness with which the sailor had expanded his fortunes. He even allowed Mattis to coax him onto the sea from time to time.

Petter proved an intelligent and handsome child, with the thick dark hair of his "adoptive" father, large blue eyes, and porcelain skin. He remained quite slender even after gaining the height of his manhood and despite a prodigious strength in his limbs. All question of who fathered the child was resolved when Christine noticed one night, as she interrupted Petter attempting to read by candlelight, that his eyes held a peculiar reflective sheen in the flickering light. Erik was the only father Petter ever knew, and their relationship remained close over the years, even after Petter left Sweden to pursue his own fortunes as an architect and master stonemason.

The Persian was true to his word and, despite maintaining a correspondence with Erik and Christine, never revealed the truth behind the mystery of the Opera Ghost or the Ghost's relationship to his reclusive friends in Sweden. When Gaston Leroux visited the Persian at the end of his life to discover the mystery behind the Opera Ghost, the Persian faithfully told the tale up to the point where Erik "died of love." The Persian knew that, when Leroux investigated the bowels of the Paris Opera House, he would find a skeleton precisely where Erik was rumored to be buried.

Without understanding what he found, thus would Leroux discover the answer to the mystery of the disappearance of the notorious Whitechapel murderer and also, finally, close the book on the Opera Ghost.

–END–

36122985R00217

Made in the USA
Middletown, DE
12 February 2019